T0354801

Star Struck

Star Struck

Stephanie Costley

authorHOUSE®

AuthorHouse™
1663 Liberty Drive
Bloomington, IN 47403
www.authorhouse.com
Phone: 1 (800) 839-8640

© 2015 Stephanie Costley. All rights reserved.

No part of this book may be reproduced, stored in a retrieval system, or transmitted by any means without the written permission of the author.

Published by AuthorHouse 05/12/2015

ISBN: 978-1-5049-1185-6 (sc)
ISBN: 978-1-5049-1186-3 (e)

Library of Congress Control Number: 2015907457

Print information available on the last page.

Any people depicted in stock imagery provided by Thinkstock are models, and such images are being used for illustrative purposes only. Certain stock imagery © Thinkstock.

This book is printed on acid-free paper.

Because of the dynamic nature of the Internet, any web addresses or links contained in this book may have changed since publication and may no longer be valid. The views expressed in this work are solely those of the author and do not necessarily reflect the views of the publisher, and the publisher hereby disclaims any responsibility for them.

Dedication

This book is dedicated to my husband, Travis, my one and only true Prince Charming.

Chapter One

It is a warm late-July evening. Aimee and I are on the couch flipping through the channels on the television. It has been a challenge so far finding anything that catches our attention. An empty pizza box from Jack's Pizza Palace sits on the coffee table as does a bottle of Barefoot Moscato. It is the sweet, delicious wine flavor of the South and a favorite among college girls.

I take another sip from my wine glass.

"So are you seeing Kevin tonight?" I ask Aimee as she glances over at me.

She shrugs her shoulders. "I'm not sure. I think he and some of his fraternity brothers were going out."

"Oh," I murmur.

I don't mind it being Aimee and me for a change. She always has something planned with Kevin. I can't actually believe they are taking a breather from each other. I really don't have time for a guy. Boyfriend. Significant other. Whatever you prefer to call it. To be honest, I really couldn't care less to make time for one. All I think about is school and work. Majoring in biochemistry and aiming to be an oncologist takes up so much of my time. My grandmother always said I had my head in the right place. There are times when I wish I did have a guy to hang out with, but then I remind myself that, deep down, I know I'm still not completely ready to trust yet.

Aimee sighs as she continues to press the channel button on the remote control. "It would be lovely if they could have a good movie on tonight. Something erotic like *Basic Instinct*. It's boring sitting around here."

1

I giggle at her as I push a small piece of hair behind my ear. "Geez, thanks, Aimee. I enjoy spending time with you too."

"Well, you know how I am. I'm not used to sitting still for too long."

I roll my eyes at her. "Maybe you should do it more often. Then it wouldn't be so hard."

She shoots me a smile. "Hey, you wanna get out for a little while? Maybe go to Triangles Char Bar or something?"

I shake my head. "Nah, I'm good. I really just want to sit back and relax. I'm still tired from work."

"Oh, come on, Jo. It couldn't have been that busy today. It's Tuesday, for crying out loud."

"Maybe this weekend. I'm just not in the mood."

Here it comes. The third degree. I can always tell when Aimee is going to start with me about getting out more.

"You always say that. Jo, you really need to do something besides school and work. You need to get out and have fun. Meet someone. Go on a date. You are too fun and beautiful to be sitting around here every weeknight and weekend."

I sigh. "Okay, let's change the subject. Turn it to Channel 3 so we can watch the news."

She hits the number three and puts the remote down. "See? That's exactly what I'm talking about. It's like you're my mother or something. I mean who *really* cares about the news at twenty years old? You should be caring about shopping, dancing, guys, and getting shit-faced."

"Well, I just so happen to *care* about what's going on in our world. And yes, I do have an interest in all those things, minus getting shit-faced, but it's just hard for me to find the time."

She gives me another one of her notorious eye rolls. She's a veteran at that. "Yeah, you look real busy right now, Jo. I'd say it's about time that you *make* time."

The six o'clock news begins with the lovely news anchor Samantha Stone. Long blonde hair, big blue eyes, and a body to die for. Yep that's her. I'm sure she holds the full attention of hundreds of male viewers. After news coverage regarding gas prices, a robbery, and the hopes of a future addition to James Island Elementary School, a box depicting a picture of Chase Hartford pops up in the right hand corner of the TV screen. I feel my body sit straight up with 100 percent interest. No ADD moment happening here.

Samantha Stone says, "We have some interesting news for you from the world of Hollywood. Chase Hartford, the popular actor from numerous award-winning movies, is coming to Folly Beach and Charleston to begin working on a new TV series, *The Crane Files*. He will play the character of Foss Crane, a newbie cop to the Charleston County Police Department, who works on solving murder cases that have been deemed unsolvable. The shooting of the series will begin next week and will last for about ten months."

My heart moves to my throat and swells. I feel like I'm suffocating. Chase Hartford! *The* Chase Hartford! *Oh my God! I can't believe it!*

Aimee turns to look at me with surprise in her eyes. "I take it you care *a lot* about that! Holy crap, Jo! Chase Hartford! Chase Hartford is coming to Folly Beach! This is unbelievable! You know how long you've had a crush on him!"

I'm finding it hard to talk. "Since ... since high school."

"Yes! This is awesome! Oh my God! What if you meet him?"

I am in a daze. The image of him from the screen is still floating around in my head. His dark, messy-styled hair, his sleek tan build, and most important, his smoky blue-gray eyes.

Aimee brings me back down to planet Earth with a shout. "Jo?"

I quickly turn toward her. "What?"

She grins and cocks her head to the side.

I smile shyly, a bit embarrassed. "Oh. Sorry."

"So like I was saying, what if you were to meet him?"

I get up to clear our mess from the coffee table and head to the kitchen. "Oh, whatever, Aimee. Do you know how many girls are going to be following his every move when he's here? The number that will try to go after him? It's insane. I'm not going to think like that. That was a dream back when I was in ninth and tenth grade."

"So," she says with a shrug of her shoulders.

I continue, "Well, it's different now. I'm mature. That was a silly teen dream. It's no different from millions of other girls around the world. Besides what would someone like him possibly see in someone like me, even if I were to meet him? I mean look at all those gorgeous actresses and singers out there. I'm sure he would much rather be with someone in his own league. Maybe Samantha Stone will interview him when he comes to town. She would be perfect for him."

I stand in the doorway to the kitchen with my eyebrows raised and an amused twist on my lips as I look over at Aimee, still seated on the couch.

Her eyes are as big as golf balls, and her mouth is wide open. "You're kidding me, right? Are you listening to yourself? This is ridiculous."

"No, I'm not kidding, and yes, I can hear myself perfectly. I am no different from any other girl. Like I said, it was just a ridiculous teen dream."

With that, I turn and walk into the kitchen, hoping to end the pointless conversation.

My alarm clock buzzes in my left ear. I reach over and hit the snooze button. It's become an early morning habit. Just a few more minutes. I do not want to have to leave the comfort of my bed to get ready for work. It's Wednesday. In the middle of the week is when we start to get really busy at the cafe.

Nine minutes pass, and the alarm is telling me again that it is time to get going. I turn it off and head for the shower.

Aimee is in the kitchen, making a bowl of oatmeal. As I come through the doorway, she asks, "What are your hours today?"

I grab a mug out of the cabinet and pour myself a cup of coffee. "Ten to five. It's going to be a long day."

She takes a seat at our small kitchen table. Steam from her bowl caresses the air. She takes a sip of orange juice. "That sounds dreadful."

I sit in the chair across from her, coffee mug in hand. "Yeah, but I don't mind. I enjoy trying to make all the money I can before fall semester starts. Senior year is going to exhaust me. I can already see it."

"Yeah, I know. I have methods two this fall and then student teaching in spring. I can't believe that we are going to be college graduates next May."

I smile at the thought, but my expression is erased when I remember that I will have another four-to-six years of school before I finally become a doctor. Well, at least I will have the first four years behind me. My smile returns.

"So what are you thinking about doing when we graduate, Aimee? Where do you want to be?"

"I wish I knew for sure, but I guess if it were totally up to me, Kevin and I would be engaged, and I would have a job in Charleston. We'd get married in a year and then start having kids within five years." She smiles.

I shake my head with a silly smirk on my face. "Sounds like you have it all figured out. Are you sure he's the one?"

She nods while eating her oatmeal. "Definitely."

I find it amusing yet scary that she can be so sure.

I arrive at work on time as always. I clock in and tie my apron around my waist. Ramona, the owner, and my fellow employees, Amanda and Zach, are busy with customers. I go over to the counter and relieve Zach so he can clear some dirty tables. The bells over the cafe doors give a continuous ring as people enter and exit. The sound of music pours from the cafe jukebox. We are steady for the next several hours. Coffee. Lattes. Sandwiches. Soup. Salad. It seems that we are making and serving nearly everything on the menu.

Several of my friends walk in and have a seat at one of the booths near the large front window of the cafe.

"Hi, Kelly. Alex. Vivi. How are y'all?"

They throw me a smile and answer in a chorus of "Good."

"So what have y'all been up to?"

Kelly rests her elbows on the table. "Oh, you know, the usual. Beach. Shopping. Sleeping. Pretty much everything you do during summer break. What about you? You never get out. We never see you anymore."

I push a strand of hair behind my ear and start to drum my pencil on my waitress pad. "Just work."

Vivi says, "Well, we're planning on spending the day at the beach this Saturday. You want to come with us? It'll be fun."

I smile and nod. "Sure. I'm actually off this Saturday, so yeah, I'll go with y'all."

Alex gives me a big smile. "Awesome. You need to get out and do something. Have fun. Meet people. Meet guys."

I sigh, looking down at the pad. "Yeah, I know. I'm trying. It's getting a little better day by day."

I quickly take their orders and head over to the counter to put it in. The cafe has calmed down since the lunch rush has passed.

Ramona walks over to me while I am preparing drinks. "Hey, Jo, I need to see if you could do me a favor."

I turn to face her. "Sure what is it?"

"Do you think you could close with Zach Sunday night?"

I nod. "Of course. I'd be glad to help."

She smiles at me and continues, "Thanks so much. I know that Sunday night isn't our busiest time, but you know how I don't like leaving one of you up here to close alone."

"No, I understand. It's not like I have anything planned."

She cocks her head to the side. I know what's coming. I know what she's about to say. "Jo, are you okay? I mean I know that it hasn't been that long since the incident, but you know that if you ever need to talk, I'm here for you."

I give her another nod and sigh. "I'm fine, and thanks."

Chapter Two

I'm so cold. Why am I so cold? I struggle to open my eyes. It's a blur. I can't see anything. My head is pounding. Where am I? I'm able to focus. There are trees. Pine trees above me that seem to touch the night sky. I realize that I am cold from the moist ground beneath me. I hear music nearby.

A sharp pain runs through my body. I reach up and rub my head, trying to soothe the ache that seems to bounce from one side of my temple to the other. I notice blood on my hand when I pull it away. Oh my God! What has happened to me? Why am I here?

It takes a minute for me to lift myself to a sitting position. I examine my surroundings. The woods. Why am I in the woods? It's dark. I'm cold. I'm hurting. The pain is unrecognizable. I look down and notice that my jeans are around my ankles, and I am stained with blood. I fight for air. I can no longer breathe. Then I scream.

"No!" I sit up. I am covered in sweat. I look around. I'm okay. I'm in the comfort of my bedroom. It was a dream. A dream of a real-life nightmare that I can't get out of my head. I begin to cry uncontrollably.

My bedroom door swings open, and Aimee runs in.

"Oh my God, Jo! Are you okay?"

She sits on the bed and grabs me in her arms. She gently rocks back and forth, running her hand through my hair.

"Shhh. It's okay. I'm here. You're all right. Shhh."

She knows. She knows it happened again. She knows it's hard for me to escape it.

7

It's Thursday. Mrs. Sanders, my advisor at the College of Charleston, finishes filling in the remaining boxes on my fall-semester form. She hands it over for me to sign.

"Well, you're all set, Miss Dawson. Two more semesters, and you'll be out of here and on your way. Are you excited?"

I smile at her, giving a brief nod. "Yeah, I am. Not thrilled about more college, but I will be glad to get these years behind me."

She smiles in return. "Oh, no doubt. And you said that you are planning to attend MUSC after you graduate with your bachelors?"

"Yes ma'am."

She sits back in her chair.

"Great choice. I know you will do great, Joanna. You have all the requirements to continue your education there. A perfect SAT score, 4.0 GPA, and you've earned all As in your courses here. That takes a lot of hard work and dedication on your part."

"Yes ma'am. Thanks."

"Well, I don't need to see you again until it's time to schedule spring semester. You can take care of all your graduation fees then. Of course if you need anything before then, please don't hesitate to call or stop by."

"Thanks, Mrs. Sanders. I really appreciate it."

We stand and give each other a quick handshake. I grab my bag and head out the door.

The sun is extremely hot, and there isn't a cloud in the sky. It's Saturday. I'm relaxing on Folly Beach with Aimee, Alex, Vivi, and Kelly. A girl's day out. A much-needed girl's day out. Aimee's right. I should take time for things besides just school and work.

Aimee applies a little more sunscreen and turns to us.

"So, Jo and I were watching the news earlier this week and saw that Chase Hartford is coming to town to film a TV series. Did y'all hear about it?"

Kelly, Vivi, and Alex give simultaneous nods with big smiles on their faces.

Kelly sits up in her lounge chair. "Can you imagine the chaos that's going to break out? It's going to be insane. The girls around here are going to clobber him."

Alex cocks her eyebrows with a mischievous grin. "I'd like to do a lot more than clobber him."

We all break out into laughter.

Aimee looks over at me.

"Yeah. Jo has had one of those teen-star crushes on him since high school, but then again, I don't know many girls who haven't."

I roll my eyes at her. "Right. Like I said before, who doesn't have a crush on him? He's amazing to look at."

Vivi speaks up. "I wonder where he is going to be staying while he's here."

Alex replies, "Well, you know it's going to be somewhere luxurious. Out of all the luxury hotels in downtown Charleston, I'd have to guess Planters Inn."

"I'm just still trying to get over that out of all the places to shoot a TV series, they chose Folly Beach. Weird," Kelly says.

I take a sip of my water. "Well, one thing's for sure, the girls around here will definitely find out where he's staying, and he won't get any peace."

Aimee agrees. "True story. Nonfiction. Being famous and coming to a town this small has its disadvantages."

Ah, her famous "true-story, nonfiction" line. I crack a smile at her.

"Hey girls, why don't we all go to Trio Club tonight? I've noticed a lot of new faces in town since fall semester is starting soon, and there's no better way to meet hot guys than dancing," Vivi says excitedly.

I turn my attention to the waves coming closer to shore. I just don't have the excitement in me about meeting anyone. Not like they do. Not right now. It's getting better. Just like I said, it's getting a little better every day, but today is not *the* day. It's going to take one small step at a time. Baby steps.

Vivi calls my name to awaken me from my trance.

"Jo? Jo?"

"Sorry," I murmur.

"So, do you want to come with us tonight?" Aimee asks.

I always hate saying no when they ask me to go out with them. I make up some lame excuse about being tired or having the early shift at work. But this time, I really do have a reason to say no.

I shake my head. "No, actually, I am supposed to have dinner with Grandpa Dawson tonight. I haven't seen him in a few weeks, and he's cooking baked spaghetti—my favorite."

I notice the disappointment on the girls' faces. I see it every time I tell them no. I'm afraid that one day I'm going to get the "we're-not-going-to-ask-you-anymore" look. I'm totally surprised I haven't seen it already.

Alex asks, "How is your grandpa?"

I shrug and reply, "He's all right I guess. He's still having a hard time with Grandma's death. It's not as bad, but he still struggles some. I'm sorry, y'all. I know it would be fun, but I really do need to go visit him. I promise that I will go next time."

They all shoot me a smile, and Aimee says, "Tell him hello for us."

I nod. "I will."

It's seven o'clock as I park my BMW coupe in my grandparents' driveway. I turn off the ignition and sit for a moment, staring up at the old farmhouse. So many memories of the times I had with my grandparents invade my thoughts. On the white porch swing, my grandma taught me how to ride the little horsey to town. She taught me how to plant flowers around the porch. Grandpa and I used to play UNO on the steps, and he would take me fishing. I caught my first fish with him, a five-pound bass. I remember how proud he was. I'll never forget those moments and will always cherish them.

I gently knock on the front door. Within a matter of minutes, my grandpa swings it open to greet me with a huge smile on his face. "Jo!"

He grabs me in his arms and gives me one of his big bear hugs. Even though it's only been a few weeks since I've seen him, he hugs me like it's been much longer.

"Hey, Grandpa. I've missed you these last few weeks. How are you doing?"

He pulls away and closes the door as I step inside. "Ah, I'm doing well. I've missed you too. How have you been? How is work?"

We begin walking into the dining room.

"I'm doing good. Work is keeping me busy. It won't be much longer, and it will be back to school."

The table is already set when we enter. I shoot him a smile. I can't believe how well he has done on his own since Grandma passed. I'm so proud of him. For a while, I was really concerned and didn't believe he would come through. He proved me wrong. He is strong for an old, gray-haired man.

"Here, let me get your chair, Jo. I have everything ready for us. I figured that way we could enjoy more time together."

He pulls out my chair, and I have a seat.

"Thanks. It looks delicious. You know how much I love your baked spaghetti, and the salad and garlic bread look tasty as well. I wasn't expecting this."

He takes his seat and smiles.

"Well, you know how well they go together, and I had a wonderful woman to teach me. I'm glad I took the time to learn a lot of this stuff. I realize just how much a woman is taken for granted and the importance your grandma had in my life."

He gazes down at his hands. I reach over and take them in mine. "You're doing very well. I'm so proud of you."

He nods. "Yes, I am. You don't have to worry about me, Jo. I have my moments, but it's getting better."

We bow our heads and hold hands as Grandpa says a quick prayer. I decide that it's the perfect time to change the topic of conversation because I don't want him to feel sad during dinner. We have talked about Grandma so much in the past that I know how it can take Grandpa from feeling better to remembering how lost he has been without her.

"Well, I'm all ready for fall semester. I met with my advisor Thursday and scheduled my classes."

"Are you still planning on attending MUSC after graduation?"

I nod as I drizzle dressing over my salad. "Yes sir. I'm excited about it, but nervous about all the work I have ahead of me."

"Don't let that bother you. I'm proud of you. Your mom, dad, and grandma would be proud of you too. Most importantly, Sam would be proud. This is what you've always wanted."

He always has the most comforting and inspiring words. It's been hard not having my parents, younger brother Sam, and my grandma here to see me work toward achieving my dream.

"Thanks. The next thing I need to think about is whether I want to move to Charleston or just keep making the twenty-minute commute. I really like working at the cafe, but I'm sure I will be doing a lot of research along with my course work, and I don't want to be too overstressed."

"I have a feeling that you will probably stick around here."

He throws me his grandpa smile.

"What gives you that feeling?" I ask.

He shrugs his shoulders as his fork dives into his spaghetti. "It's just a hunch."

"It may be best to stay here until I finish at MUSC. I mean, if I land a job at St. Jude, then it would mean a whole new move to Memphis. That would be a huge change for me."

Grandpa agrees. "Yes, it would, but a good one. Joanna, you've been through so much in such a short amount of time. You deserve it. You deserve all the great things that God has planned for you, and I know that He has an amazing plan."

I put my fork down on my plate and sigh. I look around the large dining-room table and at the empty chairs. More memories flood in. I want them to. I don't fight them back.

"When I pulled up tonight, I sat in the driveway for a moment and thought about all the great times I had here with you and Grandma. I remember swinging, planting flowers, playing UNO, and going down to the pond to fish."

I sigh again as I look over at my grandpa. His eyes are filled with a mixture of happiness and sadness.

"I just never thought that I would lose so many people that I dearly love at such a young age. But then again, who ever really thinks it would happen to them? I remember their deaths like it happened yesterday. They're all so crystal clear. The phone call that you and Grandma received when the plane crashed, Sam's last words when losing his fight to leukemia, and the sweet flowery scent of Grandma's hospital room when she lost hers to breast cancer."

"Joanna, you have to keep moving forward. You must stay strong. I honestly believe that God knows you are going to do something great. I also believe that He knows I need you to be here with me, since they are all gone."

I smile at my grandpa and fight back the tears I feel forming in my eyes. "I know. You're right. I will keep moving forward, and I will continue to be strong. For us. You're all I have left."

He reaches out and grabs my left hand. He gives it a tight, grandpa squeeze. We nod at each other.

"I tried to steer us from having a conversation like this, but obviously failed," I murmur.

Grandpa sighs. "It's okay. It's good for us to talk about everything—how we're feeling, and how we're handling it all. You're right about their deaths feeling like they happened yesterday." He stares down at the table and continues, "There are mornings when I wake up and think that Annie is sleeping beside me or downstairs making coffee. I guess you could say there are many times that I pretend she's here."

We sit quietly for what seems like an eternity. My memories rush back to Thanksgiving dinner. Mom, Dad, Sam, and I would make the trip from Highlands, North Carolina, to Grandma and Grandpa's every year to celebrate. The dining-room table would be covered with the most delicious food, all prepared by my grandma. There would be beautiful centerpieces and decorations around the room. Numerous candles would be lit, and a lovely prayer of thanks would be recited by my grandpa. I smile as I picture us all crowded around the table, exchanging conversation and drowned with laughter.

Grandpa says, "Well, on a happier note, someone is having a birthday soon. Correct me if I'm wrong, but I do believe it is the big one. The number twenty-one as a matter of fact."

I nod. "Yeah, that's the one. Lord knows what all of my girlfriends are going to try and drag me out to do. At least I have a few weeks to come up with an excuse."

I shoot my grandpa a pouty smile.

He shakes his head.

"Now, Jo, you need to go out and celebrate. Have fun. Don't shut out your friends, and don't shut yourself down from having a great time with those that care about you."

"I know, all I hear from Aimee is that I need to get out, have fun, and meet someone. I don't want to admit it to her, but I can to you." I look up at him, and I can see the concern in his eyes. "I'm just still so scared."

He sighs. "I understand that, but it has been almost a year. Now I'm not saying that you should get out there, meet some guy, and rush into a relationship. I'm just telling you that there are some great guys out there that have good intentions. Pardon me for putting this so bluntly, but you can't let that asshole take away your chances of being happy and falling in love."

He's right. I know he's right. Everyone is right. I have to try harder to push the rape to the back of my mind. Not to forget it, but to move past it. It has interfered in my life for so long now. I was innocent, drugged, and had my virginity taken away from me so violently. It's not my fault. It never was, and it never will be.

"I still have dreams about it. I find myself back in the woods, but I'm always alone. I guess my mind is trying so hard to bring him into the picture so I can see him in hopes to reveal who he is."

Grandpa cocks his eyebrows and asks, "Are you still going to see Dr. Black?"

I nod and reply, "Yes sir. I'm actually scheduled to see her next week."

"Well, do you feel the sessions with her help you in any way?"

"Yeah, I think they do. I mean I have progressed a lot, but she is still trying to convince me to do the same thing that you and the girls are pushing for."

"It's just not healthy for you to focus on school and work all the time. I know that it is all important to you, but it's also important to your health and life to get out and enjoy good times. You are young. College is supposed to be the best years of your life. I just don't want you to sit around while all your friends relish this time, and you look back one day and regret it."

"I know. I'll try. I promise. I'll remember our talk the next time they invite me to do something, and I will try very hard to go."

Grandpa smiles and gives me a wink.

"That's my Joanna. Now, I do have something special planned for your birthday next month, so I am going to go ahead and snag you for myself that day. That is, if it's okay with you?"

I give him a big smile.

"Sounds great. Are you going to tell me what you have planned?"

He shakes his head.

"No chance in that. After all you have been through, I want your twenty-first birthday to be one that you will never forget. Of course I'll plan it early enough to where if you make plans to go out with your friends, then you will have time to do that too."

I reach over and give him a hug. "Thanks, Grandpa. You're the best."

We exchange smiles and continue talking through dinner.

Chapter Three

It's eight thirty Sunday night. Zach and I are cleaning up the cafe. We have thirty more minutes until closing time. The only other sound besides us is the music coming from the cafe jukebox. The Cranberries are singing "You and Me." An oldie but a goodie.

Zach grabs a hand full of dirty dishes. "I'm going to the back to wash these up."

I nod with a smile. "Okay."

I begin placing clean mugs and plates behind the bar when I hear the bells ring above the cafe doors behind me. I push some folded napkins to the side of the counter and shout, "Welcome to Ramona's!"

A voice replies, "Thanks."

It can't be true. I'm hearing things. The voice is all too familiar. He's not here. He can't be. I close my eyes and take a deep breath. I turn around and feel my throat drop to my feet. I find myself gazing into the most gorgeous, blue gray eyes. They are so big and bright. I have to be dreaming. This is a dream! All those years of hoping, dreaming that I would have the opportunity to meet him, and here he is! Standing right in front of me!

I struggle to speak. *Come on, Jo. Say something. Don't stand here and look stupid.* I finally let words escape my lips. "Y-You're welcome."

I still feel overwhelmed with his presence. He's right here in front of me. I could reach out and touch him. I've always wanted to touch him. I've always wanted to see him. Talk to him. Get his autograph. Geez. I need to get it together.

I shake my head in an attempt to clear my thoughts. "I'm so sorry. You'll have to excuse me. I'm back to earth now."

He smiles. "No it's okay. I understand. It happens."

I smile back at him studying every inch of his godly body. "I'm so, so sorry. It's just not every day a famous movie star comes into our little cafe. What can I get you?"

"Well, I'd like a regular cup of coffee with milk and three sugars."

Oh my God! He takes his coffee the same way I take mine!

"I'm pretty tired from my flight and have some work to do so I need a little pick me up."

"Regular coffee, milk, and three sugars coming right up."

I turn around trying to keep my hands steady enough to make his coffee. I am finding it so hard to complete such a simple task. I take slow breaths in and out, trying to keep myself composed and under control.

He seats himself at the bar. "So, are you a long-time resident of Folly Beach?"

I gently place his coffee mug in front of him and reply, "Yeah, I guess you could say that. That is if you consider ten years long enough to be a resident."

He takes a small sip and then gives me a small smile. "Now that's a good cup of coffee."

I can't take my eyes off of him. His dark hair is styled in that messy way that is all Chase Hartford. His black T-shirt hugs his muscular arms and chest. I turn my attention back to his dreamy eyes.

I swallow a small lump that has formed in my throat at his compliment. "I'm glad you like it."

"Well, I bet Folly is a nice little place."

He stares back at me. I try hard to act normal.

"It is. I mean we have a lot of tourists that like to come and load up on seashells out at the beach when they are vacationing in Charleston. Folly is a very small place. But we like having the tourists because it helps keep the cafe busy."

He looks around. He is our only customer. "You guys must be getting ready to close up."

"We close at nine, but please take all the time you need. It's always this quiet on Sunday nights. I know you would probably like to have a little peace and quiet before all the craziness of your arrival kicks in around here."

He smiles and nods. "Thanks. I appreciate that. I heard there are a lot of college students that live around here. Do you go to school?"

"Um, yes. I'm a senior at the College of Charleston."

I watch him take another sip. I am so mesmerized by how his lips form around the edge of the mug. *Come on, Jo. Remember, you have to keep it together. Don't look like an idiot in front of him.*

"What are you studying?"

"Bio-chem."

"Oh really?"

"Yes. I plan to attend MUSC after I graduate in May."

"And what are you going to do in the science field?"

"I want to be an oncologist and work with children who are fighting cancer."

He cocks his eyebrows and smiles big. "Wow, that's very impressive."

I blush at his words. "I-I, um, had a little brother, Sam, who died when he was eleven from leukemia. I spent a lot of time with him at St. Jude for radiation and chemotherapy treatments. Sam made friends with several other sick children there. He met a boy named Andrew who was the same age. I would watch them play together with their toys and battle each other in video games. I found it amazing that, even though they both had a terminal disease, they found laughter in life. I knew after Sam passed that I wanted to be a doctor and battle cancer."

I gaze into his blue gray eyes and notice a sense of sadness.

"I can't imagine how hard that must have been for you and your parents to go through."

I sigh, knowing that I really don't want to depress him with my sad stories and life history. It really isn't the topic of conversation you plan on having with your hot, teen-movie-star crush. "Well, actually it was just me and my grandparents. My parents died in a plane crash when I was twelve years old. Sam was eight at the time of their death. It wasn't long after that when the doctors discovered that he had cancer."

I shouldn't have done that. I shouldn't have told him all this. What am I doing? I never open up and tell some stranger, Chase Hartford or not, about my devastating life. This is very unlike me. Pull it together, Jo.

"Shit, that's so much to have been through." His voice is crippling. His eyes even more so.

"Yeah, but I know there are others out there that have suffered far worse."

He stares at me with this look in his eyes. I would love to say that it almost seems to be one of admiration and amazement, but I know that it is really just a look he is trying to hold as he decides where to go next in the conversation. Or at least I think that's it.

"Okay, let's change the subject. Maybe something on a lighter note. How long have you been working here?"

Good. He wants to talk about something else.

"Three years. I started my freshman year."

"That's a good while. You must really like it here or something." He smiles again. *Damn. He needs to stop doing that. It is hazardous to my concentration and possibly my health.*

"Yeah, I do. Ramona, the owner, she's great. I think I may just stay on here and work as much as I can when I start at MUSC. I have been considering moving into Charleston, but the commute really isn't that bad. Plus I hope I will have a move to Memphis in my future."

"Oh yeah. That's where St. Jude is located. I hope you do too. Especially if it's what you want and what you're working so hard for."

I never imagined having a conversation with Chase Hartford about my future. What am I thinking? I have never imagined having a conversation with him, period.

He sits back in the barstool and throws his hands behind his head in a relaxing position.

"Do you work here every day?"

I shake my head.

"No. I usually work five days out of the week. Ramona asked me to close with Zach for her tonight, and I agreed so I could have next weekend off. It will be the first weekend in a long time. They are the busiest, and I make the most money in tips."

"You mean there's someone else here?"

"Um, yes. Zach is one of our waiters and busboys. He's in back washing up some dishes. Probably mopping. Things like that."

"It has been so quiet in here, I thought it was just you and I. Is he a college student too?"

I nod. "Ramona likes hiring college students. Well, the ones she can depend on at least. I've known Zach for a long time. He's a good friend. We went to middle and high school together."

He nods back.

"I see. So he's not a boyfriend that I have to worry about."

What? What did he just say?

"Uh ... no, I don't have one." I murmur.

Another big Chase Hartford smile. I look down at my nervous hands and smile. I decide to ask him some questions to get a break from him hammering me for information. Not that I mind, but I really don't know where this is going.

"So, what about you? Did you find a safe place to stay away from all the crazy girls in Charleston while you're here?"

Really, Jo? Do you actually think he is going to tell you where he is staying or something?

He leans forward, resting his elbows on the bar. I wonder if I've asked the wrong question. He would probably prefer for no one to know where he is staying. At least for now. I'm sure he would like to keep it quiet for as long as possible.

"Actually I'm not staying in Charleston. I knew that's exactly where the paparazzi and my fans would expect me to be."

I cock an eyebrow at him and smirk. "Oh, you're good. You've been in this long enough that you have some tricks up your sleeve."

He giggles. It makes my body numb.

"Yeah, I have learned a lot of tricks from this business. I'm actually staying out in the country on the outskirts of Folly. I hope it will keep under wraps for a while. At least long enough for me to get settled. Eventually they find out where I'm staying, and if it gets too out of control and stressful, then I just move on to somewhere new. I'm crossing my fingers that I can manage to stay where I am now."

"I know it has to be hard for you. Does the bad outweigh the good in what you do?"

He takes a minute to think with a contemplating look and replies, "No, I wouldn't say that. I mean, there's a lot of wonderful things about this career, but the bad does try to catch up."

"Well, I hope everything goes smoothly for you here. I'm sure that even for a small beach community like this, things can still get out of control."

"Do you go to Charleston any to eat or party? I was wondering what places were good to chill at while I'm here."

I really feel the least educated on the places in Charleston to go party and eat, since I always give excuses to not go with my friends. Apparently he should be talking with them. "Um … there's Triangles Char Bar and Silver Dollar if you're looking for drinks and live music. Silver Dollar has pool, if that's your game. For great music and dancing, there is Trio Club and Club Light."

"What about eating?"

I think for a minute because I hardly ever eat in Charleston. I prefer eating at home, grandpa's, or the cafe.

"Um … I really don't eat much in Charleston, but I know of several places that people talk about a lot. For casual dining, there's The Mellow Mushroom, if you like pizza. There is Coast Bar and Grill, if you like seafood. Um … for fine dining, which is definitely not something I ever do, there is Magnolia's for your Southern cooking and Bocci's if you prefer Italian."

The kitchen door swings open, and Zach walks in. He sees Chase and me at the bar. He stops in shock.

"Holy shit! Chase Hartford! Jo, Chase Hartford is in the cafe!"

Chase and I look at each other and roar with laughter. Zach still hasn't moved from his spot. It's like his feet are cemented to the floor.

I turn to him and say, "Yeah, I'm pretty aware of that, Zach. We've been talking for the last half-hour."

Oh crap, it's already nine! I haven't been paying attention to the time.

"Well, I was wondering why I hadn't seen you in back."

He finally walks over to Chase and extends his hand for a shake. "Hi. I'm Zach Jones."

Chase welcomes the shake. "Nice to meet you, Zach."

Chase turns his attention back to me. "Jo and I haven't officially met, but she has been keeping me company over coffee."

I feel my cheeks turning red. I smile at him. He's right. I never told him my name. Then again, he never asked for it. Almost everyone in town knows who we are, so Ramona never felt that name tags were a necessity. Then again, I'm sure the tourists would appreciate them. Okay, ADD moment; back to the convo unfolding before me.

Zach says, "I see. I was just coming to let you know that everything's done in back and it's time to lock up."

Zach then turns to Chase. "I don't want to rush you or anything, though, so take your time. I don't mind staying a little longer if you and Jo want to chat some more."

Chase shrugs. "No I know it's been a long day for you guys, and I'm sure you both would like to get out of here. I have several things I need to do tonight. We start shooting tomorrow."

He rises from the barstool and tries to hand me some money to pay for the coffee. I don't want him to go. I want him to stay. I want to talk with him all night. I shake my head and refuse to take it. "The coffee's on the house. Welcome to Folly."

He smiles at me, and then turns his attention back over to Zach. "It was nice to meet you, Zach."

Zach nods and smiles. "Yeah, man. Nice to meet you too. Come back."

Chase nods and glances at me. "It was nice talking with you, Jo. Thanks for the excellent cup of coffee. I hope to see you again very soon."

He smiles his big, sexy smile. I feel my legs turn to jelly. My cheeks are an even deeper red than before. I know because I can feel it. The heat radiating from them is intense. I smile back.

"Nice talking to you too."

With that he turns and exits the cafe.

I walk into Aimee's and my apartment. I am beaming from ear to ear, still thinking about the time I spent with Chase at the cafe. I remember every word we exchanged. Every smile. All the times I blushed beet red.

"What's going on with you?" Aimee asks as I close the door behind me.

I scream out with excitement, "I met Chase Hartford!"

Aimee springs from the couch with a complete look of total amazement. "No way! You're joking, right?"

I shake my head with an even bigger grin on my face. "He came into the cafe for coffee. I waited on him, and he sat at the bar and talked with me until it was time to close."

She walks over to me still in shock. "No way! You're lying!"

I shake my head again and set my purse down on the nearby armchair. "I promise you! Ask Zach. He was there too."

Aimee grabs me and squeezes me tight. "Oh my God! I can't believe it! You are so lucky! You have to tell me what y'all talked about! Spill it now!"

She pulls me to the couch, and we have a seat together. She sits Indian style, waiting with an impatient look on her face.

I take a breath, preparing myself for the hundred questions I know she will ask as I try to tell her about my experience with the sexiest guy in the world. "Well, we talked about places to eat and dance in Charleston. He asked me questions about myself and told me a little about him."

She throws her hands up. "No no. I need details. That's not details."

I sigh. "Okay. He asked me if I go to college. I told him yes, and he wanted to know what I am studying. Then we ended up talking about Mom, Dad, and Sam, which was weird because that's not the topic of conversation I ever thought I would have with him. He asked me about working at the cafe, and then we talked about eating and dancing."

"Where is he staying? Did he tell you?"

I shake my head. "He didn't tell me exactly. He just said that he is staying on the outskirts of Folly and not in Charleston because he knew that's where everyone would expect him to stay."

"When do they start shooting the series?"

"Tomorrow. And no, he didn't tell me where, in case that's your next question."

She rolls her eyes at me. "Geez, Jo. You obviously don't know how to ask the right questions. I mean, did you find out any useful information? Did he say anything like coming back to the cafe or where he may go to party?"

"No, he didn't say anything about that, but he did say he hoped he'd see me again very soon." The blushing returns, and I raise an eyebrow at her.

"What? Are you serious? He said that to you?"

I nod. "Yes. Right before he left."

She starts jumping up and down on the couch. The vibration from her bounces me a little. I start to laugh. "Calm down, Aimee. It's really not that big of a deal."

She stops and grabs a hold of my shoulders. "Are you crazy? It is a big deal! He must have enjoyed your little chat together if he leaves with those words. I think he likes you." She gives me a wink and lets go of my shoulders.

I wave my hand at her.

"Oh, Aimee, he was just being nice, that's all. I didn't take any meaning from it."

"Well, you are crazy then. I certainly would. I bet he's going to come back and see you. He'll probably come for coffee every day you're there."

"Oh, whatever! So not true! I'm sure he'll come back for coffee, but definitely not to just see me." I stand up and go over to collect my purse. "I'm going to try and go to bed. Hopefully my nerves will settle so I can sleep. I'm still trying to get over the fact that I talked with Chase Hartford tonight." I wink at her with a smile. "Goodnight, Aimee.'

She smiles with a wink back. "Sweet dreams, Jo."

Monday is here. It's been slow at the cafe. I've only waited on ten customers, and I've already put in five hours. I look up at the clock above the bar and notice that it's four o'clock. Most likely there will be a small rush for supper.

I'm standing at the register, ringing up the bill of a customer, when a man walks in holding a beautiful flower arrangement. The vase is a clear, aqua blue, and it is overflowing with a mixture of daisies, roses, and tulips, surrounded by baby's breath.

The man turns to me and says, "Good afternoon. I'm looking for a young lady by the name of Jo."

I say, "That's me."

He smiles and hands the vase over to me. "These are for you. Enjoy."

What? No way. There has to be a mistake. I never get flowers. Who on earth would want to waste their time sending me flowers?

I walk to the counter around back and set the vase down. The flowers are gorgeous and have the sweetest scent. I pull the little white envelope from the floral pick. On the front, my name is written perfectly. My heart beats hard against my chest as I prepare myself to open it. I take a slow, deep breath and close my eyes for a minute. I gently take the card out of the envelope and open my eyes to read:

> *Jo*
>
> *Greatness will come from the sadness you've endured*
>
> *You are an inspiration*
>
> *I can't wait to see you again*
>
> *Chase*

Chapter Four

Well, I've made it to Thursday. I am exhausted after working for a week straight and can't wait to have this weekend off. Most of the night crowd has paid and cleared out of the cafe. I am busy helping Amanda roll silverware in napkins. We have been talking about all sorts of things. It gives us a little bit of girl time.

"Good evening, ladies."

The voice coming from behind us is all too familiar. I take a breath in order to prepare myself to look into his dreamy eyes again. This time I am able to hold myself together a little better than the last.

I turn around with my biggest smile. "Hey, Chase."

Amanda looks like she could faint any minute. I reach over and hold her steady by the arm.

"It's okay, Amanda."

She sighs. "Oh my God! I can't believe this! Chase Hartford!"

He smiles. "In the flesh."

I giggle. I don't know why I'm trying to act so composed. I mean, I'm still having a slight problem controlling my emotions about seeing him as well.

She pulls herself together and asks, "How do you like Folly Beach?"

He replies, "It's nice and small."

She smiles, still a little shaken up. "Awesome."

She continues to stand there and stare at him. No doubt she is entranced by his godliness.

He looks over at me. "I'm sorry; I don't mean to be rude, but can I speak with you for a moment? I really don't have much time. I have to be back on set."

I nod. "Sure."

He wants to speak with me? Alone? Oh, geez. I tense up, afraid of what he is about to say. *What if he's here to tell me that he made a mistake sending me the flowers? Or what if he's here to ask me out? Shit! That's impossible. I can understand sending flowers as a nice gesture, but asking me out? Not a chance. I'm not ready for anything like that, anyway. I don't care if it is Chase Hartford.*

He reaches over to shakes Amanda's hand. "It was nice to meet you, Amanda."

She accepts his hand in hers. She blushes. "You too." She turns and walks to the back.

"I hope she didn't think I was being rude."

I shake my head. "No not at all. Um ... I wanted to say thank you for the beautiful flowers you sent me Monday. I was very surprised."

He smiles that big, Chase Hartford smile again. The one that I would make my heart skip a beat on the cover of magazines.

"You're welcome, and I hope you liked them."

"I loved them. They were a perfect Southern mixture." I grab another napkin and begin rolling more silverware. "So what's going on? Is everything okay?"

He nods. "Of course. I was just wanting to stop by and ask you to accompany me for dinner tomorrow night."

What? Dinner? Holy crap! No he's not! I was wrong! He is asking me on a date! This can't be happening! This is way too good to be true!

I gulp, and it takes me a second to answer, "I'd love to."

What, Jo? What the hell happened to not being ready for this? Even if it is Chase Hartford? That was a complete 180.

He smiles again. *Damn, he sure does love to do that. I love for him to do it too. It makes my blood rush through my body and gives me feelings I have never felt before.*

"Wonderful. Can I pick you up around six?"

"Sure. My address is ten-twelve Madison Avenue. Aimee and I live in apartment thirty-three."

"Okay, great."

"Um ... how should I dress?"

"Wear a nice dress if you have it. We're going fine-dining tomorrow night."

He gives me a wink. "Can't wait. See ya," he says.

I get one more smile as he turns to leave.

I'm standing in front of my bathroom mirror, giving myself one last glance before Chase's arrival. My long, brown hair flows in big, loose curls just above my boobs. My red-and-tan sundress is sexy, yet simple. It hugs every curve that I possess. My nude sandals and clutch purse give it just the right touch. It's been a long time since I pulled something like this out of the closet. I'm sure it will work.

I check over the light amount of eyeshadow I have applied to enhance my hazel eyes and the blush on my cheeks. I have apparently tried my best to go for the natural look. Less is definitely more. I apply a small amount of lip gloss and smile. I'm still trying to come to terms that this is happening. It seems very quick. It's almost as if I expect to wake up to realize that it has all been just a dream.

The chime of our doorbell rings. I take what seems like the hundredth deep breath since talking to him yesterday and walk out of the bathroom.

When I open the door, he is standing there, as handsome as ever. He's wearing a pair of khakis with a light-red polo shirt. The seams of his sleeves are tight around his muscular arms. His hair is styled in his signature messy way, and his eyes are larger than life.

We smile at each other.

"Hi," he says in a soft tone.

I look down at my sundress. "Hey. I wonder how we managed to do this."

We both laugh. He throws up his hands. "I don't have a clue, but what I do know is that you look great."

The light shade of pink on my cheeks is overcome with red by my blushing at his compliment.

He holds out his hand for mine. "Ya ready?"

I nod as we walk out, closing the door behind us. Waiting outside the apartment complex is a black limousine. It takes me by surprise, even though I wasn't sure what to expect. The chauffer, dressed nicely in his black suit and tie, opens the door, and we slide inside. The interior is covered in black leather. A flat-screen TV with a surround system is mounted in the corner. There's a mini bar and a small refrigerator in the other corner.

As the limo pulls off, I ask, "Do you have your bodyguards with you?"

"I do most of the time. Boss is riding up front with my chauffer. I have three more waiting at the restaurant for us."

"Oh, I see. Does it get tiring? You know, constantly having men around trying to protect you?"

He shakes his head. "Not really. I get my privacy and everything, but I've needed them many times."

I smile at him. "Do you mind me asking where we're going?"

He gives a mischievous grin. "No, I don't mind, but I'm not going to tell you. I'm sure you will enjoy it."

Oh, no doubt I will. After all, I am eating out with him.

"How did filming go today?"

"It went well. We've almost completed the first episode. I'm excited about it."

"I can't wait to see the show. You'll definitely get a lot of viewers from Folly Beach and Charleston, since the director decided to film here of all places."

"Yeah, I can pretty much count on this area for a high viewer rate. I'm leaving for LA in the morning to promote the series there. I also have a photo shoot for a magazine article they are running. Busy weekend ahead."

He's leaving for Los Angeles? Why do I all of a sudden feel my heart drop?

"How long will you be in LA?"

"I'll be back Tuesday. James, our director, wants to wrap up the first episode as soon as I get back."

I nod. After a fifteen-minute ride, the limo pulls to a stop on the side of the road.

"Well, here we are."

The door suddenly opens with the chauffer holding the door, and Boss waiting. I step out first and spot the restaurant sign. I turn to Chase and smile. "Magnolias?"

Chase smiles back and grabs my hand. "Indeed. Fine Southern dining for a fine Southern girl."

He's a charmer. My heart swells at his words.

"Boss, allow me to introduce you to Jo."

Boss reaches out to shake my hand. "Miss Jo. It is a pleasure. My guys and I are going to make sure that you and Chase have a pleasant dinner together."

I smile. "Nice to meet you, Boss, and thanks."

Wow! What a good feeling!

Chase and I approach the door, with Boss right behind us. Three other muscled men, Zane, Lincoln, and Mac, are standing at the entrance to Magnolias. They welcome us and speak with Chase for a moment while he keeps a firm grip on my hand. I glance around at the busy, downtown Charleston street. Cars are flying past, and people are walking the bars.

We enter Magnolias and step up to the hostess stand. A young girl with long, blonde hair and big blue eyes greets us.

"Good evening and welcome to Magnolias."

She stops for a moment and drowns in Chase's sexiness.

Chase says, "Good evening. We have a reservation for two under Hartford."

For two! The two of us! Hell yes! I just love the sound of it!

She glances down at her reservation sheet.

"Um … yes, Mr. Hartford. You requested private dining?"

Chase nods. "That's correct."

She continues. "We actually reserved the Wine Room for you, since we don't have private rooms for two. It's located in our Upper-Level Gallery if that is all right?"

"Of course. Thanks."

She smiles and points to a well-dressed young guy next to her.

"Wonderful. This is William. He will take you to your table. We hope you enjoy your dining experience at Magnolias."

He smiles. "Thanks again."

Chase still has a firm grip on my hand as we follow William, along with Boss, to the Wine Room. We carefully climb the spiral staircase behind William. He leads us into a room large enough to accommodate thirty-six guests. There is a beautiful bay window overlooking Charleston's historic district. The wood detail is extravagant, and the walls are painted a hunter green. The tables are covered with beautiful white-linen tablecloths, and fresh flower arrangements are perfectly centered. Relaxing vibes of classical music flood the room. I'm not quite sure if it's Mozart, Bach, or Beethoven. William leads us to the table by the window.

"Here you are, Mr. Hartford. Ma'am."

Chase politely pulls out my chair for me to have a seat. I smile. How thoughtful. He has a touch of Southern gentleman in him.

As soon as we are seated, William says, "We have an extensive list of fine wines if you are interested. We have two different dinner menus for you to choose from tonight. Your waiter is Logan. He will be with you shortly, and our executive chef, Daz, will be preparing your meal. Enjoy your evening."

We both nod and thank him.

"Thanks so much for asking me to dinner. This is amazing."

Chase smiles. "It's my pleasure. I'm glad that you accepted the invitation."

Our waiter, Logan, approaches our table. He is wearing a long-sleeve, button-up shirt with the cuffs nicely rolled above the wrist, a brown Firenza banquet vest, a red tie tucked neatly inside, and brown slacks.

"Good evening. Welcome to Magnolias. My name is Logan, and I will be your personal waiter tonight. Have you dined with us before?"

Chase and I both shake our heads.

"No, it's our first time," Chase says delicately.

"Well, we are glad to have you. Would you be interested in looking over our wine list tonight?"

Oh no! I still have a few weeks until I am of legal drinking age. What if he cards me? I mean, it's not like I've never had a drink in a bar before without being carded, but here … Oh, the embarrassment! I turn my attention to Chase, not really sure how to answer. I raise an eyebrow at him and shrug my shoulders.

Chase asks, "Is there a wine you can recommend?"

Well, of course he has no worries; he is twenty-five. Maybe he just knows that it will be cool, since he's so famous and all.

"If you would like a fantastic summer wine, I would recommend the Far Niente Chardonnay Napa 2010. It's a California chardonnay that has the aromas of Meyer lemon and fig. It has a rich texture with flavors of ripe citrus and melon."

"Does that sound good to you, Jo?"

"Um … sure. Sounds lovely."

My nerves are shot! He's going to card me. I just know it. A fancy restaurant like this, they just have to cover their ass.

Logan nods. "Great. Would you like it by the glass or bottle?"

Chase replies, "I'll take your word that it's fantastic, so we'll have a bottle."

"Very well. Here are the two menus that are available for your dining experience tonight. I will give you some time to look over them while I grab your wine."

He hands us the menus and walks away.

"Are you okay, Jo?"

I nod and gulp. "Yeah, I'm fine. I was just a little nervous. I won't be twenty-one for a few more weeks, so I just knew he would card me."

I feel a little embarrassed admitting how I felt.

Chase chuckles. "I understand. It's fine. No worries. I've got you covered."

Apparently so.

"So, you have the weekend off. Any big plans?"

I shake my head. "Not really. I'm sure my friends will hound me to go dancing and bar-hopping with them tomorrow night. They usually do."

"You make it sound like that's a bad thing."

"I don't know. I really don't go out much. The party scene hasn't been my thing for the last year."

He leans back in his chair. "Oh? Why? That is, if you don't mind me asking."

I sigh.

"It's mostly because of school and work."

"You said mostly. There's another reason in there that you're not sharing."

I can't do this. I can't tell him the real reason why I have had such a hard time partying with my friends. He has heard enough of my sad life story. I am certainly not going to bore him and ruin our perfect evening talking about my disaster over dinner.

I throw my hand up at him. "It's nothing really. Maybe one day we can talk about it."

"Okay. I respect that."

"Thanks."

I smile at him. He is so caring and seems so gentle. Why am I here? Why me? Why not some other girl?

He looks down at the menus.

"I guess we need to decide what we want to order. Any ideas of what menu you want to choose from?"

I glance over menu one and two. They both look extremely delicious, and both are high-priced. As I skim the selections I say, "I don't know. They both look amazing. I guess I'm going to lean more towards menu one."

Chase smiles.

"You know, that's exactly what I was leaning towards."

Ah, not only do we take our coffee the same way, but we also pick out the same menu. Genius. I could definitely say that so far we are compatible.

Logan returns with our bottle of wine. He pours us both a glass of the perfectly chilled beverage and sets the bottle down in an ice bucket.

"Did you have time to make a decision on the menu?"

We both nod, and Chase responds, "We are going with menu one."

"Perfect. What would you prefer, ma'am, the creamy tomato bisque or Wadmalaw field green salad?"

I respond. "The salad please."

"Okay. And for your entrée?"

"I'll have the buttermilk fried chicken breast."

"Outstanding. Now that is served with pepper-cracked biscuits, mashed potatoes, collard greens, cream-style corn, and sausage-herb gravy."

I nod. "Sounds wonderful. Thanks."

Logan then turns his attention to Chase. "And for you sir?"

"I'll have the same."

Wow, Jo! Okay here's another indicator of compatibility. We order the same menu item.

Logan gently takes the menus.

"Once you are finished with your entrees, we will serve our Magnolias sweet biscuit. It's an orange-custard anglaise, fresh strawberries, and freshly whipped cream. Our executive chef, Daz, will have your meal prepared shortly."

We both thank him as he turns to leave.

Chase picks up his wine glass. "I would like to make a toast."

A toast? Seriously? A toast to what?

I pick up my wine glass and watch as the pink chardonnay whirls around. I am nervous about what he is going to say.

"Here's a toast to us. May we enjoy this time together, just chilling and getting to know each other better."

We smile and bring our glasses together to a gentle cling. We take a small sip and place them back down on the table.

"Thanks. That was very nice," I say.

"So, I know that during our talk last Sunday night at the cafe that I got to know a little bit about you. What else can you tell me?"

"What would you like to know?" I ask.

"Well, where you're originally from? What brought you to Folly Beach? Really, anything you want to tell me. I'm very interested."

He's very blunt. I am melting in my chair. I feel that soon there will be a puddle of me on the well-cleaned carpet below. He's interested. *Very* interested, I might add.

"I'm originally from Highlands, North Carolina. I was born and raised there. When we lost our parents in the plane crash, Sam and I moved to Folly Beach to live with our grandparents. I attended James Island Middle School, and then moved on to James Island Charter High School. Sam died my sophomore year of high school. My grandma, Annie, died early last year. My grandpa, Thomas, still lives in their old farmhouse in the country outside of Folly Beach. I go to visit and eat with him as often as I can."

Chase says, "You know, you seem to be a very strong girl to have been through all you've been through. I want you to know that I really admire you."

I smile. "Thanks. I admit it's been real hard, but I have a goal to accomplish in memory of my brother. I really believe that's what keeps me going. I find myself angry that he had to die so young. I find myself angry about a lot of things, but then, come to realize that there's nothing I can do to change what has happened to those I loved so much."

"I can't imagine. You don't have to talk about this. I'm sure you would rather discuss something on a happier note. How did you like living in Folly Beach at a young age?"

I reply, "It was an adjustment from waking up to the mountains to getting used to the coast. I soon learned to like it. I had Sam at the time and my grandparents. They were so good to us. There was nothing they wouldn't do for us."

"Did you already have friends there, since you would visit your grandparents before?"

I nod. "Yeah, Sam and I both had a great group of friends. We would see them over the summer and during school breaks when we would visit. Having them made it a little easier for us to move there, but we missed our friends back home."

"Do you keep in touch with any of them?"

"I do. Several of them have moved to other states to attend college. We text and talk a good bit."

"What about school? Were you involved in any sports or activities?"

"Actually, I was. I played softball in middle school, and I was a cheerleader all through high school."

"Softball and cheerleading, huh?"

"Yeah, but my favorite sport is football."

He raises an eyebrow and smiles. "Really?"

"Yeah."

"You didn't play?" he asks jokingly.

I laugh. "No! My grandpa would have had a heart attack. He was doing good just to let me put on a cheerleading uniform."

Chase laughs in return. "Ha. Grandparents can be a trip. What about college football? Any favorite teams?"

"I love watching Georgia."

He gives me a look of shock.

"Why Georgia?"

"Both of my parents graduated from UGA. My mom was from North Carolina, and my dad from Folly. They met on campus."

"Oh, okay. So that's where they fell in love. I understand. They are a good team. I'm just not a big football guy. I hardly ever have the time to sit and watch like I would like to. What about clubs? Were you involved in anything like that in high school?"

"I was on the debate team, a member of the Beta Club, yearbook staff, and student council. I was also valedictorian."

"Wow! That's very impressive. So I'm here with a very smart and talented girl working hard for a future in fighting cancer."

I'm beet red again. *I wonder how many times my cheeks have turned red since I've met him?*

"I wouldn't say that, but the future in fighting cancer is definitely true."

We both take a moment to sip more wine. Logan returns with our salads. The greens look delicious and are covered with lemon-lingonberry vinaigrette.

Logan asks, "Is there anything I can get the two of you? Can I pour you more wine?"

Chase replies, "We are good. Thanks, Logan."

Logan nods. "Enjoy your salad. Your entrees will be out shortly."

I grab my napkin and gently place it in my lap like the well-raised Southern girl I am. I pick up my salad fork and get ready to dive in.

Chase quickly asks, "Do you mind if we say grace?"

What? Grace? He wants to pray. I am shocked! I mean, I think it's so awesome that he wants to bless our food, but I just didn't expect it.

I gently put down my fork and nod.

"Are you comfortable with me doing it?" he asks.

I reply. "Yes, please do."

We bow our heads and close our eyes.

"Dear Father in heaven, I just want to take this opportunity to thank you for all the blessings in life. Thank you for allowing me to meet such a wonderful girl of whom, in such a short time of knowing her, I admire so much. I ask that you guide her in her ambitions and continue to be with her through all walks of life. I thank you, Lord, for this food, and pray that we strive to make your presence known in the lives of others. For it is in your most gracious name I pray. Amen."

Wow. I'm lost for words. He is wonderful. Who would have thought that he would take the time to pray on our dinner date?

We lift our heads, open our eyes, and smile at one another. I reach for my fork again to attempt to eat my salad.

"Okay, so let's turn the table around. What about you, Chase? Tell me some things about you. I mean I know the crazy stuff that you read in magazines, but I want the real story. Straight from the source."

He chuckles at me. "Is this an interview?"

I laugh back. "No. As a fan, I'm interested."

"Oh, so you're a fan, huh?"

"Not just any fan, a long-time fan."

He stops chuckling, and we smile. For the brief moment of silence, I feel myself getting lost in his blue-gray, dreamy eyes again.

"Well, what is it you want to know about me, long-time fan?"

I shrug my shoulders. "Anything you want to share. I'm all ears." I take a bite of my salad.

"Okay, let me re-ask the question. What do you not know about me already?"

"Not a whole lot."

"Then why don't you tell me what you know, and then I'll fill you in on the rest."

I put down my fork. "You're really asking me to do that? It's going to make me sound all stalker and stuff."

He bursts into laughter. I can't help but laugh with him. "Yes, I'm really asking you to do it."

I sigh. "Okay, if you fear for your life afterwards then I will completely understand."

He laughs more. I knew I would have fun, but I'm having such a great time with him.

"Your full name is Chase Deacon Hartford. You were born on April 10, 1989, in Louisiana to Bradley and Linda Hartford. You have an older sister, Mary, and a younger brother, Cameron. You enjoyed modeling as a child, and eventually turned to acting. I know all the movies you have starred in and all the TV shows you were a guest star on. I have every clipping and article from every magazine you have ever been in. I know all the awards you have won during your career. Your hobbies are reading, traveling the world, and supporting various charities. Now, is that enough to portray me as the perfect stalker or what?"

His eyes are wide in amazement. "It does freak me out a little bit."

Oh shit! I knew I shouldn't have told him all this! I've completely blown it! I'm such a dumbass!

He smiles. "I'm just kidding."

I smile with embarrassment. "I can keep going, but why should I tell you things you already know."

"Okay so you do know a lot about me. Now let me think what you don't know that you need to know."

He sits with a contemplating look on his face.

"I can answer that. I want to know *you*."

Oh my God! I just said that out loud! Where the hell did that come from? My brave side must be coming out. Damn it, Jo!

His contemplating look turns to serious. I'm not sure how to read his expression right now. I gulp and look down at my hands.

He says, "I want to know you too, Jo."

I pick my eyes up to meet his. We hold each other's stare for a moment.

Suddenly Logan appears with our entrees.

"All right. We have your entrees all prepared for you."

He sets the plates down.

"How was the salad?"

Chase replies, "It was great, Logan. Thanks."

"I'll take those out of the way for you. Can I pour you both some more wine now?"

I nod. "Yes, please."

Logan adds some wine to our glasses.

"Is there anything else I can get you?"

We look around the table and shake our heads.

"I believe we're good for now, Logan," Chase answers.

"Splendid. I hope you enjoy your meal. I'll be back to check on you in just a little bit."

He turns and exits the room.

Chase and I start to dig into our fried chicken. It's the best that has ever touched my taste buds. My grandma would be envious of this recipe.

We continue talking and laughing through the remainder of our dinner and wine. The dessert was to die for. We decide to stay longer and drink coffee. I can honestly say my first fine-dining experience was definitely intriguing. I could get used to it.

Chase pays the bill and gives Logan a generous tip. The time has slipped away from us. We enjoyed our time together so much that we didn't realize we had already spent four hours in the private dining room. Logan leads us out and back, down the spiral stairs. Boss follows.

As we exit the restaurant, several girls catch a glimpse of Chase. They rush over with pens and napkins, hoping to get an autograph. Boss protects us while the other bodyguards keep the girls at a safe distance. Chase speaks with them for a brief moment and agrees to sign autographs. I find it sweet that he takes time for his fans. He grabs a hold of my hand, and we dive into the limo. The chauffer closes the door, and we are off to my apartment.

When we arrive, Chase tells Boss that he wants to walk me up and that he will be back shortly. I am excited, yet nervous. I don't know what to expect from him when we reach my door. I contemplate whether I should invite him in or not. Will he come in? Will he leave right away? I know that he has an early morning flight, and that he needs his rest.

We reach my door, still holding hands. I don't want to let go. I want to feel it wrapped in mine forever. They fit so perfectly together.

I turn to face him.

"Thanks so much for everything tonight. I really enjoyed every minute of it."

He smiles. "I'm so glad that you did. When I get back from LA, we will definitely have to get together again. That is if you want to?"

I nod and smile back. "Of course. Just let me know."

He reaches in his pocket and pulls out his iPhone.

"Here let me get your number so I can call you when I get back in town."

Oh my God! He wants my number! My number is going to be in Chase Hartford's cell phone!

I pull myself together and call out my number.

I watch as his fingers delicately type my name under his contacts and my number.

"Okay, great. I'll text you later so you will have mine."

I nod.

"Well, I guess I'm off. It was wonderful spending time with you tonight."

There go my cheeks again. There goes a big gulp down my throat. Can I be any more obvious about how nervous I am?

"I can't wait for next time."

His smile gets bigger. "Me either."

"Have a safe flight."

He nods and grabs a hold of my right hand. "Thanks. Good night."

He leans in and gently places a kiss on my right cheek. My body turns to mush. Mush like the oatmeal that Goldilocks finds in the bear family's bowls. He pulls away, and our eyes meet. Hazel and blue gray. What a mixture. He slowly lets go of my hand, and I watch until he is out of sight.

Chapter Five

It's Saturday morning, and I'm lying in bed reliving every moment from last night. The smiles that Chase and I exchanged. The conversation. My hand in his. The soft kiss he planted on my cheek. The way his voice said good night. I could lie here all day and picture it over and over.

I glance over at the clock. It's nine. I never stay in bed this late, even on the weekends. I'm surprised that Aimee hasn't barged into check on me and get a full description of every word said and move made last night.

Suddenly my cell phone starts to ring. I sit up and grab it off the nightstand. I look down and see that it's a number I don't recognize. I hit the answer button.

"Hello."

"Good morning, sunshine."

His voice brings a bright smile to my face. That and the fact that he called me *sunshine*!

"Chase. Good morning."

"I didn't wake you did I?" he asks.

I sit even straighter up in bed and prop against my pillows.

"No, of course not. I've just been lying here thinking. Are you on the way to the airport?"

He replies, "I am. I just wanted to call so you would have my number instead of texting it. I also wanted to wish you good morning and to tell you again how much I enjoyed last night."

My smile gets bigger and brighter.

"Aw, thanks. That's sweet of you. I really enjoyed it too."

"There's another reason I was calling too."

"Really? What's that?"

41

"I want to encourage you to go out with your friends if they decide to party tonight. You said you haven't been in the party scene for the last year. I need you to brush up on some dancing, since I plan on taking you to do just that when I get back."

"Well, I might just see what they have planned. You better believe I'm an excellent dancer, so you don't have to worry about that. The only thing you do need to worry about is me having the nerve to get out on the dance floor in front of you."

He laughs. "Oh, come on, Jo. You can certainly dance around me. I'll bust some moves with you. I love it."

I laugh back. "Okay sounds like a deal."

"All right well I'm going to go. I'm about five miles from the airport. Have a great weekend. I'll see you as soon as I get back."

"Sounds great. Be careful and have fun in LA."

"Thanks I will. Talk to you later."

"Bye."

"Bye."

I hang up and take a breath. I'm so excited I got to hear his voice first thing this morning. I add him to my contacts. His name looks amazing listed on the screen. I put my phone back down on the nightstand.

There's a knock on my door. It's Aimee. She is here to do exactly what I predicted earlier.

"Come in, Aimee."

The door swings open. She stands there with a cup of coffee in hand. Steam rolls from the top of the mug.

"Morning, Jo. I was wondering if you were going to wake up anytime soon. I'm not used to you staying in bed like this, ya know. I brought you some coffee."

I smile at her.

"Thanks. I'm wide awake this morning. I really don't need it, but I'll certainly take it."

She hands me the cup and sits down at the foot of my bed.

"All right so you know why I'm here. Spill it. Tell me everything about dinner last night."

I take a small sip and set the coffee to the side.

"It was wonderful. It was everything I would have dreamed of for a first date with a famous, sexy movie star."

She smiles, waving her hand at me to keep talking. "Keep going."

I reply, "Well, he wanted to know some more about me. We talked about him. The food was fabulous. We had wine with dinner and stayed late, talking over coffee. He signed a few autographs for some girls when we left. Then he brought me home."

"What time did you get home?"

"It was around eleven thirty."

"Wow! You mean y'all spent four hours at Magnolias?"

I nod. "Yeah, we kind of got carried away with conversation."

"I'd say so. Did he come in when he brought you home?"

I shake my head. "No. I thought about inviting him in, but I knew he was leaving this morning on a flight to LA, so I didn't ask."

"Any juicy details about the goodbye?"

I blush. "He gave me a kiss on the cheek."

She rolls her eyes with disappointment. "A kiss on the cheek? Seriously? That's it?"

"Well, so sorry to disappoint, Aimee. I, on the other hand, happened to like it. His lips. They were so soft and gentle."

I think back again to last night. Oh, wonderful it was!

Aimee leans forward and smirks.

"Yeah, well, imagine those lips on your lips. Next time fill me in on the goodbyes when a granny kiss isn't involved."

I roll my eyes back at her. "Oh, whatever. I thought it was sweet. He seems to be a real gentleman. You know the kind of guy that doesn't move fast."

"It's not like if he was the type of guy that liked to move fast that you would shoot him down or anything. I mean, for crying out loud, he is Chase Hartford."

I shrug my shoulders. "I don't know. I mean, even with him, I wouldn't want to do something that I would later regret. I want him to respect me."

She shrugs her shoulders as well. "So he's off to LA, huh?"

"Yep. He has a ten o'clock flight. He'll be back Tuesday."

"Okay. Well, thanks for sharing. Like I said, next time try to have more juicy details. It would certainly make it more interesting."

She stands and walks toward the door.

I ask, "Do you and the girls have plans tonight?"

She turns to look at me. "Yeah, we're going to Trio Club."

"I think I'm going to join y'all."

She raises her eyebrows. "Really?"

I smile with a nod. "Yeah. I feel like dancing."

She smiles back at me. "Awesome. We're leaving around ten tonight."

"Great. Sounds fun."

The heat from all the bodies at Trio Club almost makes the dance floor unbearable. Aimee, Alex, Kelly, and I are happily demonstrating our best moves. The disco balls spin, throwing cosmic colors all around us. Carly Rae Jepsen's "Call Me Maybe" blares from the surrounding speakers. Aimee and I throw our heads back and roll our eyes around while Carly Rae sings her "this is crazy" line, along with our fake phone imitation to our ear during "so call me maybe." *I am loving this!* I have almost forgotten how good it feels to be out partying with my friends. I can feel sweat beading all over my face.

Aimee screams over the music, "Let's go get a drink!"

I nod as she pushes our way through the dancers. Alex and Kelly follow.

The bartender meets us as we approach the bar. "What can I get you ladies?"

Aimee replies, "We need four Bud Lights please."

He lines up the four beers and pops the top on each. "That'll be eight bucks, ladies."

We each hand him some money as Alex says, "There's nothing like ladies night and two-dollar Bud Light."

We all smile and walk over to a nearby table.

Kelly takes a sip from her bottle and asks, "So, Jo, when was the last time you talked to Chase?"

"This morning. He was getting ready to catch his flight to LA."

"You should text him a picture. He wanted you to get out and enjoy yourself. Show him how much fun you're having."

I smile.

"Oh, why not. Why don't y'all come over here and stand by me. I want all of us in the pic."

Alex and Kelly come to stand beside Aimee and me. I hold my Galaxy out to snap the picture.

"All right, ladies. Say cheese."

We all say cheese simultaneously with big smiles, and my phone flashes as it takes the picture.

I check it. The four of us look amazing, standing together in our sexy dresses. The girls give a look of approval. I pull Chase's name up under my contacts and type a text message to go along with the picture.

"Girls' night out! Having a blast! ☺*"*

I press send. There's a quick response from Chase.

"Wow! U ladies look awesome! Glad ur having fun Jo ☺*"*

Oh, a smiley right back. I smile down at the text. I type a response.

"Thanks & thanks for the advice. Didn't realize how much I've missed this ☺*"*

"No problem! Can't wait 2 be back 2 c u ;)*"*

Wow! Now a wink! I'd give anything for him to be here, right now, winking at me with one of his big, dreamy, blue-gray eyes. My heart swells with each pulsating beat. I am blushing and have no doubt it is noticeable even in the faint light of the club.

"I can't wait 2 c u too! ;) *Hope ur enjoying L.A."*

"I am. Be bk on the east coast soon. Get home safe tonight ☺*"*

"Sounds gr8 and I will ☺*"*

As I place my phone in my clutch, all I can think about is how Tuesday can't get here fast enough.

It's Tuesday night, and I haven't heard from Chase yet. He never told me exactly when he would be arriving back at Folly Beach today. I reprimand myself for not thinking to ask him. No. It's probably a good thing I didn't. I wouldn't want him to think I'm desperate. Suppose he didn't tell me for a reason. Maybe he decided, while in LA, that he would like to get back and have some time alone. Time to think. Think about the short time we have spent together and how it is pointless. Pointless to share his time with an average girl who has been through hell and is just another fan. I try to rid my head of the thought.

I glance over at my clock. It's six thirty. I suppose I could shower and try to relax. My brain is not able to focus right now on what I will wear to see Dr. Black tomorrow. The only thing that has my wheels spinning is if and when I will hear from Chase.

As I close my closet door, I hear the chimes of the doorbell. Probably Kevin. He is supposed to come over tonight. Suddenly I hear Aimee scream. I bolt for my bedroom door and swing it open. I run down the hall as fast as I can to the living room.

Aimee is standing there with her hands over her mouth, and in the doorway he stands. I don't know if the swift beats of my heart are evidence of my qualifying Olympic dash from my bedroom or the sight of him looking as handsome as last Friday night. I smile through heavy breaths.

Aimee turns to look at me. She is still flabbergasted that Chase is at the door. I wonder if she will be able to speak. That will be a first. Ha! I laugh inside.

"Chase. What a surprise," I say as I continue panting.

He smiles his big makes-my-body-melt smile.

"Hi, Jo. Sorry I didn't call. I wanted to surprise you."

I need to put blushing at the top of my list for things I do best.

Aimee finally removes her hands from her mouth and says, "Oh my God. I'm so sorry. I am so embarrassed. I didn't mean to scream. I just didn't expect to open the door, and it be you. Are you all right? Can you hear okay?"

Chase laughs with a nod. "Yeah, I'm fine. My ears are used to the screaming."

"I really am sorry." Aimee's embarrassment is expressed greatly. "I think I need to try this the right way."

She reaches her hand out to Chase. "Hi. I'm Aimee Smith."

Chase takes her hand. "Hi, Aimee. It's nice to meet you."

She is about to melt into a puddle. Just like me and every other girl that has had the opportunity to touch his heavenly skin.

I walk over next to them. "It's great to see you made it back safely. How was LA?"

He turns his attention to me. "Wonderful, thanks. I really hope you don't mind that I stopped by without calling."

I shake my head with the corners of my mouth stretched far enough to touch my ears. "No, not at all. I'm glad you're here."

I study him. His plain white T-shirt is tight-fitting, with his dark denim jeans hanging just off his waist and long enough to brush the straps of his brown flip-flops. *Man, he has gorgeous toes. Go figure!*

"I was headed for a walk on the beach and wanted to stop by and see if you'd like to join me?"

Wow. First a surprise visit, and now a walk alone on the beach. What do I make of this? I look down at my clothes. I'm wearing an old Earth Day T-shirt and gray sweatpants. Oh, he shouldn't see me like this. I realize that now I am embarrassed by my appearance.

"In case you're wondering, you look great just the way you are."

Damn! He noticed.

"I'd love to go with you."

I step over to the door and slip on my black Rainbow flip-flops.

Aimee smiles at us.

"Well, I'll let you two get to it. Nice to have you in town, Chase. Good luck with the show."

He nods and smiles back at her. "Thanks, Aimee."

She turns and heads for the kitchen.

Chase and I head out the door and walk down the breezeway to the elevator together. When we reach the parking lot, Chase pulls out a set of keys and walks up to a silver Toyota Prius. There is the beep of the security lock, and he opens the passenger-side door. He waves his hand to the seat and says, "Ladies first."

I smile at him and slide in. He closes the door and, within seconds, he is sitting in the driver seat next to me. I gaze around at the inside of the car.

"Is this yours?" I ask.

He shakes his head while putting the key into the ignition. "Nah. I do rentals when I travel, unless of course I am flying to one of my homes. I have cars at all of my residences. The rentals really help keep me undercover. This is the last thing most people would expect me to drive."

I wonder how many homes he has now. Not that I care or that it matters. Just curious, since I really don't know *everything* about him, and the fact that it has been a few years since I kept up with him and all the star gossip.

"So what cars do you drive? That is if you don't mind me asking."

He glances over at me. "I don't mind, Jo. You can ask me anything."

I don't know how to respond, or if I should at all. My eyes meet his. We hold our stare for a brief moment. I smile again and look away nervous.

"I have several cars. I have an Audi Q7 in LA because it seats seven, and my friends and I go partying in it a lot. I have a Mercedes SL63 coupe in Key West because it's perfect for living at the beach, and a Hummer H2 in Denver because it's great for mountain life. Oh, and I have an antique 1966 Ford Mustang at my home in LA for cruising."

"I love old Mustangs. I've always wanted one. A red one."

"That's funny because my Mustang is red."

He shoots me a quick smile while focusing on the road. *Oh, another thing that makes us compatible.* This just keeps getting better and better.

"So, apparently you have homes in all these places because you enjoy them."

He nods. "Yeah, for sure. They are just a few of my favorite places. There's just something about being in the middle of the crazy city life with all the huge clubs, fancy restaurants, and architecture. Then there's also something about waking up to the sound of the waves and feeling the sand between your toes. And looking out at a fascinating mountain range first thing in the morning, fishing next to a ravaging stream, and roasting marshmallows on a fire pit."

I sigh, thinking how I've only been to Virginia, the Carolinas, and Florida. I'm sure I couldn't count on my fingers and toes all the places he's been.

"That all sounds amazing. I wish I could say I've been to those places, but I haven't."

"So where all have you been?" he asks.

"Well, I've been to Jamestown and Williamsburg, Virginia. My parents took Sam and me to see the way of colonial life. I've been skiing in Virginia. The mountains in North Carolina are pretty, but are nothing compared to the ones in Colorado. I've been to Florida, but never to any of the beaches."

"We might have to change that one day."

He looks at me with softness in his eyes. His face serious.

He pulls up at the Folly Beach State Park area and slowly coasts the Prius into a parking spot. With no other cars or people in sight, the beach looks stranded. I'm sure that's a good thing, and it makes him feel comfortable being without Boss and his other bodyguards. I wonder how often he does venture out without them.

I am suddenly distracted by the alert of a text message coming from my phone. I reach down in my bag and pull it out. I smile over at Chase. He has turned off the ignition and is eyeing me.

"I'm sorry, let me see who this is."

"No, please, don't mind me. Go ahead."

I look down and notice that it's from Aimee.

"Okay, I know that I shouldn't be bothering u right now but I must say he is ten thousand times HOTTER in person and u r one lucky bitch! ;)"

Great, Aimee, thanks. Why couldn't she wait and tell me this when I get back? The last thing I need is to be stuck in a texting convo with her. Geez. I text her a quick message.

"I'm very aware, and thanks! We just got to the beach. See u later tonight ☺"

There. Hopefully that will let her know that I am in no mood to text, and I will certainly not turn my attention away from the hottest guy on earth. I put my Galaxy back in my bag and decide at that point to leave it in the car.

"It was Aimee. I'm ready now."

"Is everything okay?"

"Sure."

"All right, let's go for a stroll. Wait just a second, and I'll get your door for you."

He jumps out quickly. Obviously he is showing his gentleman side again. First the chair at the restaurant, then the simple, sweet kiss good night on the cheek, now opening and closing doors. This is far more than I ever imagined with him. It's safe to admit to myself now that even though I was always overcome by his sexiness that I really felt that he would be the world's biggest asshole with all his money and fame. He has proven that part of me wrong. *Shame on you, Jo, for thinking that.*

When the door swings open, he reaches out for my hand. I smile and welcome it. Even as he closes the door, he holds on to it tightly. He's not letting go? My heart beats rapidly.

We walk over to the sand and slide off our flip-flops, still hand in hand. His is so warm, and it engulfs my own. There is a gentle breeze blowing with the sweet smell of summer. His dark messy hair blows with it.

"Isn't it beautiful out here?"

I nod and reply. "Yeah. When I come here I think about all the wonderful times Sam and I had when we would come to visit my grandparents. He loved the beach. We would build these magnificent sandcastles together and go ghost-crab hunting at night. Even after my parents died, and Sam was sick with leukemia, we would still come out here and spend time together. We had so many laughs, the two of us. He was a very special kid."

I feel the sadness swell up inside me while thinking of my little brother. However, it doesn't seem to be as suffocating standing here with Chase. It's almost as if there is a comfort inside of me with him that I have never felt before. It's odd.

Chase gives my hand a gentle squeeze.

"I wish I could have met him."

"I wish you could have too. He would like you a lot. My parents would too."

We slowly head a little closer to the shore and begin walking in the direction of the Folly Beach Pier.

"Jo, you know how I told you earlier that you can ask me anything?"

"Yeah."

"Well, I want you to know that you can also tell me anything. Anything and everything you want to share. I have never met a girl like you. I'm so captivated by you. I want to know so much about who you are."

"I can't believe you don't think I'm crazy or something. I've been pretty messed up for quite some time."

It's true. I have been. The loss of my family has been extremely hard for me over the years, and then the rape just made things even more unbearable.

"I don't think you're crazy. You're strong and courageous. You have a dream in life that you are very compassionate about. I envy that."

"I'm weaker than you think, and I'm certainly not courageous. I'm afraid. I fear being hurt. I fear my future and all the things in it, even though I want them so badly."

We continue at a slow pace, still hand in hand. Never in a million years have I imagined I would be here in this moment with him.

"What are you afraid of that could hurt you?" he asks with a concerned tone.

I reply, "The future. My dreams. Falling in love."

He stops and turns to face me, not letting go of my hand.

"I wish I knew enough to understand why you fear those things. I believe that they should all be something to look forward to. They should all be things to go after."

I shrug my shoulders. "Look I don't want this to sound cheesy and all, but I'm still finding all of this so hard to believe. The fact that you are here, but most of all that you are here with me. I'm just an average girl that has a lot of issues, normal ambitions, and I honestly don't understand why you would even remotely want to take the time to get to know me. Deep down, you must think I'm just another fan or a real nutcase."

He shakes his head. "No. No. I don't think that at all. There's something different about you. Something special. I knew that the very first night we met at the cafe. I was drawn to you. Your life. Your ambition."

I shake my head.

"I don't understand. This is all so confusing. I don't know what to think or how to feel."

He grabs my other hand. We are standing at the edge of the water, looking into one another's eyes. Oh, the hazel and blue-gray together. Again what a combination. I'm sure it's a wonderful one.

He sighs and glances down at our hands. "I may not understand where this is going, but I do know one thing. Despite what I do know about you, there is something you are hiding. Something that has you trapped."

What? I stand there, bewildered by the words that have just escaped his lips. *He acts like he's here to save me.* No, he's here to film a TV series and move on with his life. He's not here to worry about me and my problems.

"Chase, I don't expect you to save me from anything, and I definitely don't want to drown you in all my personal matters."

"I want you to open up and tell me what is making you afraid of all the wonderful things you should experience and have in life. You can trust me."

I sigh and ask, "Haven't you heard enough depressing details about my life?"

He shakes his head again. "No, and I want to know more. Deep down, I know there's more. If only I knew. I want to help. Whatever it is that happened to make you shut out the possibilities of feeling and falling in love, I want to know. You're young and beautiful, and you deserve it more than anyone."

I can feel tears form behind my eyes. I fight them. I can't cry. He can't see me cry. The words he has just spoken are chiseling away at my heart. No one has ever said anything like that to me before. I can trust him. Can't I?

Chase looks down for a spot to sit in the sand. I sit beside him.

"Last year, I went to a party with Aimee, Kelly, and Alex. It was right before the end of fall semester in December. We were out at a barn in the country off of Chandler Road. There was a big bonfire. There was a huge crowd of people. Most of them we knew from campus, but the occasional strangers would stop by and scope out the party. We were all drinking, of course. Later on that night, I started feeling a little queasy from having too much. I wanted to get away from everyone because I knew I was about to be sick. I walked off away from the fire toward the woods. I didn't want anyone to see me to save my embarrassment."

I take a breath trying to pull myself together to finish. "This guy appeared out of nowhere and asked me if I was all right and needed any help. I was so drunk. I felt funny. Dizzy. Confused. I told him that I thought I would be okay, and that I just needed a break from the party. I couldn't get a good look at him because it was dark. All I remember after that is waking up in the woods. I was lying on the ground. I was cold, and my head was throbbing. When I finally realized where I was, I sat up and noticed that my pants were down around my ankles, and there was blood."

Chase's face has a strong look of hurt and anger. His eyes are filled with remorse and pain. I see it in them clearly.

"I was raped. I was raped by some random guy that the police figured had watched me at the party and spiked my drink."

Chase pulls me into his chest. His embrace is calming. It's comforting. I feel safe in his arms. I want to stay there forever and drown in his smell.

Melt in his touch. But is that really the right thing to want and the right thing to feel?

"I lost my family to things I had no control over and my virginity to someone I did not know or love."

He lays his head on mine as I sink further into his chest and shoulder.

"I'm so sorry that this happened to you. I wish I could erase it for you. I wish that I could make it all go away."

"I'm dealing with it. I'll be all right. It's getting better day by day."

He pulls me away and rests his hands on my shoulders. He looks into my eyes. "You didn't deserve this. It's not your fault. Any of it."

I nod. "I know. Really, I do."

"Thanks for telling me. I don't want you to feel pressured to tell me things that make you uncomfortable."

I nod again. "I know. I want to tell you. I just don't want to overwhelm you with all my problems. I don't want to turn you away. I've been afraid that you might really think I'm some crazy, screwed-up girl."

"No, never. I would never think that. Did they ever find out who the guy was?"

I shake my head. "No, they didn't. He was extremely careful. He used protection and discarded it so they weren't able to run any tests or anything like that. I've been going to counseling for that, along with the deaths of my family."

He pulls my chin up with his hand to where our eyes meet. The blue-gray sends a welcoming shiver down to my toes. I am paralyzed. I am lost in them. He scoots in a little closer to me.

"I'm here for you. I'm here to listen to whatever you need to talk about. It doesn't matter what it is. I will never judge you."

I give him a small smile. His hand is soft.

"Thanks. That means a lot."

He leans in and plants a sweet, gentle kiss on my cheek. I close my eyes, savoring the touch of his lips on my skin. This is heaven. He slowly pulls away, and, with his arm draped around my shoulder, we sit together quietly and stare at the calm ocean.

Chapter Six

I flip through the pages of *People* magazine. Soothing spa music pours from the speakers in Dr. Black's waiting room. I am nervous. Nervous about my session with Dr. Black. I haven't seen her in several weeks, and so much has happened. I can't help but wonder what she will say about everything. About meeting Chase. Spending time with him.

Dr. Black's office door opens, and a young married couple walks out. She bids them farewell and glances over at me and smiles.

"Joanna."

I place the magazine back on the rack and walk over. "Hey, Dr. Black."

She points to her office. "Please come in and have a seat."

I walk into the huge office and sit down on the couch. This room has been like my second home since last December. There was a time when I thought they would have a bed permanently placed for me in here or just admit me to the nearest psych ward. Fortunately, it never came to that. I had her. She helped me through it all. She helped me mostly through the tough beginning. Now it's about staying on the recovery path.

Dr. Black is dressed in a black skirt that just brushes the tops of her knees. Her white blouse is accented with a black, beaded necklace, and her pumps are to die for. Of course I'd fall all over myself if I even attempted to wear them. Her hair is placed neatly in a bun at the top of her head. Quite the psychologist look.

She sits down in her big leather armchair across from me and smiles. "So, Joanna. How have you been?"

I reply, "Good. Doing well."

"Well, that's wonderful to hear. What has been going on the last few weeks?"

I shrug my shoulders. "Pretty much the usual. Work. I am registered for fall semester. It starts the end of August."

She nods. "Great. I know you're excited about this being your last year before transferring to MUSC. Are you thinking about what you plan to do in May, as far as moving goes?"

"I'm leaning towards staying at Folly Beach. I figured, since I already make the commute to campus now, that it's not going to be any different once I'm at MUSC. Plus I enjoy working at the cafe, so I'd like to stay on there as well."

She writes on her big legal pad as I chatter away. She looks up above the frames of her glasses. "Having any fun? Going out with the girls?"

I nod. "Yeah, actually I went out last Saturday night dancing."

She looks up and smiles brightly. "That's awesome, Joanna. Great news. Good to hear that you are getting out and enjoying yourself. No doubt that was a big step for you."

"Well, I had a little encouragement, but I did have a great time."

She repeats, "Encouragement?"

"Yes. I had someone encourage me to get out and try to have some fun with the girls. I went, and I was glad I did. I had almost forgotten how good it felt to cut loose."

"And who is the person responsible for this?"

Oh, dear. I wonder how she is going to respond once I tell her. "You probably won't believe it."

"Please do tell," she says.

"Chase Hartford."

I say his name like I'm admitting to my mother that I've been talking to the bad boy across town. It's just the fact that he is this famous movie star, and every girl wants him. People get the impression that famous people fall in and out of love quickly. I know what Dr. Black is thinking: I'm just another one of them. Another fling on his list of women.

"I see. So you've met him already?"

"Yes. Just a little over a week ago."

"What all does he know about you, Joanna?"

I'm afraid to tell her. What will she say? Even though she's my doctor, she has also been like a mother figure to me. She has helped me through so much. Will she think I'm crazy for telling him about all the things I have been through? I don't want a lecture, and she has lectured me before, but in a caring way.

"Pretty much everything."

She nods with a disapproving look on her face. "I see. And you feel comfortable with him knowing so many intimate details about your past, your life in such a short period of time?"

I nod back at her. "Yes, I do. I know you may find that difficult to believe, but I feel like I can share things with him. He wants me to. He's not anything like I ever expected him to be."

"And how exactly did you expect him to be, Joanna?" she asks.

"Well, despite his gorgeous looks on the outside, I expected him to be this hot-shot asshole of a guy who is rich and famous. I thought him to be rude and intimidating. I know that magazines and TV make him appear the opposite of that by showing all his generous acts, but you never really know a person until you meet them. He is actually quite wonderful."

"Where did you meet him?"

Her pen moves quickly but delicately across her pad again.

"Sunday night, a week ago, at the cafe. He came in for coffee before closing."

"How soon did you tell him about your parents, Sam, and the party?"

"Well, he found out about my parents and Sam when he was at the cafe. He sat at the bar and talked with me for about half an hour. He was just curious about Folly Beach, since he had never been here before, and curious about me. I didn't tell him about the party until last night."

"What did you do last night?"

Geez. She's asking a lot of questions. Why is she so concerned? It's not like I'm talking to the devil or anything.

"He stopped by and wanted to know if I would like to join him for a walk on the beach. It was then that I told him."

"What led to you having that conversation with him?"

"He told me that I could tell him anything, and that he wanted to know all about me. He said that I could trust him, and that he could sense that I was hurting inside about something."

"Okay. I understand. So, you told him about the incident, and what did he say?"

I reply, "He hugged me and told me that he was sorry that I have been through so much. He wished he could erase it. Take it all away. He said that I deserve so much in life."

She nods in agreement. "Yes, Joanna, you do. You have been through more in your life than most adults. My main concern here is that I don't want you to get hurt. You are very aware of who he is. You know that he has had several long-lasting relationships in the past. They have all been with famous women."

I look down at my hands. My fingers are tangled together in a nervous gesture. I manage a small gulp.

"Look, Joanna. I'm not saying this to upset or hurt you. That is not my intention. I just know what you have been through over the years. I don't want this guy to take advantage of you. It doesn't matter who he is."

"I understand, Dr. Black. I also understand that there's something about the way he makes me feel. I realize that I have only known him personally for a very short amount of time, but he makes me feel open. At first I didn't really want to share anything about me, but now I honestly feel I can."

"Joanna, I'm glad he makes you feel that way. That's progress for you. However, I don't want this to turn into something that is only going to last while he's here on set, and then you end up heartbroken when he leaves."

I nod. "I understand."

She's right. What am I going to do when he is done filming, and he leaves Folly Beach? The thought had never really occurred to me. I've been so wrapped up in the few moments that we have shared together that I never let the idea of him leaving cross my mind.

She puts her pad and pencil down on the table next to her chair. She folds her hands and lays them gently in her lap. One leg crosses the other. "Now I'm not saying that you shouldn't see him and enjoy spending time with him. If it's good for you, then that's great. But what I am saying is that you probably shouldn't read too much into it and get yourself wrapped up. Just be careful and think about what you're doing. You are in control of your feelings. Most importantly, you are in control of your heart."

I nod again and turn my attention to her. "I trust him. I know that sounds crazy, Dr. Black. It's hard for me to explain even to myself. I believe he cares about me. And maybe it is in a friendship kind of way. I don't know. I just know that I have really enjoyed spending the few moments together that we have had. I'll be careful."

She smiles and sighs. "Good. I know that he was your famous heartthrob as a teen. I had one too, so I can completely relate to that. I had a huge crush on Corey Haim from the movie *License to Drive*. I believed that he was the perfect guy, and I would meet him one day, we'd fall in love, get married, and live happily ever after with all the fame and glory. What we as young girls and women don't realize is that there is so much more to it than that. We only see the good and never the bad. The bad must come with the good."

Wow. She's really stirring up thoughts I have never had before. To all good things there is a bad. She's absolutely right. Fame, fortune, and women surround Chase. They are a part of what he knows. What he lives. Could I deal with all that? Could I handle all the girls and women that want him? Throw themselves at him? *Oh, snap out of it, Jo. You're just friends. Nothing more. You have no reason to even worry about that.*

"Thanks, Dr. Black. I really appreciate you talking with me about this. I completely respect what you're saying, and I'll do my very best to make the right choices in the matter. The choices that are right for me."

She stands from her chair as I stand from the couch. She walks over and gives me a tight, motherly squeeze.

"I'm here to help, Joanna. Anyway I possibly can. If you need anything, just give me a call. I'll see you in a few weeks, and you can catch me up on what all has been going on with you, and even with Chase."

I smile as our arms fall from the hug. "Great. See you then."

I leave her office with my head spinning. Different emotions are invading my brain and my heart. All I can do is go with the flow and see what lies ahead.

I'm searching through the crowd of bodies. Girls laughing. Guys playing drinking games. Couples with their lips glued to each other. Music is blaring from every corner in the barn. My head is still throbbing. I want to find the girls. I need to find them. Where are Aimee, Alex, and Kelly? And him? I want to see if I can find him. Point him out. Catch a better glimpse.

I feel so stupid. Stupid for walking off alone. I'm a wreck from screaming and crying. Could no one hear me out there? I look a mess. I skim the crowd, trying to find my friends. Trying to find him. Whoever he is. Whatever he looks like. I try to picture him in my mind. What color was his hair? I vaguely remember him being tall and built. Why did it have to be so dark where I couldn't see him clearly? Why did this happen? Why was I so stupid? There's a faint tap on my shoulder from behind. I turn around, and there he is. He winks at me and a roar of evil laughter escapes him.

I sit up to find myself in bed. I'm covered in sweat again. Another nightmare. When will this stop? When will this go away? When will I quit trying to identify my rapist? I glance over at my clock. It's two a.m. I grab my Samsung from the nightstand and pull up Chase's number. I have to talk to him. He will make me feel better. Just hearing his voice will make it all go away.

Wait. It's so late. I hate the thought of waking him. He has to be tired from filming all day. I shake the thought and tell myself that he will understand. I dial his number with eager fingers and wait for him to answer.

"Hello."

His sleepy voice reaches my ear through the phone.

"Chase. It's Jo," I say softly into the phone.

The tone of his voice changes from sleepy to one of concern.

"Jo? Are you all right?"

I reply, "Yes. Um … no. I had a nightmare. I'm sorry I called you. I just wanted to hear your voice."

"No, it's completely fine. I'm glad you called. Was it what I think it was about?"

I look down at my porcelain blue quilt and play with a snag.

"Yes. I know I sound so childish right now. I shouldn't have called and woke you."

"I promise you it's okay. Anytime you need to call me, just do it. The time does not matter to me. Do you want to talk about it?"

I sigh. "This happens often. I have these nightmares about lying in the woods. I'm cold and in pain. I wake up screaming." After I tell Chase the specifics of my dream, I say, "I'm just a little shaken up. I'm sorry to bother you really."

"Jo, please do not apologize for calling me. I told you I would be here for anything you need. If you need to talk at two o'clock in the morning, I will be right here to listen. Understand?"

I wish he were here right now with me to listen. To hold me close.

"Thanks. I just feel better when you are with me. I'll be fine, though. I'll let you get some rest."

"Are you sure you're going to be all right?" he asks with sincerity.

"Yes, I will. I'll talk to you later. Good night."

"Good night."

I hang up the phone and put it back on my nightstand. It was soothing to hear his voice, but I feel like an idiot for calling him. I feel better, but at the same time, guilty. Guilty for waking him up when I know he is exhausted from work.

I lie back down and try to find a comfortable position. I grab my cream-colored lumbar birdcage pillow and cuddle it close to my chest. Different thoughts about my nightmare rush through my head. I'm having a difficult time shaking them. Thirty minutes pass, but I feel I have been lying here for an eternity.

I am distracted by the sound of low voices coming from outside my bedroom door. I sit up and try to make out who it is. I can hear Aimee, but who is she talking to? Kevin? It has to be Kevin. I forgot he was coming over tonight to watch a movie with her. They must have fallen asleep on the couch and now be going to her bedroom.

Suddenly there is a faint knock on my door. I respond without movement. "Come in."

The door slowly swings open, and there to my astonishment stands Chase. The nightlight next to my door shines a small glow where I can see him perfectly. He's wearing a plain white V-neck T-shirt, black sweatpants, and his feet are bare. *Damn! He's as sexy in the middle of the night as he is any other time! And he's here in my room! My bedroom! Oh geez!*

I sit up with an amazed look. "Chase?"

I pull the quilt closer to my chest, trying to hide the fact that I only have on my printed peace sign panties and an old T-shirt.

He walks over to my bed. "Hey. I wanted to come and see for myself that you are all right. I was real worried when we hung up the phone."

I smile at him in the dark. I am bewildered that he drove here in the middle of the night to check on me. I suddenly feel even more terrible for picking up the phone and calling him.

"I should have never bothered you. I didn't mean to make you worry. I'm fine. Having some trouble falling back to sleep, but I'm okay."

He points to the spot beside me and asks, "Do you mind if I lie down with you for a bit?"

Shit! What? Lie down next to me? In my bed? A lump forms in my throat. I gulp it down and look over at the empty spot and then back at him.

"I-I don't mind; it's just, I'm not fully clothed."

Man, I sound like a dork. Any other woman would jump at the chance to have him ask her if he could lie down in her bed, and I am using my seminakedness as an excuse.

He throws his hands up in a surrender gesture and says, "I promise you I won't try anything. That's not why I'm here. I'm here because I want to make absolutely sure that you're all right."

I think for a brief second and give him a nod. He walks around to the other side of the bed and slowly plops down beside me on top of the quilt. My heart starts to beat faster. He props himself up with his right elbow and uses his left hand to fluff the pillow.

"Would it make you uncomfortable if I held you?" he asks, looking into my eyes.

I can almost see the blue-gray clearly in the dark. He is so close to me. I want him to hold me. I want him to touch me. I have never wanted anyone to touch me so much. *Why, Jo? Why are you allowing yourself to feel this way? You shouldn't. You need to protect yourself. Protect yourself from hurt. It's too soon to let down your guard. Give in a little, but not too much.*

I shake my head and force another lump down my throat.

"Are you sure?"

I nod. I can't believe I'm doing this. This is not me at all.

He reaches over and pulls me close to him.

"Come here," he says in a gentle whisper.

I scoot over and lie down next to him. My back is pressed against his chest. He drapes his left arm around my waist. I can feel his breath on my ear while I struggle to catch my own. My heart feels like it could burst out of my chest at any moment. My body is going numb. I am lying in my bed with Chase Hartford. Now this has to be a dream. A dream that I don't want to wake up from. I want to hang a "Do Not Disturb" sign on my door. Boy do I feel ashamed thinking that.

He kisses me softly on the top of my head.

"I'm here. Now get some sleep."

I feel my eyes get heavy and my troubles lighten as I drift into a deep sleep in the arms of Chase Hartford.

Chapter Seven

The big twenty-one. How exactly is one supposed to feel when they reach this age? Excited? Legally able? The thought has never really crossed my mind. To me, it is just another number.

I'm getting ready for my birthday dinner with my grandpa. I promised him that I would commit myself to spending time with him before celebrating with my friends. I run my fingers through my long, brown, curly hair as I check over my red-checkered top and cut-off blue-jean shorts. It feels good to wear something comfortable, knowing that after dinner I'll be slipping into a sexy dress to go clubbing. I slide on my red Toms by my closet door and switch off my bedroom light as I head out the door.

Aimee steps out of her room when she notices me walk down the hall.

"So you'll be done with Grandpa Dawson around nine?"

I stop, turn to face her, and nod. "Yeah. I'll be back here to change so we can be in Charleston by ten."

She smiles. "Great. See you later on then."

I smile back at her and leave for the old farmhouse.

Grandpa Dawson is very excited to see me as I walk in the door. He gives me a great birthday hug.

"Happy birthday, Jo!"

He always gives the best ones. Chase may be giving him a run for his money though, with his calming embrace a couple of weeks ago in my bed. My body shivers at the thought.

I pull away and smile at him. "Thanks, Grandpa. Good to see you. I've missed you these last few weeks. Sorry I haven't been by."

He waves his hand with a shake of his head. "Ah, you know I understand you're busy. How's work?"

"It's been good. Nice to have this weekend off."

"Well, you should have it off. It's your birthday. You got big plans with the girls tonight?"

I nod. "Yes. We are going to a couple of clubs in Charleston."

He gives me his you-better-be-careful-and-make-the-right-choices look. I giggle at him.

"Don't worry. I'll be careful." I follow him into the kitchen and ask, "Is there anything I can help you do?"

He turns to face me and replies, "No. I've got everything covered. It's your birthday, and you're not lifting a finger. And guess what?"

"What?"

"Neither am I."

I give him a confused look as he chuckles his old man laugh.

"We must be going out for dinner."

He shakes his head. "Well, I hope you don't mind, but I ordered delivery."

"That sounds great. What did you decide on? You know anything works for me."

"I ordered your favorite from Mellow Mushroom, the buffalo-chicken pizza."

"Great choice!" I smile.

He smiles back. "I hope you don't mind, but I invited someone else to join us tonight."

Someone else? I wonder who. Maybe Grandpa has met a lady friend. A cute, sweet, little, old, gray-haired lady. How exciting that would be! Grandpa has been so lonely that it would make me so happy to see him with someone. I know Grandma would love for him to be involved and not miserable all the time.

"I don't mind at all. Have you met someone?" I ask with a curious look.

"I guess you could say that."

"Really? Where?"

I'm excited for him.

"At the senior center a few weeks ago, playing bingo."

I am shocked that he is just now filling me in on this very important information. I put my hands on my hips. "And you're just now telling me this?"

"Well, I wanted to make sure she was interested before I introduced her to you. Her name is Margaret. She's retired and lives in Charleston."

"I'm happy for you. This is great news. You must really like her."

He nods with a smile. "She's got a great sense of humor and can cook good too."

"I can't wait to meet her."

Suddenly there is a knock on the front door. Grandpa looks over at me with a big smile on his face.

"That must be her now. I'll be right back."

I nod and stay in the kitchen as my sweet, old grandpa goes to answer the door. I decide to grab three tea glasses from one of the cabinets. I set them on the counter, walk over to the freezer, and start dropping ice cubes into each. I hear my grandpa talking and chuckling. I turn around as he and Ms. Margaret walk in.

She's a sweet-looking old lady. She's a little shorter than grandpa, with gray hair and glasses. She's dressed all cutesy in a pair of khaki capris and button-up blouse. In her ears are pearl earrings, and a pearl necklace hangs from her neck.

"Margaret, please let me introduce you to my granddaughter, Jo."

I walk over to hug her neck. "Nice to meet you, Ms. Margaret."

She welcomes the hug and smiles. "Oh, how sweet. Nice to meet you too, Jo. Happy birthday. Thomas has told me so much about you."

I glance over at my grandpa, who is smiling so big.

"Yeah, that would be my grandpa. Please come in. You two should have a seat. I'm just preparing our glasses."

They walk over to the small kitchen table for four and sit down next to each other.

"So, Grandpa told me the two of you met at bingo a few weeks ago. You enjoy playing too, huh?" I ask.

"Yes, I enjoy it very much. It gets me out of the house," Margaret says.

"And she's a great player. You have to watch out for her. She can win some money. The balls seem to always favor the numbers on her card," Grandpa adds.

I look over and catch a smile being shared between them. It is so cute! I haven't seen my grandpa smile like that in such a long time. It's a great feeling.

I hear another knock on the door and say, "That must be the pizza delivery guy. I'll be right back."

"The money is on the table in the foyer, dear," Grandpa shouts as I walk out of the kitchen.

I grab the money and swing the door open. *Holy hell!*

"Chase?" What in the world is he doing here? I'm shocked and confused.

He smiles big, standing there holding the pizza box in his hands.

"Happy birthday, Jo."

I'm still trying to grasp the fact that Chase is standing right in front of me on my grandpa's porch. I hear footsteps behind me and turn to see Grandpa and Ms. Margaret. I glance back and forth from Grandpa to Chase.

"What's going on?" I ask, still completely bewildered.

Chase replies, "A surprise, and I'm not talking about the pizza."

Chase laughs as Grandpa gives me a wink.

I shake my head, still confused.

"Okay, I'm missing something. How did this happen?" I move my finger, pointing from one to the other.

Chase speaks up. "Well, a couple of months before I was scheduled to arrive here at Folly Beach, my assistant was looking into a place for me to stay. He knew I wanted to stay somewhere that would keep me out of the city and away from the chaos, so he happened to come across your grandpa's tenant house up the road. He took the information off the "for rent" sign and set everything up. It wasn't until after my arrival that your grandpa found out we had met and informed me that you were his granddaughter. Quite a coincidence, wouldn't you say?"

I am speechless. Not only is Chase Hartford in Folly Beach filming a TV series, but he is also my grandpa's tenant. I don't know how many more surprises I can take. "How did you know that we had met, Grandpa?"

"Oh, Chase stopped by the night he arrived to introduce himself and said Folly seemed like a nice place with nice people. Then he went on talking about this great girl he had met at Ramona's Cafe, and how she was adorable with her sweet, Southern, girl-next-door charm. He was very interested in finding out who she was, and I guess you could say I was drilled for information."

Grandpa smiles big.

Chase's cheeks turn red. *Seriously? He is blushing? I should be the one doing that at the moment.*

"Your grandpa is great company. I've heard some very interesting stories about you."

Okay *now* it is my turn to blush. I really should keep track of this. I'm sure I have broken the world record.

"Perfect. What did you tell him?" I ask.

Grandpa shrugs his shoulders. "Oh … you know the typical kind of stuff that a good ol' grandpa would share with boys that come calling on his granddaughter. Bathtub and potty moments. Pimples. The horrible one-piece bathing suit. Things like that."

The red color on my cheeks is now a sign of complete and utter embarrassment. He must be joking! "Grandpa, please tell me that you don't really mean that?"

He glances over at Chase. "I'm not sure. Chase, am I joking?"

Chase shrugs his shoulders as well and shakes his head. "I don't know."

I roll my eyes at them with a grin on my face. "This is torture. Let's eat."

Chase and I smile at each other as we all head for the kitchen.

Chase and I are sitting on the front porch. Grandpa and Ms. Margaret are inside cleaning up the kitchen. They insisted that we leave them to it and go outside to enjoy the nice summer evening. My August birthday summer evening.

"I must still admit that I am in total shock about you being here."

Chase shoots me a confused look. "Here, as in Folly Beach, or here, as in your grandpa's house?"

"Well, both, but really here at my grandpa's house. I'm sure you can replay the look of complete shock on my face when I opened the door and saw you holding the pizza box."

He smiles. "Yeah, I can see it perfectly. I can also remember the color of your cheeks when he told me that we've been talking about you." He nudges me gently with his right elbow.

I smile at the gesture. *Oh, whatever, Chase Hartford!* "Thanks for coming tonight. It really means a lot to me."

"I'm very happy to do it, and very happy to be here. Your grandpa is an awesome man. I've spent several nights out here on the porch talking to him."

Wow, really? Chase Hartford and my grandpa having chats on the front porch? This is unreal.

"He has some great stories. Stories about life, love, and you."

He turns to me with a serious look on his face. *Oh shit.*

"Okay, I have to know this. Did he really tell you things about me that I would find humiliating?"

He shrugs his shoulders just as he did earlier in the kitchen. "Let's just say that's between your grandpa and me."

He winks.

I nudge him back with my left elbow. "Oh, whatever. You two are teaming up on me. That's not fair. It's my birthday, you know."

He nods. "Yes, as a matter of fact it is, and speaking of birthdays …"

He reaches over next to him on the steps and presents a small wrapped box. "This is for you."

The wrapping is white and a pink bow is placed perfectly on the top. He holds it out for me to take. I glance back and forth between him and the box. "Chase, you didn't have to do this."

I slowly accept it.

"No, I didn't, but I wanted to."

I hold the box in my hands. I'm nervous. I didn't expect for him to get me anything. Above all, I didn't expect to see him here tonight.

"There is something I would like to say to you before you open it."

"Okay."

Now I'm even more nervous. I brace myself for what he is about to say.

"I know that we have only known each other for a short while, and that there is still so much to discover about each other."

Oh, my head is spinning.

"I really appreciate you opening up to me about all the things that you have in such a short period of time. I realize that you did it because you trust me, and I just want you to know that this gift … well … it comes from my heart."

From his heart?

I swallow, trying to push the lump that has swollen in my throat down. Something else I have probably broke the world record on. I don't know how to react. How to respond.

I slowly untie the bow and tear the wrapping. The box is white. I pull the top off and stop for a moment. I look over at him. He is sitting so close. Our knees are touching. I am numb. The matching bracelets that lie inside are made of leather, and both have a single silver plate. On one is the word "Faith" and the other "Strength." *What does it mean?*

Chase says, "I bought these for an important reason. They have a special meaning to me."

Special meaning?

"What?" I ask, dying to know.

He picks up the "Faith" bracelet and tenderly grabs my right arm. He slides it on, pulling on the leather strings to make it slightly tight, but comfortable.

"This faith bracelet is for you. It is a symbol from me to show that I have faith in who you are and in who you want to be. I won't give up on you. I want to hold you together."

My emotions are bursting at the seams. I am lost for words. If I wanted to speak, there is no way I could.

Next he picks up the "Strength" bracelet and slides it onto his right arm.

"This Strength bracelet is for me. It is a symbol that shows I vow to be your strength. I want to be there for you every step of the way. I want you to find your strength through me."

For a short moment, we sit there in silence, staring at each other. I look deep into his blue-gray eyes. I desperately want to kiss him. I can't believe I want to kiss him! Should I? Would it be the right thing to do? No. Not now. It's too soon for me. I must get my emotions under control. His gift means more to me than words could ever explain, but I'm still not quite sure how to read all of this. I'm not sure what it all means, and I don't want to get it wrong. *And, Jo, let's not forget you're on Grandpa's porch. Embarrassing.*

"Thank you so much," I say as I continue to stare into his eyes. "It means a lot."

He smiles and wraps his right arm around me.

"Happy birthday."

I smile and welcome his embrace. This is the perfect birthday.

"So, you going partying with the girls?"

I nod. "Yes. Would you like to come?"

"Nah. You should go and enjoy your birthday with your friends. I don't want to ruin an all-girls night out."

"Well, actually it's not just me and the girls. Kevin and Zach are coming too."

He raises an eyebrow. "Oh really?"

"Yes, really. Would you come if I said that I wanted you to?"

"Of course I would. How about we ride over to the house and take the limo? That way we could all ride together. Plus I would need to give Boss a call. I'm pretty sure I'll need his assistance, along with Mac, Zane, and Lincoln."

I smile. "Oh, yeah, the mafia."

He lets out a small laugh. I guess he found my title for them amusing.

"So, does that sound good to you?" he asks.

"Sounds great. I want to say goodnight to Grandpa first."

We enter Club Light. Boss is walking in front of Chase and me through the crowd. Mac, Zane, and Lincoln surround us from each side and behind. Chase has a firm grip on my hand as my posse of friends follow us to a table in a private corner of the club. Girls are screaming and trying to make their way toward Chase. They don't stand much of a chance with the muscle mafia around us. I'm a little overwhelmed by the excitement.

We all slide into the big, circular booth for eight at a VIP table and wait for service. Chase throws his left arm behind me, resting it on the top of the booth cushion. Boss and the guys continuously push girls back. Eventually the girls give up and walk away.

A waiter shows up and asks, "What can I get you guys?"

Chase replies, "I'll take a VO and Coke and whatever they want. The tab is on me, brother."

A chorus of thanks and thanks, man echoes from my friends. They start to place their drink orders.

Chase looks over at me. "And what would the birthday girl like to drink?"

I blush. "I'll take an amaretto sour."

The waiter nods. "Okay, I'll have your drinks out soon."

He turns and walks away.

Within minutes, another group of girls tries to make their way to our table. They are yelling out Chase's name and I love yous. It's insane. I mean I've witnessed the love-stricken girls wanting autographs outside of Magnolias, but they weren't all crazy like the girls here.

Kevin chuckles with his eyes in amazement. "Damn, man! I'd love that shit! Girls everywhere screaming for me."

Aimee rolls her eyes and punches his shoulder with her fist. "Oh, whatever. Shut up!"

Kevin rubs his shoulder and gives her a mischievous wink.

"It gets a little crazy. Believe me, it gets to the point many times when you like being able to go somewhere without having to deal with all that shit," Chase remarks.

Kevin shakes his head. "Nah, man. I'd eat it up! I'd have a girl on each side everywhere I went."

Chase smiles and looks over at me. His arm is still behind me on the cushion. His fingers brush my shoulder with his movements. It makes my body tingle. I begin to wonder what my friends think. Aimee, Kelly, and Alex keep giving me smiles. I just smile back.

The waiter returns with a tray holding all of our drinks. He passes them around to each of us and says, "I'll be back in a bit to see if you guys need anything else."

We all nod and give him a thanks.

"So, Chase, how long are you going to be here filming?" Zach asks from across the table.

"Um … at least another nine months. It doesn't really take that long to film a TV series, but with all the events and things I have to attend, it kind of stretches it out."

"Do you get any time off set just to relax?"

Chase nods. "Yeah. It all really depends on how things are going. I may have several days off or the weekend. Around the holidays I try my best to spend time with my family and do things I enjoy."

Alex asks, "Do you have anything lined up after you film *The Crane Files*?"

"I know that there is talk about a Cinderella movie. It's supposed to be a darker, adult version of the story. I can't say a whole lot about it because I haven't discussed all the details with the film company yet. I just heard I'm in the running for the role of the prince."

Kelly speaks up. "Oh my God, yes! I heard about that! I've always wanted them to do more of a grown-up version of the fairytale. Would love to see it!"

Chase and I look at each other and smile. *The prince. He could be my prince. Why do I feel more and more like I want to be his Cinderella? He said he would never give up on me. That he was here to save me. Save me from my dreadful past. Rescue me to embrace the things I deserve ... life, dreams, and love. Well then, that makes me Cinderella, and he can be my prince. My knight in shining armor.*

All of a sudden, "Sexy Bitch" by David Guetta and Akon blares over the club speakers. Aimee jumps in her seat.

"Oh my God! This song is the shit! Let's go, girls! We have to dance!"

She grabs my hand to pull me out of the booth. I turn and roll my eyes with a smile at Chase. He smiles back.

The next thing I know I am on the dance floor with my girls. The four of us dance together. We are killing it with our sexiest moves. I run my hands through my long brown hair and then down my sides while my hips move in a provocative way. The four of us bump and grind with our asses in a line. We laugh. I feel amazing and free.

The music changes. "Sledgehammer" by Fifth Harmony booms through the speaker system next. The disco balls throw a different set of colors around the dance floor. Lights that resemble stars begin to flash. I spin around in my dancing trance and come face-to-face with Chase. I stop and notice that Boss and his crew have created a protected area for us to dance. My nerves are shot. I want to go dance with him, but am a little embarrassed to be in a situation where so many people can look on. Chase smiles, and then grabs me. We start to move. His hands send a sensation through my body that I have never felt before. It's almost erotic. I notice that he is being careful in how he touches me and where. I feel my embarrassment slip away. I welcome his hands. I desire his touch. He gets close. I place my hands on his sides as we get closer. We move perfectly together. My mind flashes back to when he told me that he wanted us to dance one night, and that he had some moves. Damn, he was right.

We get so close that our foreheads meet. I feel his warm, sweet-scented breath on my face. I am so wrapped up in this moment. I want the music to continue playing forever. I feel myself letting go. I'm not restraining myself.

When the song is over, he grabs my hand and leads me back to our table. Boss and the guys are constantly battling girls to keep their distance.

"Okay, ladies, not too close. Let's step back. Give them some room."

Everyone is there, already seated and finishing their drinks. Chase and I slide in next to them.

Kelly speaks up. "Well, you two looked mighty hot out there. I could feel the chemistry all the way over here."

I shoot her a will-you-please-shut-up look. I then hide it quickly with a smile. She shrugs her shoulders with a what's-the-big-deal expression.

"So, Chase. We need to have a guy's night out," Kevin says.

Chase throws his hands up. "Whenever you're ready."

Aimee shakes her head. "Oh, no. I don't think that's a good idea."

"Why not? You worried about something?" Kevin asks.

"Maybe," she replies.

"And what would it be exactly?"

"I don't know. Sometimes you lose control about certain things. I like to keep an eye on you."

Kevin sighs. "Oh, whatever. Chase, man, just let me know, and we'll hit the town. We'll do it right."

Chase nods. "All right."

He glances over at Aimee. "Don't worry, Aimee. I'll look after him for you. Don't want him getting into any trouble on my account."

"Yeah, right. We'll see about that," she remarks.

The seven of us talk, drink, and dance for several hours. I have had happy birthday cheers and shout-outs. It has been by far the most memorable birthday. As I partied with Chase and my friends, there wasn't one thing I could think of to change.

It's one thirty in the morning when the limo pulls up outside Aimee's and my apartment. They get out of the car and say their thanks and goodbyes.

Aimee, being last, looks back at me. "Are you coming, Jo?"

"My car is at Grandpa's. I'm going to ride with Chase so I can drive it back home."

She gives me a smile. "Okay, if you say so. Drive careful."

With a wink she exits the car and closes the door.

Chase asks, "Are you sure you're going to be all right to drive? I can get your car to you tomorrow if you want to stay."

I shake my head. "No, I'm fine. I can just go ahead and get it now."

He nods. "All right."

The limo pulls off and heads toward my grandpa's house.

"Thanks for tonight. I had a great time."

Chase smiles. "You're very welcome, and you deserve it. I'm worried about you driving home tonight, though. You've had a good bit to drink."

"I'm okay. My buzz is wearing off. I haven't had that much to drink in such a long time."

Actually I haven't drunk like that since the rape. I don't want to think about it. I push the memory out of my head.

When I look out the window, I realize that we are beyond the town limits and getting close to my grandpa's.

"Well, I can drive you home in your car and have the limo follow. Or you can just stay and leave tomorrow."

Our eyes meet. He's serious. *Stay? Stay where? With him? I couldn't. It wouldn't look right. What would Grandpa think? Most importantly, what would he say? Oh, come on, Jo, you're not a child. You don't have to answer to anyone.*

"I-I don't know. I don't want to inconvenience anyone."

He reaches over and grabs my hand.

"If I told you I wanted you to stay, would you?"

I look down at his hand over mine. I gulp easily, hoping it will keep him from noticing how nervous he makes me. "I-I don't know if that's the right choice."

"I don't mean in that way, Jo. I just don't want the night to end. I don't want you to go. And I really don't want you driving home."

I am torn between yes and no. I fear that I will feel regret with whatever choice I make. What is the *right* choice? He said I could trust him. I want to believe him so badly. I want him to have the faith in me that he hungers for. I glance down at my bracelet. I close my eyes for a brief moment and let a small courageous breath escape my lips. Then I look over at him.

"I'll stay."

Without a word, he gives me a gentle smile that assures me everything will be all right and squeezes my hand.

The old tenant house is just as my grandmother left it. I take a look around the living room as we walk in and savor everything that was her. The Victorian antique couch and armchair are still in place. On her favorite cherrywood coffee table sits a bible and a small, framed picture of my parents. Above the couch on the wall is a large portrait of me when I was eight. I remember my grandma's excitement over it. She had me dressed in an old, white gown with a pearl necklace and a flowered headpiece that rested on my forehead. I smile. I looked just as a child should. I was sweet and innocent. I was a little girl who had no idea what tragedy was ahead in her life.

Chase walks over and stands beside me as I stare at the portrait. "She's a precious-looking girl isn't she?"

I don't turn my gaze from it.

"This was my grandma's favorite. She loved antiques and old-style clothing. She wanted a picture of me so badly when I was little dressed like I lived centuries ago. My mother thought she was crazy, but after it was taken, my mother had to have a large print of it for herself."

"Your grandpa told me that she decorated this place. It was her hobby. Anything she could find antique she bought and put it here."

I nod. "Yes, she did. It was her passion. Oh, the yard sales and antique stores she carried me to."

I think back to the weekends when she was alive and how we would drive for miles to locate certain items. I dreaded it. Now I would go willingly if she was here.

He turns to face me. "Would you like me to get you anything? Coffee maybe?"

I meet his look. "I'm fine, thanks."

"Well, I can get you a change of clothes. I have a T-shirt and a pair of sweat shorts you can wear if you'd like to get comfortable."

Oh, shit, that's right. I don't have any clothes. I totally didn't think about that.

"That sounds great. I'm dying to get out of these heels and this dress."

"Okay, I'll grab them. Be right back."

I can hear Chase rummaging through the dresser drawers in the bedroom as I walk around and examine my grandma's things. I haven't been out here in so long. Grandpa begged me to move in here instead of living in town when I started my freshman year of college, and now I'm so glad that I didn't do it. Now that Grandma's gone, living here would continuously bring back memories of her. I'm glad I'm where I can let the sadness rest. Not put it to sleep entirely but hibernate. This place is a constant reminder of her. I pick up the small frame that contains the picture of my parents. The smiles on their faces bring a smile to my own. They were so beautiful, happy, and in love. I want a love like theirs. A love like the one they shared. I run my finger over the glass. It's the only way I feel that I can actually touch them.

"I know you miss them," Chase says.

He has managed to walk up behind me without my noticing.

I give him a quick glance and turn back to the picture. "Yeah, I do. Very much. They were wonderful. I can't remember a time that they weren't so happy and in love. I'd give anything to experience a love like the one they had."

I continue to stare down at the picture. I fight back the tears.

"You will."

I look at him. I get lost again in the blue-gray of his eyes. He takes the frame slowly from my hands and sets it down on the coffee table. I can feel the tears form in my eyes. I am losing my battle against them. He sets the clothes he has brought for me down on the coffee table as well. He looks at me as a teardrop escapes and slowly begins to roll down my left cheek. He takes his hands and places them on each side of my face. With a gentle sweep of his right thumb, he wipes it away. Our eyes are locked together. My heart is calm. There are no words. He pulls me close and wraps his arms around me. I melt. A part of the guard that has secured me for so long seems to want to slip away. I realize that, all along with him, I haven't been as guarded as I hoped. We stand there for what seems like an eternity.

I finally pull away. "I'm going to change. I'll be right back."

He nods.

I grab the clothes, walk into the bedroom, and close the door. I stand with my back pressed against it and close my eyes. *What is happening to me? Why does he make me feel like this? It's a feeling I crave but try to ignore because of my fear. Take it slow, Jo. You're doing fine. You're doing just fine.*

I walk over to the bed and start to remove my pumps and then my dress. I dress quickly in his clothes, which happen to be a little loose, but better than nothing, and throw my dress neatly over the sitting chair. I find a small ponytail holder in my clutch and pull my hair into a loose bun at the top of my head. I feel comfortable and relaxed.

When I return to the living room, Chase has already changed and is sitting on the couch. He too has on a pair of sweat shorts and T-shirt. I take a seat next to him.

He smiles and asks, "Feel better?"

I nod. "Thanks for earlier. I didn't mean to have a moment in front of you."

"Jo, you can have all the moments you want. Anytime you're with me, I want to hold you together through them."

I smile and look down at my hands. They are nervously playing with the seam on his shorts that I am wearing.

"Thanks. Everything that you have done has meant so much."

We sit there, quiet for a few minutes. I feel like we have so much to say, but don't really know where to start.

Chase moves a little closer to me like he is trying to find a comfortable position.

"Can I ask you a personal question?" he asks.

"Sure."

"Have you ever had a serious boyfriend? You know, a guy that you believed was the one?"

I wonder about the meaning behind his question and where the conversation may go. Why not tell him about it? I've been open about other things. I should certainly be able to talk to him about this. "I dated a guy named Jake for almost a year. He was the new guy at my school senior year. He was charming and had the personality and good looks that girls would die for. I thought for a short time that he was the one for me, but realized later that I had it all wrong."

"What happened?" he asks with a look of curiosity on his face.

"He wanted more than I could give. He was experienced and wanted things at a fast pace. I was surprised he hung around as long as he did, being that I wouldn't screw him. I consider him serious because we were together for a good while, and we spent the majority of our time together. It eventually just didn't work."

"So you haven't dated anyone since then?"

I shake my head. "No, not really. I've been out with some of my college guy friends, but no serious relationships."

He nods his head in an understanding way.

"I haven't been very successful when it comes to guys and love. I loved Jake, but couldn't give him what he wanted because I wasn't ready at the time. I knew what I wanted to stand for. I wanted to be the respectable girl that made the right decisions. So I broke up with him. Then, last year, I was raped by a heartless stranger that strips me of the belief that there is actually someone who finds me worthy of love. The one thing I wanted to save of myself to give to someone that I knew I really loved and loved me in return was taken away."

I continue with an angry scowl on my face. "I just don't understand why I had to lose so many precious things in my life in such tragic ways. I suppose you could say that's why it's taking me so long to get over them. It's so difficult to see the good when you've experienced so much bad shit."

Chase reaches over and gently takes my left hand. "It'll be over one day. You will keep the memories of your family and lose the dread of that son of a bitch that has caused you pain."

I try to give him a positive smile, even though it's hard with all the negative thoughts running through my mind. "I hope you're right. Besides, that's all I can do is … hope."

"You know I've had several relationships with girls that proved to me that there is so much about love that we can't comprehend. I realized that what I was looking for was never present. I wanted a true love, and I sought it in all the wrong places. I went after it with girls who were famous like me, only to discover that I was headed toward a dead end. An end that held emptiness and not happiness. What I find so strange, yet amazing, is that we look for things and cease to recognize it when it's right in front of us."

Why does he say things like this? I don't know how to take it. He's so caring and gentle. He sends me flowers and takes me out to dinner. He holds my hand, swallows me in his hugs, and buys me a bracelet. He wants me to stay with him because he doesn't want the night to end. He's worried about me driving home. I don't know how much more of the confusion I can handle. Does he want friendship, or more? The part of me that yearns for more with him is growing, but yet I find myself wary of what Dr. Black said. The next nine months will go by quickly, and he will soon return to LA. What will I do then? What will he do? Forget everything and move on?

"I can't express this to you enough, so I'll say it again. You can trust me. I will never do anything to hurt you, and I would never do anything that you don't want. I know this is all so weird, but I have never been so drawn to anyone in my life. There's something about you that wants me to be and stay grounded."

He points to my bracelet and then to his own. "Faith and strength. I want you to remember that. I have faith in you, and I want my strength to give you strength. I want you to see that there are people that know you're special and wonderful. People that care and want so much for you. Your grandpa. Me. I never once imagined that I would meet someone like you when I came here. You have no idea how thankful I am that I did."

I want to cry. I want every tear that I have held back all these years to find freedom. They need release. Never in my life has anyone said the things he has just said to me. Never have I felt that someone had so much confidence in me in overcoming so many heartbreaking ordeals.

I burst into tears. I cover my face with my hands and cry into them. I am embarrassed, but so touched. Chase grabs me gently and pulls me into his chest. He wraps his strong arms around me as I bury my head into him.

"Shhh. It's all right. I'm here."

His voice is so soft and caring. It gives me great comfort. I wrap my arms around his waist and move my head to his left shoulder. For a few minutes I sob, and he continues to hold me. He's so warm. I melt into him. I don't want him to let me go. Why do I battle my feelings? *Because, Jo, you don't know what he wants.* How do I find out? *You will know when the time is right. It will be up to you.*

I pull away and wipe my face. He looks at me with tenderness in his eyes. It's not pity but hope. The hope I am searching for. The hope I need.

"I'm sorry that I do this to you all the time. It seems that we always talk about your past, and all it does is bring out the pain in you."

I shake my head. "No, Chase. It's good for me. I just feel terrible burdening you with all of this. I want to be this strong, happy girl that isn't so scarred. I'm afraid that eventually it will push you away. Away from whatever this is."

I point between the two of us.

He rubs my hand. "I'm not going anywhere."

Chapter Eight

I wake up to the smell of coffee and bacon frying. The last time I woke up to this smell was when my grandma was alive. She would cook the best breakfast. I look around and remember where I am. I slept so well. It must have been because Chase was so close by. I jump out of bed and pull on his sweat shorts. I head into the bathroom, wash my face, throw my hair back up into a bun, and walk out. I notice that Chase has neatly folded the blanket he used on the couch and placed it on top of his pillow. I smile.

I walk into the kitchen to find him standing over the stove. He looks so sexy standing there with his bare feet. He takes a fork and flips the bacon over.

He turns and sees me in the doorway.

"Good morning, sunshine. How did you sleep?"

"Good morning. Very well, thanks. And you?"

He shrugs. "Pretty good. I mean a couch is never the best place to sleep but, ya know."

He smiles and gives me a wink. *Melt! Just what I need first thing in the morning!*

I walk over next to him to see what he's been cooking. He has whipped up some scrambled eggs and pancakes along with the bacon.

"It smells delicious. I didn't know you could cook."

He nods. "I love to cook. The coffee is ready. Would you like a cup?"

"Yes, but I can get it."

He shakes his head. "No, I got it. Consider this a belated birthday breakfast from me."

I smile and have a seat at the small kitchen table.

He walks over and grabs a mug from the cabinet.

"How do you take it?" he asks.

"Three sugars and milk."

He smiles at me as he prepares it. "No other way to have it."

He walks over and sets it down on the table in front of me.

"Eggs, pancakes, and bacon?"

I nod in approval. "Yes, please."

After he fixes his coffee and both of our plates, he sets them down and sits across from me. He says grace before we dig in.

"So you have a whole nother day off. Any plans?" he asks.

I grab us a couple of napkins and pick up my fork to enjoy the wonderful breakfast he has prepared.

I shake my head. "No. The first thing I have to accomplish is survive the twenty questions my grandpa is going to ask when I pick up my car."

Chase lets out a laugh. "I hope he'll take it easy on you."

I laugh back. "You and me both. What about you? What do you have going on today?"

He takes a bite of his eggs and a sip of coffee behind them. "I have a few scenes to shoot, but then I'm just going to relax around here."

"Sounds nice. I guess I could be productive and do laundry, straighten my room. Maybe catch up on some reading."

"Would you like to get together again sometime this week?"

"I'd love to. I'm working the early shift every day this week, so just let me know."

"All right. Great. Maybe I'll cook us dinner."

"Wow, you do like to cook."

"It's a secret of mine. I don't share it with many people. I'm actually pretty good at it."

I nod in agreement. "I can tell. This breakfast is delicious. The last time I had a breakfast this good was when my grandma was alive. I'd come and spend the night or the weekend with her and Grandpa. She would always cook this big spread for me."

"Well, I'll have to cook you my specialty this week."

"And what is that exactly?" I ask.

"Steak. I can grill a mean steak. Twice-baked potatoes and salad. Does that sound good?"

"Awesome. I look forward to it." I smile.

"Me too," he says with a smile in return.

Grandpa walks out of the house as Chase's limo pulls out of the driveway. He stops at the steps as I throw my dress, heels, and clutch in my BMW.

"Well, I noticed your car in the drive this morning and was wondering when you would come to get it. Did you have fun last night?"

I nod with embarrassment, wondering what is going through his mind. I knew that he wouldn't let me get away without some conversation.

"Yes sir. Sorry. I hope I didn't worry you."

"No it's fine, Jo. You're not a child. Just making sure you're all right."

"I'm fine, Grandpa. I promise. I just had several drinks last night, and Chase felt that it was best for me not to drive my car home that's all."

"I understand. You headed home?" he asks.

"Yes sir. I might come back later, though. I may decide to go out to the pond and fish for a little while. I have some things on my mind."

"Are you sure everything's all right?"

He looks concerned.

"Everything's great."

I hope that the tone of my voice and the smile on my face reassures him that everything is really all right.

"Well, I'm going into town to play bingo tonight at the senior center. I'll be gone a while. There's some leftover pizza in the fridge if you get hungry while you're here later."

I smile again, thinking of Chase walking in last night with the pizza box in his hand.

"Okay, thanks. Have fun and be careful."

He smiles back. "All right. Love you, dear."

"I love you too, Grandpa."

I get in my car, fire up the engine, and head home.

As I enter our apartment Aimee hangs her head out of the kitchen and demands, "In here right now, girlfriend. We have to talk."

Her head is gone, and then she's at the door again. "His clothes look good on you, by the way."

She winks and disappears again into the kitchen.

I sigh, roll my eyes, and set down my things. *Shit. She wants details. As always.*

I walk in. She is making a cup of coffee for herself. "Would you like a cup?" she asks.

I shake my head as I sit at the table. "No, thanks. Chase made coffee and cooked breakfast this morning."

She spins around with a grin. "Coffee and breakfast means sex happened last night."

She cocks her eyebrow as she sits across from me.

"No, Aimee, there was no sex last night. Looks like I'm going to have to disappoint you again."

"Girl! What is wrong with you? You spent the night with Chase Hartford, and you come home without having slept with him?"

I nod. "Exactly."

"So you're telling me that you spent the night with him and not a single thing happened between the two of you?"

"That's exactly what I'm telling you. I slept in the bed, and he slept on the couch."

She sits back in the chair and murmurs. "That is really boring. There wasn't even a kiss?"

"No. Not even a granny kiss," I reply with a smirk on my face.

She rolls her eyes. "I don't get it. Can you not see the sign?"

I give her a confused look. "What do you mean?"

She sits forward. "He's very into you. He picked you. You are so blind. He takes you to dinner, you go for a walk on the beach, he comes to make sure you're okay in the middle of the night after a nightmare, and then your birthday last night. Oh, and please don't let me forget to point out the gorgeous flowers he sent you the day after he met you."

"I'm very aware of all the things he's done, but that doesn't mean I have to run off and sleep with him. I'm just being cautious. I don't want to make a mistake. Besides, he could be doing all this because he just wants a good friend while he's here."

She shakes her head. "I seriously doubt that. That's a lot to do for someone that you've only known for a month. You are blind, girlfriend, and you need to open your eyes."

All of this coming from my wild, sometimes bad-decision-making best friend. *What if she's right?*

"I'm scared. I don't want to get hurt. He's only here until filming is over. What happens when he leaves? I stay here as a damaged, heartbroken girl while he goes back to living his life the way he did before he met me?"

"You can't think that way. You just have to give things a chance and see what happens. You can't ignore what's happening around you. I can feel the chemistry between the two of you when I see you together. The last thing I think he's after is friendship."

I shrug my shoulders. "I don't know. It's all so confusing, just like everything else in my life."

"Where did you get that?" she asks as she points to my bracelet.

I look down at my right wrist and begin to play with it. "Chase gave it to me for my birthday."

"Really? So what is the meaning behind 'faith'?" she asks with a serious look of curiosity.

"It's a long story."

"Tell me. I want to hear it."

"Well, he knows what all I've been through with losing Mom, Dad, Sam, and Grandma. I even told him about the rape. I'm still shocked at myself for telling him so much, but every time I've been with him, I've felt myself being more open. He's been a great listener and very supportive of my feelings."

"Another sign," Aimee says.

"He gave me this as a reminder that he has faith in me to break free of the sadness of the past that holds me hostage. He has one identical to mine, except his has the word 'strength.' He said that it signifies the strength that he will carry in himself to help me discover my own."

Aimee's mouth falls open. She seems speechless. Wow. I'm impressed. This is the second time she seems lost for words where Chase is concerned.

"H-Holy shit. He told you that?"

"Yeah, when we were sitting on the front steps at Grandpa's last night before going out."

"Look, Jo. You have to let go. Let go and embrace what's right in front of you."

"I'm trying. I am. It's like I feel deep down inside that his words and actions mean he would like to be more than friends, but I'm afraid of acting on it and ending up disappointed. It just all seems too good to be true. I have feelings for him that are so different from the star-struck ones I had as a teenage girl. I'm actually getting the opportunity to *know* him. I'm eager to show how I feel about him, but I'm not sure how. My feelings scare me. It's like I believe I shouldn't feel them."

I have an epiphany. What if Chase is waiting for me to make the first move? What if, out of respect for me, he is using his strength to hold himself back from doing something he is afraid will cause me to run? *Holy shit! He's waiting for me to have the strength and faith to let go of the pain and see him right in front of me!*

"You just have to do it. Trust how you feel and act on it. You have to give it a chance."

She couldn't have read my mind better or put it into better words!

I smile at her. I can't remember the last time that we had a heart-to-heart. I'm so lucky to have her as my best friend. What would I do without her? Even if she is crazy and irrational most of the time.

"I'll think about it. I promise. Thanks for the talk."

I get up from the table. "I'm going to get some laundry done and clean up a bit."

She nods. "No problem. I'm going to Kevin's parent's for lunch today, so it will be some time later before I get back."

"All right. Have fun."

She smiles. "I always do."

I'm sitting on the dock at my grandpa's pond. I'm wearing one of my favorite old brown tank tops and a pair of cut-off blue-jean shorts. My bare feet dangle as I focus on my fishing line. I think about Chase. I reflect on all the things that Aimee pointed out during our talk. We have spent a good bit of time together, and he has done some sweet things. The bracelet being the sweetest of all. I look down at it on my wrist. It brings a smile to my face and a feeling in my heart that I have wanted for so long. I have got to quit ignoring it.

I hear thunder in the distance and notice dark clouds in the sky. I should have checked the weather before coming out here. I had no clue there was rain in the forecast.

The beep of a car horn startles me. I turn around and see Chase's limo. The door opens, and he jumps out. He waves and then sticks his head in like he's talking to his chauffer. He quickly shuts the door and heads toward me in a small run. The limo drives off. I wave with a huge smile on my face. *What is he doing here?* He's dressed in blue jeans and a white T-shirt again. Must be his favorite, most relaxing thing to wear. I love how attractive he looks in something so simple. I breathe and try for a minute to push his godliness out of my head.

"Hey. Trying to catch a fish?" he asks.

I nod. "Yep. So far no luck."

He kicks off his flip-flops and sits down next to me. He lets his perfect feet dangle in the water beside mine.

"I should have known with you being a Southern girl that you like to fish."

I look at him. Dark strands of his hair brush the top of his right eyebrow. I try hard not to get lost in his eyes again, even though I want to.

"I definitely like to fish. I learned from the best. However, you couldn't tell that now."

We chuckle together. "I like it too. I do it all the time when I go to Denver. There's the perfect stream on my property, and every time I go, I catch a huge mess of fish."

A huge mess of fish. He sounds just like my grandpa.

"Grandpa and I came out here all the time when I was little. I caught my first fish with him."

"Really? What was your first catch?"

"A five-pound bass. It doesn't sound like much, but I will never forget my excitement and the look on my grandpa's face."

"No, that's a pretty good-size fish for a little girl."

Suddenly my line jerks a little, and the bobber starts to make ripples in the water. I slowly start to reel in my line. The fish isn't tugging too hard, which tells me that it's not going to be a big one. Chase looks on with a smile on his face. I keep reeling until the small fish is hanging above the water. I glance over at Chase with a smirk.

"It's a little brim," I say as I grab him with my right hand. I work gently on freeing his mouth of the hook.

"You know I find it sexy when a girl is not afraid to take a fish off the line."

I'd rather not look at him. The word *sexy* just escaped his lips. I just blush.

"It's just a fish. There's nothing to be afraid of. I just want to make sure I get him off in time so he can be free and swim away."

"Well, I had this one girlfriend who would never touch a fish. It grossed her out."

I'm not jealous at the mention of his ex. Instead I am happy with the fact that I can do something he finds sexy that she couldn't do. *Shame on you, Jo.* I smirk at my mental scolding of myself.

I finally manage to free the little guy off the hook and reach down into the water to let him go.

"So I guess it's safe to say that fishing trips were not your top pick of things to do with her?"

He smirks and shakes his head. "Not at all."

I smile at him. More thunder roars in the distance, and the dark clouds seem to spread all around us. We both stare up at the sky.

"Looks like a storm is coming," he says.

"Yeah. Don't you just love pop-up summer storms?"

I turn to face him.

He shrugs his shoulders. "I don't know. What's to love about them?"

"Well, for one, they catch you by surprise, and two, they are so much fun to play in."

He gives me a funny look. "Fun to play in?"

"Yeah. Haven't you ever played in the rain?"

"Um … once when I was a kid, but not lately."

"Sam and I used to do it all the time. We'd come out here and play in the mud. He loved for me to chase him. He was so fast. I remember the sound of his laugh. It was like music. It's one of my last fun memories with him."

There's another roar of thunder, and then the rain starts to fall. It comes down in huge drops.

We are soaked within a matter of minutes. We look at each other and laugh so loud. Chase holds his head back and opens his mouth to catch some of the drops. *Hotness! Damn, I want to be a raindrop!*

He looks over at me with a playful grin.

"Okay, I'm going to give you until the count of ten to run, and then I'm coming after you."

"What?" I ask with a look of surprise.

He starts to count without answering me.

"One, two, three …"

I set my fishing pole down, jump up from the dock, and start to run as fast as I can. He starts counting a little louder where I can hear him.

"Four, Five, Six …" He counts faster. "Seven, eight, nine, *ten!*"

I look back to see him running after me.

"That's not fair! You cheated!" I scream to him behind me.

The rain is not slacking. It falls heavily.

I stop when I realize I'm far enough away from him. I look below and notice how quickly the dirt beneath me has turned into mud. I reach down and grab a pile of it in my hand. He stops dead in his tracks.

"You wouldn't?"

I give him the same playful grin he gave me on the dock. "Oh, I would, and I will."

I use my softball-pitching arm and throw the mud at him. It splatters him right across the chest. A clump sticks to his shirt. He looks down in shock and then back up at me. He points his finger at me and shakes his head with a I'm-going-to-get-you look on his face with a big smile.

He grabs some mud and throws it in my direction. I start to run from the massive wet ball that propels toward me. A small clump hits my back. I turn around to see that he has started running toward me. I reach down to the ground for more. We both grab a small handful. He approaches me. I take it and rub it on his face. He tries to fight me and manages to get some on my face as well. We laugh uncontrollably. My stomach hurts from the laughter. I hold it as we stand there together.

We look at each other. Our laughter stops. Water drips from his hair and off his face. His soaked, mud-stained, white T-shirt hugs every muscle in his chest and arms, so I can see them perfectly. He looks so sexy standing in front of me in the rain. I realize that, at this very moment, I want him so much. I want to show him that I want him. I'm not afraid of what may happen. My fear is gone. I have to take the chance. The chance that Aimee was talking about.

We look into each other's eyes as the rain pours continuously around us. He steps in closer to me. We hold our gaze and say nothing. I lift my right hand to touch his cheek. It is soft. He grabs my hand gently as it stays on his cheek, and he closes his eyes. My heart pounds rapidly and does not skip the first beat. It wants this. I want this. He opens his eyes to look back into mine. I lean forward as he leans down. I close my eyes softly, placing my lips on his. When I pull away, he is looking at me with an expression that speaks to my heart. His heart is telling me that it wants this too.

He grabs my face and tenderly kisses me. His lips are so soft and swallow my own. Our tongues intertwine. Our breathing gets heavy. The kiss is long and hard, but placid. He reaches down with his right hand and pulls me in closer to him. I run my hands up his wet back. I can feel his heart pulsate against my chest. There's a storm engulfing us, but we're in heaven.

Chapter Nine

Chase and I slowly pull our lips away from each other. As we do, we drown in each other's eyes instead of in the rain.

He places his left hand under my chin. "I feel like I've waited an eternity for you to do that. I've wanted it so badly in just the short time we have known each other."

My heart drops, and I gulp. *It's true. He was waiting for me to make the first move.*

I gaze deeper into his blue-gray eyes. "I've wanted to, but I was afraid."

"You're not afraid anymore?" he asks.

I shake my head. "No."

He leans in and kisses me again. This time it's just a sweet touch of the lips. He pulls away again with a small smile. "So, we're standing here in the pouring rain, soaked, and covered in mud. What are we going to do?"

We look down at our muddy feet and clothes.

I shrug my shoulders. "I'm not sure."

He looks down the dirt road that leads to the tenant house. It's only half a mile away.

"Well, we can't get any worse off than we already are. I'd say let's go for a little walk."

He motions his head in the direction of the house. He reaches for my hand. I take it with a smile, and we begin to walk together.

"Would you like to stay for dinner?"

I nod. "I'd love to."

"I'll cook you another one of my specialties."

"I'm looking forward to it."

"You said you were working the early shift this week. What time do you go in?" he asks.

"Nine thirty. It's early enough to get things set up and ready for the lunch rush."

"I'm surprised that Ramona doesn't serve breakfast there. I bet she would do pretty well if she did."

I agree, "Yeah. She has thought about it, but couldn't really decide if she wanted to do it or not. The cafe is her life. It's been in her family for a long time. She spends so much time there I'm sure not having to rush in the mornings is a nice for her."

"What do you serve there for lunch?"

"A variety of things. We have soups, salads, and sandwiches. Nothing fancy."

"Any recommendations?"

"The vegetable soup is fantastic. It's my favorite. We have a green salad that is very tasty, but only if you have it with Ramona's secret dressing. And the best sandwich to me is the turkey specialty. It has lettuce, tomato, and there's a sweet sauce you put on the bread. Delicious."

"I'll come for lunch one day this week to see you and try something out."

I smile. He can come every day for lunch and see me if he wants to.

"Make sure you bring Boss. It gets pretty busy, and I'm sure you'll need him. School starts back week after next, so Folly gets a little crazy. You'd be surprised at the number of students who want to stay here."

"I'll make sure he's with me." He gives me a smile.

It's not long before we reach the house. The silver Toyota Prius is parked in the driveway, but the limo is nowhere in sight.

"Where do Boss and all the other guys stay?"

"They are staying in a house close by. We are spread out, and I like it that way. It kind of throws the fans off guard, and I get my privacy. They're not too far when I need them."

"Smart move. Like I've said before, you have a few tricks up your sleeve."

He gives me a wink. "You remember things well."

We walk up the steps to the porch and stand by the front door.

"So, what do we do now?" I ask, as we are standing there still covered in mud and not wanting to track it all in the house.

Chase looks around as if he's thinking for a solution to our problem. "I got it. Wait here," he says.

He goes back down the steps and grabs the water hose that sits on the ground at the edge of the porch. He unwraps it from the wheel, turns it on, and drags it up the steps with him.

"A little bit of water in the house is a lot better than some mud. Are you with me on this?"

I push the small lump that has immediately formed in my throat down to my gut. I nod with a nervous look on my face. *Calm down, Jo. Everything's going to be fine. You can handle this.*

He hands me the water hose. He pulls his soaked T-shirt off and throws it down on the porch. *Holy shit! I want him to be standing in the rain like this and not under the dryness of the porch.* I notice the small beads of water on his chest. I want to touch him. I want to drop the hose and watch my hands explore him. I fight the urge. He unbuttons his jeans and strips them from his body. *Double holy shit!* My heart can't handle this! He has on a pair of black Armani boxer briefs. They sit low on his waist and hug him in every way that would make any girl face-plant the floor.

He carefully takes the water hose from my hand and rinses his hair, face, and body free of the mud. I am savoring every minute of this gorgeous sight. I watch as the water runs down every inch of his body. I find it very erotic. *Erotic?* A part of me feels dirty and ashamed for seeing it this way, while another part of me wants more.

He hands the hose back to me and says, "Okay, so I may be wet, but the mud is gone. I'm going to run in and grab us a couple of towels. I'll be right back."

I stand there with the hose in my hand, still in shock at what I have just witnessed. I want him to do it again. *Another mud fight maybe? All right, Jo, quit having naughty thoughts.* I smile. Oh, how I love to scold myself and find amusement in it.

He returns with a white towel wrapped securely around his waist and another in his hand. He sets it down on the chair next to the door. He then takes the water hose from me and stands waiting. *Oh damn! It's my turn! No way! I can't do this!*

He can sense my hesitation. He rests his left hand on my shoulder to reassure me. "It's okay, Jo."

I nod as I push an even bigger lump down my throat. *Yeah, Jo. It's okay. A bra and underwear are no different from a bathing suit. Get it together. You can do this.*

I let out a small breath and try to relax as I pull my tank top over my head. My white, lacy Victoria Secret bra highlights my boobs nicely. I drop my tank on the porch and then start to unbutton my shorts next. Another small breath escapes my lips. I pull them down and display my matching panties. I slowly step out of the shorts as they rest on the porch boards.

I start to reach for the water hose, but Chase pulls it away.

"Do you trust me?" he asks.

He wants to rinse me! The erotic feeling that I had watching him has returned inside of me. I want him to do it. I want him to be the one in control of the water that rinses the mud away from my body.

I nod and feel the anticipation build inside of me.

He places the hose above my head, and the water falls around me. It is cool and crisp feeling. I close my eyes and run my fingers through my hair and over my face, feeling the mud fall freely. Suddenly I feel his hand on me helping the water wash me clean. I open my eyes and look deep into his as I help his hands and the hose do the work.

Once I am clean, he drops the hose and grabs my towel. He opens it up and swings it around my shoulders bringing it to a close at my boobs. I hold the ends together as he rubs his hands on either side of my shoulders, drying me. He stops as we stare deeply at each other. We both lean forward and fall into a deep kiss. Our tongues explore each other's mouth. I devour him. The taste of him.

We slowly pull away, and he says, "Let's go in. You're shivering."

He quickly turns off the water, and we turn and enter the house, closing the door behind us.

I'm in his clothes again, except this time I also have on a pair of his boxer briefs. I like the way they look and feel on me. Of course they are loose. I find a hair dryer in the bathroom and dry my hair. I run a brush through my loose curls and head for the living room. I hear the sound of music coming from the radio in the kitchen. I walk in and see that Chase is covering chicken breasts with strips of bacon. He notices me in the doorway.

"Good and dry now?" he asks.

I nod. "Yes, thank goodness. It was fun, though."

I smile.

He washes his hands and smiles back at me. "Yes, it was."

He opens the oven and slides the dish holding the chicken and bacon inside.

"So, what are you making?"

"It's smothered chicken breast. The chicken is cooked with bacon and then smothered in sour cream and mushrooms. Goes great with rice and steamed veggies. I hope you'll like it."

"Well, it certainly sounds delicious."

"It's going to be a little while."

Another song starts on the radio. He walks over to it and turns up the volume. "I love this song. Have you ever heard it?"

I shake my head. "No. What is it?"

"'Hold Me Together' by Royal Tailor. It's real good."

He grabs me and pulls me into him. He wants to dance. We slowly move across the small space in the kitchen. I feel my cheeks turning as he starts to sing along. He actually has a pretty good voice. "Can you hold me together? Can your love reach down this far? Can you hold me together cause without you holding my heart I'm falling apart."

I pay close attention to the words as the song plays on. They are perfect. Perfect for him. Perfect for me. Maybe even perfect for us. He wants to hold me together, and I realize I want him to do just that. I want him to hold my heart because without him I know now I would fall apart.

He continues to sing the song through as we keep dancing slow. I feel myself melting at the sound of his voice and the lyrics of the song. My left arm is resting on his shoulder, and my hand at the nape of his neck. My fingers play in his hair as we look into each other's eyes. Strands of his dark, messy, styled hair rest on his eyebrow again. The look he has in his eyes cripples me.

"You sing very well. Yet I feel I should be singing these words to you."

He smiles. "Oh really?"

I nod.

"So, will you?"

"Will I what?" I ask nervously.

"Will you let me hold you together?"

Oh, thank God! I thought he was asking me to sing. It was just a statement. I'm so glad he didn't take it seriously.

"Yes. I will let and want you to hold me together, Chase."

His smile widens, and the blue-gray brightens. "Good. I was hoping you would say that."

Within seconds, we are embraced in another long, tongue-tying kiss. The music plays on, and I feel my heart opening up and holding together. I am no longer falling apart.

Aimee and Kevin are sitting on the couch when I walk into our apartment that night.

She shakes her head at me. "Another day in Chase's clothes, huh?"

I do my famous eye-roll at her, which she has become used to over the years. However, I'm still not the veteran that she is.

"Hey, Jo. How's it going?" Kevin asks.

"Good, Kevin. How are you?"

He smiles with a nod, his arm resting on the couch cushion behind Aimee's head. Her big, nosey, I-need-to-know-everything head. "Just chilling."

"What happened this time?"

I sigh, somewhat aggravated that I can hardly make it in the door without being asked five hundred questions. My grandpa isn't even this bad.

"Let's go have a chat in my room. Sorry, Kevin, but this is strictly girl talk."

He throws his hands up. "Totally fine with me. Now I can turn off this stupid girly shit we've been watching and find something entertaining for a change. Maybe the Dallas Cowboy Cheerleaders are on. You know, football season starts soon. Take as long as you need."

Aimee punches him in the shoulder and rises from the couch, giving him one of her go-screw-yourself looks. She follows me into my bedroom and closes the door. We sit down on the bed. I can see the eagerness all over her face. She must know that I have something interesting to tell her this time. No granny kiss or boring stuff.

"So?" she says with a nod of her head and her hands in the come-on-and-tell me motion.

"It happened," I say calmly.

"It happened? You totally had sex with him?" she says excitedly and loud.

I wave my hands. "Aimee, shut up! No I didn't have sex with him. Geez, that's all you think about. I kissed him."

Her face turns to the disappointment I was expecting. "What?"

"I kissed him." I repeat myself so she hears me correctly this time.

"Look when you brought me in here, I thought you were going to tell me something that would leave me extremely hot and bothered, but I'm sorry to say that just a kiss doesn't quite do that for me."

I shrug my shoulders. "Well, I guess that shows where we're different."

"I can't believe you just said that." She has an astonished look on her face.

"I'm sorry I didn't mean it rudely, just honestly. I'm trying to tell you about what I consider one of the most amazing moments in my life, and all you can think about is me having sex with Chase."

"Look, I'm sorry. I don't mean to throw all of that at you. I've just seen you so unhappy and alone for such a long time that I'm ready for you to experience love and passion."

Geez could she have said that any cheesier? She is making me feel like I'm in a session with Dr. Black. I'm not depressed or anything.

"I understand. I just want to take it slow in a way. I just kissed the guy."

"Okay so wait a minute. *You* kissed him?"

"That's what I just said."

She smiles. "Holy hell! You've experienced a breakthrough. You made the first move. I'm so proud of you, Jo! Impressed actually."

I give her an achievement smile. "Thanks. I'm pretty impressed with myself too."

"Okay, so details on the kiss. How was it? I mean, is he an awesome kisser?"

"Well, first the *kisses* were beyond what words could even describe, and yes, he is amazing."

She giggles and bounces on my bed like a little girl. "Kisses? Damn, girl, when you do something you do it right! This is unbelievable! I am still trying to grasp that this is happening. So, is it official? Are you two a couple?"

I shrug my shoulders again. "I don't know. I guess. We really didn't talk about it."

"Well, in my book, if you kiss more than once and all on the same day, then something is definitely hitting the relationship status."

"I feel like that's where we are or where we're headed. I'm not 100-percent positive."

"You're 100-percent positive when the 'I love yous' come in."

I shake my head as my eyes widen. "I'm not ready for that. It's too soon."

"But do you?" she asks.

"Do I what?"

"Love him?"

For a minute I struggle to answer. "I have feelings for him in that way, but I'm just not ready to express that side of me yet."

She nods. "You will soon, or he will beat you to it. Especially if he's been waiting on you to make the first move. Once a girl shows a guy that she's interested, he takes it from there."

"Sorry, but I'm not familiar with that type of relationship. My high-school boyfriend made the first move and expected sex and then some son of a bitch rapes me."

"Well, I have a feeling you're about to become very familiar with it. Just remember what I said before. You have to go with it. If you really want it in your heart, then it's meant to be. I hope that your first real experience with love is everything it should be."

I smile at her. Even though she aggravates me so much, I love how she can turn from being completely annoying during a conversation to understanding and encouraging.

"Thanks again, Aimee. Another successful talk."

I reach over and grab her neck. We share a best friend's hug.

"You're very welcome. I love being here to help and get the scoop." She smiles.

Chapter Ten

It's Wednesday, and I'm trying hard to focus on getting everything ready at the cafe for the lunch rush. We have about fifteen minutes until it's time to unlock the doors to the public. Ramona walks behind the counter and adds a new roll of receipt paper to the register. Her red hair shines under the light. Her glasses hang from its cord around her neck. She is struggling to fit the paper in.

"Glasses, Ramona."

"Oh, yes. Thanks, Jo."

She reaches down and puts them on. She needs to be reminded at times to use them. Bless her.

"So, what's going on with you and this movie-star guy? Oh, what's his name ... Chase?"

I smile, thinking about her age and how she doesn't keep up with all the hunks that grace the big screen. Well, maybe Bob Barker, but not Chase Hartford. Well, maybe not even Bob since he retired from *The Price is Right. Dang I really liked that show.*

I turn to her.

"How did you know about that?" I ask.

She shoots me a don't-you-know-I-hear-things look. I get it. She's given that look to many people in town.

"Oh, well, he's nice and everything. We've been spending a lot of time together."

She smiles. "Yeah, that's what I heard. I also heard that he is a very attractive young man. Watch yourself, Jo. He is a big star."

"I know. I know. Believe me, I've heard that already."

"Well, you know what your grandma would say if she were here. I'm sure she'd like him, but you know how she worried about you."

I nod as I start rolling silverware in napkins. "Yes ma'am. I know."

"You should tell him to come have lunch here with us at the cafe."

"Oh, I have. He's coming by today. I told him about your special dressing and the turkey specialty."

Her eyebrows rise, and she grins. "Thanks for the advertising. Maybe it will pay off. We can have a picture taken of him here at the cafe and send it into the paper. But then again, we know he's not coming here for the food." She winks at me.

I laugh at her. "Ramona, you are a true mess."

I look up at the clock and notice that it's eleven. Time to open up. Zach walks over to the door with the key.

"Are we ready to rock and roll?" he asks before inserting the key into the lock.

Ramona replies. "Let's do this."

Zach unlocks the door and flips on the open sign in the window. Kelly comes rushing in and makes her way to the bar. She is holding something in her hand.

"Hey, Kelly. What's up?" I ask.

"Girl, you are hot news!" she says in an excited tone.

I give her a confused look.

"What are you talking about?"

She sets a magazine on the bar counter.

"This!"

"Holy shit!" I exclaim.

On the cover of *Star Gaze* is a picture of Chase, and then in the corner a small picture of the two of us at Club Light. The title reads "Chase's girl. Who is she?"

I am shocked. I can hardly speak. *Oh my God!* I wonder if he's seen this. I start to worry about what he is thinking if he has. *Oh no! This can't be good!*

"Jo, please! What's going through your mind right now? You have to tell me!" Kelly begs.

"What's going through my mind right now is that this is probably not a good thing. I bet if Chase has seen this he is having a stroke."

I am afraid. *Fear again. Great!*

Kelly shakes her head. "No, this is freaking awesome! You're on the cover of a national magazine!" Her excitement escalates.

I don't know what to think, how to feel, or what to say. I am trampled by so many emotions coming over me at once. *I'm so stupid! Why didn't I think about something like this happening?*

I open the magazine and turn to page thirteen. According to the table of contents, it is dedicated to Chase Hartford and his mystery girl. I try to read the article. I'm so nervous that I find it hard to concentrate. Part of the article reads:

> *Chase Hartford was spotted last Saturday night having a great time at Club Light in Charleston, South Carolina, with a mystery girl and her group of friends. They enjoyed drinks and some time on the dance floor together. It has also been reported that, prior to their night of partying, Chase took her to the exquisite and popular Magnolias restaurant in downtown. So, the question is and remains who is this lovely gal that has Chase swooning? Well, we aim to find out and will keep all you love-stricken and heartbroken fans updated with any information.*

My head is spinning. What the hell am I going to do? What will Chase do? Will he be calm and cool or overreact?

Kelly shakes my arm to pull me from my thoughts. "Jo? Are you all right, Jo?"

I shake my head. "No, I feel nauseous."

She rolls her eyes. "Are you kidding me? How can you possibly be worried about this?"

I place my elbows on the counter and cup my hands over my face. *Oh my God.* "Kelly, this is serious. This is so, so serious. What is he going to say? I mean he just got here, for crying out loud. The media is all over this and will stay on it. This is not what I wanted. I didn't want to bring attention to him or myself for that matter."

Kelly murmurs, "Well, I'm sorry, honey, but this is the sort of thing that happens when you are seen with one of the most famous movie stars on the planet. The thought had to have crossed your mind at some point."

I shake my head. "Honestly, not really. I guess you could say that I didn't think they would care too much about the average girl next door."

"Seriously? They love the average girl next door more than anything else! You're not some hotshot female movie star. You are different. Very different from the type of girls he is used to dating."

She's right. I am *very* different. I just hope that if he's gotten hold of this information that he is all right. It's worrying me so much.

"Why don't you text him and see if he's heard?" Kelly asks.

I could. "No. I want to talk to him personally. Facial expressions are hidden through text messaging, and I really need to see how he is responding to this."

She shrugs her shoulders.

"Whatever you say. But I think you need to accept this. If you're going to continue to see him, then you're going to have to get used to it."

I nod, knowing she is right again. But it's not just me that has to accept it, it's Chase too, and I desperately need to know if that's something he is willing to do.

The cafe is busy with our usual lunch customers, and even some new faces. There are several college freshmen and their parents seated at the booths and tables. I am nervously awaiting Chase's arrival. I'm also nervous about the chaos that may break loose when he walks in the door. Amanda and the new waitress, Zoe, are running from table to table, making sure their customers are happy and well-served.

I walk over to the register to ring up one of my customers, and I hear the bells ring over the door. I close my eyes for a brief moment and breathe. I look up and see that it's Chase. He's here. The squeals of a few college girls in a corner booth can be heard. Boss and Lincoln are standing next to him. The college girls jump up and head in Chase's direction. They each hold a napkin in their hands. I'm having flashbacks now from our first date at Magnolias. I watch as Boss and Lincoln tense up, but relax once they see that they only want an autograph. Chase takes a pen from Boss's hand and signs away. He chats with them for a second and even gives them a hug. He's so sweet. I smile, pushing the magazine cover and article out of my mind for a brief moment.

The girls walk back over to their booth, giggling and talking about their autographs. He looks over and sees me standing behind the register. We smile, and he walks over. "Hey. I've missed you the last couple of days."

He gives me a quick gentle kiss on my left cheek.

"Me too. Can we talk for a sec?" I ask.

He nods with a look of concern. "Sure. Everything okay?"

I glance over at Ramona. I had already filled her in on the situation and how worried I am. She gives me a nod that assures me she will watch my tables while I talk with him. I give her a thank-you smile. She winks.

I grab the magazine out from under the register and walk over to the employees' area, where we can have some privacy. Boss and Lincoln stand close enough, in case Chase needs their security.

"Have you seen this?" I ask as I hold it up.

He nods with a small laugh. "Yes, I have. I saw it this morning when Boss and I stopped at the store. Why? Does it bother you?"

I shrug my shoulders. "I don't know. I'm just shocked. I'm embarrassed to admit that I never really thought of something like this happening. At least not so soon."

"Welcome to my life. It comes with the territory. I had no doubt the media would be all over you. And I must admit myself they have really jumped to it this time. I'm surprised they have already been watching me so closely, being that I haven't been here long." He steadily watches my facial expression as I glance down at the cover. "Are you all right?"

"I guess. I was just real worried about whether you had seen it or not, and how you were reacting."

"It doesn't bother me. It's just another thing you get used to in this business. I don't want it to upset you, however."

I love how he is more concerned about how I feel than anything. I wasn't really sure what to expect from him.

"I just didn't want it to scare you away from me. I didn't want them to push something like this to where you think you are making a mistake with me. I'm no Megan Fox or Emma Stone."

He smiles. "No, you are not them, but you are someone I care about very much. They can write what they want and take all the pictures of us together that they want. I don't care. They're going to do it anyway, and there's no way to stop them. They can let the whole world know how crazy I am about you."

My heart melts at his words. *He's crazy about me, and I'm so crazy about him!*

I smile. "Thanks. I feel better."

He smiles back. "You're going to have to get used to it because they are going to see us a lot of places together. And the insane thing is that, most of the time, we won't even know they're there."

A lot of places together? What does he mean? LA? Key West? Denver? All around the world? I'd go anywhere with him, and they can write about it and post pictures in every magazine and paper they want. As long as I'm with him, it doesn't matter.

He wraps his arms around me and pulls me close. "Don't worry about it, okay? I can handle this. It's going to be all right. I'll hold you together. Remember? I would never be ashamed or hesitate to admit how I've fallen for you."

Our eyes lock. He stares into the hazel color of my eyes as I stare into his blue-gray. The end of the world could take place right here right now, and I would go happy. Happy because of the words he has just spoken. Happy because I know that they are true. Happy because I feel what I do in my heart.

"Are you ready for some lunch?" I ask, knowing that I need to get back to work.

He nods. "Yeah. We need to grab a bite. I have to be back on set in an hour. Where's your section? You're the only waitress I want."

He smiles big.

I smile as well. "Follow me, sir, and I shall show you to your table," I say, all waitress-like.

Boss and Lincoln follow closely as I lead the way. I reach a back table and point. "Here you are. What may I get you gentlemen to drink?" I ask in a professional manner.

Boss replies, "I'll take a water."

Lincoln says, "Me too."

I look at Chase. "Make that three waters."

"All right I'll be back in just a sec."

Chase and I smile at each other again as I turn to walk away.

Ramona is behind the counter, serving a customer. "Everything all right dear?" she asks me as I collect three glasses to fill with ice and water.

"Yeah, it's all good. Perfect, actually."

"Well, I'll tell you one thing." She turns to face me. "They definitely weren't lying when they said he was hot."

She gives me another wink. The third one today.

I am shocked by what she has just said. I had never imagined hearing the word *hot* escape the lips of a woman who is old enough to be my grandmother. It makes me giggle.

I finish preparing the glasses and head back over to the table where Chase, Boss, and Lincoln wait.

I set the glasses down carefully.

"All right, guys. Here you go."

A chorus of thank yous comes from the table.

"Now what can I get y'all to eat?" I ask.

Chase replies first. "I'll have the turkey specialty."

He smiles, looking up at me.

I hold my pen above my pad and smile back. "Everything on it?"

He nods. "Yes, please."

I turn my attention to Boss. He orders, "I'll take the club with mayo and mustard. Everything else, but hold the onions."

I write down the order on my pad and then wait for Lincoln.

"And I guess I'll just have soup and salad."

"Sounds good. What soup would you like? We have vegetable and homestyle chicken noodle today."

"Vegetable will work."

"And would you prefer green or Caesar salad?"

He thinks for a moment.

"Green."

"Dressing?" I ask.

Chase leans over and says, "Go for Ramona's special dressing. Jo recommends it."

We smile at each other again.

"Okay, I'll try that out."

"All right. Thanks, guys. I'll have your food out shortly."

I put the order into the kitchen and wait on some of my other customers. Every once and a while, I glance over in Chase's direction. He and the guys are talking. Girls constantly go up and say hello, wanting autographs and hugs. Some even want a picture taken with the famous Chase Hartford. All this happening right here at Ramona's. A month ago, I never would have imagined this would be a part of my life.

Nearly an hour later, Chase walks over to me.

"I have to head out. James is hoping to get a few scenes done today."

I nod. "Okay."

"Call you later?" he asks.

"Sounds great."

He leans in and gives me a soft kiss on the lips. There are people all around. I can feel them watching. He smiles when he pulls away. "Bye."

"Bye," I say in a whisper.

He leaves with Boss walking in front and Lincoln close behind. All I can think about is how I can't wait for his call.

I'm curled up in my sitting chair next to my bedroom window, reading *Pride and Prejudice.* I consider it the greatest novel of all time. I find my thoughts drifting from what is happening between Elizabeth Bennett and Mr. Darcy to waiting for my cell phone to ring. I'm dying to hear Chase's voice. He has been so busy with shooting this week that the closest I have been to him is through phone calls and his visit for lunch today at the cafe.

It's eight fifteen. I can no longer concentrate, so I put the novel aside and walk over to my bed. I decide to call my grandpa to help ease my anticipation of hearing from Chase.

"Hello?" He answers through the phone.

"Hi, Grandpa. How are you?" I ask.

He sounds excited to hear my voice, even though it's only been a few days.

"Jo! I'm good, sweetheart. How are you?"

"I'm good. I just wanted to check on you and see how the bingo game went the other night."

"Oh, I'm making it. I won a hundred dollars playing. Pretty good, huh?"

I smile. "Wow! Yeah, that is good."

"So, have you been seeing Chase a lot?"

Oh, the mention of his name. It is everywhere.

"Yes sir. He came by the cafe today and had lunch while on break from shooting."

"I really like him. He's such a good guy. He came by last night and visited with me for a little while. He was on his way home from the set and decided to stop by and chat. I enjoy talking with him."

It really moves me that Chase takes the time to visit my grandpa. There are very few guys that would want to spend time with an old, gray-haired man. I find this part of his personality very attractive and appealing. It says so much about who he is.

"Well, that's nice. I'm glad he came by to see you."

"All right. I'm not going to tie you up on the phone. I'm sure you have plenty to do. School starts next week, and I know you're working hard at the cafe."

Good old considerate Grandpa. He has a heart of gold.

"Speaking of the cafe, why don't you come by tomorrow and eat lunch with me."

"I'll do that. What time do you have your break?" he asks.

"Well, the lunch rush usually lasts until around one, so you could come by then if it's not too late."

"No, that'll be fine. I'll be there, and we'll eat."

"Great. See you then. Good night. Love you."

"Ok. Good night, Jo. Love you too, sweetheart."

As soon as I hang up with Grandpa, my phone starts to ring. I look down and grin from ear to ear when I see his name.

"Hey, Chase."

"Hey. I'm sorry I'm just getting around to calling you. I've been wanting to hear your voice since I left the cafe. I was going to call an hour ago, but we had a slight problem on set."

He's been wanting to hear my voice since then? Melt!

"Is everything okay? It's nothing bad is it?" I ask with concern.

"No it's not bad. Everything's fine. We just had an electrical problem, but it's fixed, and we are ready to start back shooting tomorrow."

"Oh, well, that's good to hear. What time is your call in the morning?"

"I need to be there around six because the whole crew is eating breakfast."

"Sounds nice."

I'm a little jealous. I want to eat breakfast with him again.

"Didn't you say that every day this week you go in at nine thirty?" he asks.

"Yeah, every day and off Sunday."

"Do you want to join us for breakfast in the morning before you start your shift? I'd love for James and the rest of the crew to meet you."

What? He wants to introduce me to the director and crew?

"I'd love to." I smile into the phone.

"Great. I can pick you up in the morning around five thirty."

I think about my schedule.

"Well, I work until four tomorrow afternoon. How will I get to work and get home?"

"Um … I can either drive you to work and pick you up when you get off, or you can just drive my car and come back to the set."

"Okay. I guess we can talk and figure it all out in the morning."

"That'll work. I can't wait to see you in the morning. I've missed you this week. We have definitely got to plan something this weekend together. Maybe Saturday night, since you're off on Sunday."

My heart drops at his impatience to see me and his confession of how he's missed me.

"Are you not filming this weekend?"

"Yeah, but only for a little while Saturday, and then I'm taking off Saturday night and all day Sunday."

Hell, yes! We're definitely going to make plans!

"Awesome. We can talk about what we want to do this weekend tomorrow morning too."

"Good deal. So, I'll see you."

"Yes. I'll be ready at five thirty."

"Good night. Sweet dreams."

"Good night," I say and then sadly push the end button when I pull the phone away.

I'm walking out of the woods. Tears are running down my face. I am cold and in pain. My arms are folded across my chest as I try and warm myself from the chill of the winter breeze. I can see the barn and the bonfire in the distance, but not clearly. I struggle to walk. My legs are weak and sore. My female organs feel as if they have been torn inside of my body. I try to fight my loud sobs. They echo around me. I can hear the faint sound of music playing.

I need to make it there. I need to make it to the protection of the barn. My friends are there. Worried. Worried about where I've gone. At least I hope they are.

I am suddenly grabbed from behind by these strong arms. A hand goes over my mouth to keep me from screaming. I struggle to breathe as the tears flow faster down my face.

"Listen, bitch." He talks in a whisper. "You better run and not turn around. You better not try to find me or find out who I am. Because if you do, and I find out, and I will, I promise you will regret it. I know who you are, and I'll make your life a living hell. Do you understand me, you stupid little bitch?"

I can't control the sobs that are trying to fight through the strength of his hand. I'm afraid. So afraid. Is he really going to let me go?

He pulls my hair hard with his other hand. "I'm sorry, I can't hear you. Do you understand?"

I nod as his hand stays, covering my mouth.

"Don't you forget it."

He pulls his hands away to free me. Without looking back, and with my tears falling uncontrollably, I run like hell.

Chapter Eleven

I'm standing at Chase's front door. It's midnight, and I can't shake the nightmare I have just experienced. It seemed so real, and it was by far the worst I've ever had. I knock gently, but loud enough to where I hope he can hear.

The door swings open, and I am awestruck. This time, with his white undershirt he is wearing a white pair of Armani boxer briefs. The white looks amazing on his tan body. *Complete and utter hotness stands before me!* I know I've seen him minus the T-shirt, but I'm finding it difficult to breathe.

"Oh my God, Jo. What's wrong?"

He looks down and notices the bag I am holding.

"I had a nightmare," I murmur.

"Him again, huh?" he asks in a sorrowful tone.

I nod. "I haven't had one since the night you came and stayed with me. But this one … this one was different. I've never had one like it before."

He takes my bag from my hand and opens the door wider. "Come on."

I walk in as he sets it on the floor and closes the door. He wraps his arms around me tight. "I'm so sorry. I'll take care of you. I'll protect you from him."

I sigh and say while standing there with him, "I know you can. That's why I'm here."

We pull away, and he places his hands on my cheeks, holding my face to where our eyes meet. "Do you want to tell me about it?"

I shake my head. "Not tonight. Maybe another time. I just really want you to hold me right now."

His face is sweet, yet serious. "Well, I can definitely do that. Let's go."

He reaches down and grabs my bag, then my hand, leading me to the bedroom.

We crawl into the bed, and he pulls me close. This time he gets under the covers with me. I lay my head on his chest and listen to the beating of his heart. It is such a soothing sound. It relaxes me. My fear is released with his touch, his embrace.

"I don't want to be anywhere else but here with you," I say with a courage inside of me that I thought would never exist.

He leans up, and my head falls gently on my pillow. He props himself on his right elbow and pushes a small strand of hair off of my forehead with his left hand. I notice his bracelet. *He wears it to sleep?* He looks down at me with a soft, sexy expression. A tingling sensation runs through my whole body. I yearn for him.

"I'm so glad you came to me tonight," he says in a whisper.

I can feel the warmth of his breath on my face.

"I need you, Chase."

I lift my hand to rub his cheek. His eyes close for a second at my touch, and then he opens them, gazing at me. "I need you too."

He leans down and starts to kiss me hard. Our tongues move rapidly. I raise my right leg and he pulls me closer into him under my knee with his left hand. I feel like I can't get close enough. My hands explore his hair, neck, and then his back while we continue to kiss. I find the bottom of his shirt and start to pull on it, wanting to strip him of it. He stops kissing me and pulls it quickly over his head, throwing it behind him to where it falls on the floor.

Our breathing increases as he kisses me more. He runs his hand under my shirt and rubs my stomach. I quiver. His tongue feels so good in my mouth. He moves his hand slowly and gently from my stomach to my side, going up, my shirt moving with it. I want to take it off. He stops, looking down at me again. I sit up and pull off my shirt. I feel sexy and confident in my pink bra and pink-and-white-striped sleep shorts.

I grab him. I devour every inch of his mouth. I moan because I want him so bad. I need him. I need him in *that* way. The way I've never had anyone. Yet I am so angry at myself for feeling this way. What am I doing? It's too soon. I know it is. I can't allow this to happen. I'm not ready. Yes, I am. No, I'm not.

His hands explore me, and then he moves his kisses to my neck. My hands move all around his back. His breathing deepens as our bodies get closer and closer. I want this, but I don't want this. I need to stop. I need to control myself. Why am I allowing myself to feel this way? I can't give in now, no matter how strongly and deeply I feel for him.

Suddenly he pulls away. *What is he doing?*

"Stop. Wait," he says through heavy breaths.

"What's wrong?" I ask.

He shakes his head.

"I'm sorry, Jo, but I can't do this. Not now."

"What do you mean?"

"It's not right. It's too soon. You need more time. I need more time."

Wow! I'm impressed. I am also relieved that he stopped before things went further. I am thankful because there is no telling what I would have allowed myself to do.

"Chase, do you want to be with me?" I ask.

"Yeah, I do very badly, but if we do this now, I'm afraid we will both regret it."

I sit up to where I am closer to him and nod. "You're right. This is not the right time. It's too soon."

"I'll regret this because I still feel that you're not ready. I want you to know that you are making the right choice. I'll never forgive myself if I do this with you now."

"I'm not ashamed to admit that I liked it, but a big part of me is disappointed that I did. It's almost as if I believe I shouldn't want this or feel the way I do about you."

He nods. "I understand. It is taking so much of my strength right now not to let this happen. I have to gain control of what I want to do and think about what's best for you. The big part of me knows that this is not how it should be. We need more time."

He moves in closer to me. "I just know that I want it to be special for you. For us both," he says.

He gently strokes the left side of my face with the back of his hand. "I want to give you so much more than here and what this would be. When it happens, I want it to be where we wake up the next morning in each other's arms, and we know it was right."

"Chase, I've never had the feelings for anyone that I have for you."

A true confession. I'm getting good at this.

"That's what I'm afraid of. I feel the same way about you, and I don't want a heated moment to turn into a rash decision."

Why does love have to be so confusing? It has been nothing but that for me. I fell for a guy in high school that desired sex more than anything, and I wouldn't give it to him. Now I find a part of me wanting to hand myself over to the hottest guy on earth, and he is telling me no. Not now. Not yet. I know I should respect it.

"It means the world to me to hear you admit how you feel about me, but it's also a good reason for me to not let this go on tonight. You're so beautiful and sexy, and I want you in every way imaginable except this way. My feelings for you are so different. You're different."

"I'm feeling things I never have before."

"I understand, and you feeling that way is definitely a start. I've made many mistakes in my life with girls and love. You're not one of *them*. What I have with and feel for you is so different and so much deeper. I refuse to let a mistake happen here."

I nod. "You're right. I don't want a mistake to happen either, but I must admit that I really enjoyed what was just happening."

He smiles in an attempt to hide his serious side. "Yeah, well, the actions were very pleasant and encouraging. And, yes, making love is like that. I want to make love to you. Countless times. I want you to remember them all, but the first is most important."

"You want to make love to me?" I ask.

He gives me an are-you-crazy-what-do-you-expect look. "Of course I do. More than I could ever explain right now."

I just did it! I just broke the world record! I honestly believe I have blushed more than any other girl on the planet and have swallowed the biggest gulps conceivable.

"But right now I just want to hold and kiss you. I want you to be here with me in the sweet and innocent way that builds the need inside of us to do and want more."

I nod. He's right. I must wait. We must wait. It will happen when the time is right for the both of us.

We lie down, and he pulls me close. He runs a finger across my lips and then covers them with his own. We kiss endlessly and passionately as the darkness folds around us.

I despise grocery shopping. I'm bad about going when I'm hungry, and the next thing I know, my buggy is filled with items I did not intend to buy, and my wallet takes the punch for it. Luckily, I'm at our local store to pick up only a few things. Chase wants to enjoy another night in, away from the crowds of Folly and Charleston, so I am on the job to collect our ingredients while he finishes up a few scenes on set.

I carefully look over the steaks in the meat department, trying to find the best-cut filets. I can honestly say I've never had one, and Chase is aiming to show off his fabulous grilling skills. I certainly won't object. He's quite the chef. Something I never once thought he would be. I smile at how sexy it is that he likes to cook so much. And to top it off, he's cooking for me.

As I'm standing there, rummaging through the wrapped filets, a woman walks up next to me and starts doing the same. She looks to be in her early thirties, with short, blonde hair and brown eyes. She's wearing a cute summer dress and flats. I glance over and give her a quick, friendly smile. She smiles and then does a double-take. It makes me feel a little unsettled, so I turn my attention back to my hunt.

"You know it doesn't have to be so difficult," she says.

I turn to face her and give a confused look. "I'm sorry?"

"Picking out meat. It's actually easier than you think."

"Oh. I guess. I don't do it often, so right now I'm definitely struggling."

"Well, I do it all the time. Maybe I can help. What are you looking for?" she asks.

I look down at the list that Chase made for me. "Um … filet mignon or at least the closest I can get to it."

"Yeah, well you can go with these." She picks up a pack of two. "But if you really want the mignon then you'll have to get the butcher to cut them up for you. They wouldn't have a cut like that out here. It's a little fancy for this size store."

I feel a little embarrassed. "Oh. Thanks for your help."

I pick up my shopping basket and start to head in the direction of the bell to grab the attention of one of the butchers.

"No problem. Big dinner date?" she shouts after me.

I turn around and nod.

"I'm taking it that you're not the one cooking," she says.

"Right. He is. I'd probably grill a steak dry."

We giggle for a second.

"Well, I would love to find a guy that would cook for me. Consider yourself lucky."

I smile.

She extends her hand out.

"I'm Stacey. I'm here on business, so I'm not very familiar with the area or the people."

I take her hand and give it a quick shake. "Jo. I'm from here, and believe me, there's not a whole lot to see, and we run a little short in this area on guys that like to cook."

"Thanks for the heads up."

"So what type of business are you here on?" I ask.

"Writing. I work for a company up in New York. There's big news going on around Folly Beach, and I'm here to find out all about it."

I have a perfectly good idea what news she is talking about: Chase. He is the only *big* news that this small town has ever had. I feel that this is a cue for my exit.

"Well, whatever big news you are here to dip into, I wish you luck," I say in a short-and-sweet tone.

"Thanks. I never run into much trouble. I'm real good at getting all the information I need for my story."

She smirks and walks away.

Shit! I need to remain calm. Could the *big* news she's after be finding out who Chase's mystery girl is? Is that why she's here? *Please tell me I'm wrong!* I wonder if she has seen the magazine with Chase and me on the cover. She *did* give me a look like she recognized me. *Shit! Shit! Shit!* I quickly speak with the butcher, get the perfect cut filet mignons, and then hurry through the store marking off the remaining items. I can't get to Chase's fast enough.

Stephanie Costley

Chase has already wrapped the filets in bacon, and now I watch as he spoons his secret marinade over them. They look mouth-watering.

"So, I want to tell you about a little experience I had at the grocery store."

He glances over at me with a curious look. "Something bad happen?"

"I'd define it as weird. Maybe even unsettling."

"I have a feeling I know what this conversation is going to be about, but I'd rather you enlighten me. Will you grab us a couple of beers out of the fridge, and we can sit outside and talk about it?"

I reach in and grab two Bud Lights and follow him out to the back patio, where the grill is heated and ready. He places the filets carefully on the rack and closes the lid. We sit on the patio chairs and pop the top on our beers.

"Well, I was in the meat department, desperately searching for the perfect cut filets when this woman started making conversation with me. She helped me with the steaks, and then when I started to walk away she asked me if I had a big dinner date. I didn't know if she was just trying to be friendly, or if I should be alarmed by anything. I found out that she is a writer that works for a company in New York, and she's here on business."

Chase takes a sip of his beer and continues to listen.

"She told me that there is big news going around in Folly, and that she is here to find out all about it. Her name is …"

"Stacey. Stacey Phillips," Chase says, cutting me off before I can get her name out myself.

My eyes widen as I hear her name escape his lips. "You know her?" I ask.

He nods. "Most definitely. She's a beast when it comes to her job, and believe me, she *will* find out everything she is here to dig up."

"How long have you known her?'

He replies, "Forever, it seems, but she has only been writing stories about me for the last couple of years. A fierce one she is."

"Well, there we go. The *big* news is you."

He shakes his head. "Oh, no no. The big news is *you*." He points to me with his beer in his hand. "You didn't realize that?"

I shrug my shoulders. "It crossed my mind, but I didn't want to overanalyze anything she said."

"Did you tell her your name?"

"Yes, and right now I feel like a complete idiot for doing that. She introduced herself, but it was before she told me why she was here. Damn, why didn't I see all that coming?"

"It doesn't matter. She would find out anyway. You didn't do anything stupid or wrong."

"I don't like this."

"What? That she knows your name, or that you're the big news?"

"Neither. I'm not prepared for this. I don't know how to handle whatever it is."

I am so stressed at the moment wondering what Sneaky Stacey is going to do with my name.

He puts his beer down beside his chair. "Will you please come here?"

I put mine down as well and walk over to him. He takes my hand and pulls me into his lap.

"I know this is hard for you, but I'm here to help you handle it. I remember how I felt the first few times I had to go through it. I hated reading lies about myself. I hated that they knew every single move I made and word I spoke. Eventually I got used to it. I mean, I still get upset over some things, but you can't let it control your life. You just move on."

"But that's so easy for you to say because you've been around it so long. I, on the other hand, do not know how to deal."

"That's why I'm here. You let me take care of things. The last thing I want is for you to be stressed over this."

"Well, I'm sorry, that's a little impossible right now. Stacey knows my name. She has an advantage over me."

He shakes his head. "No, she doesn't. You have an advantage over her."

I'm completely confused. How in the hell can that be? "And how is that exactly?" I ask.

"You have to show her and every other gossip writer that you're strong, and that what they say or write about you does not bother you in the least bit."

I slightly roll my eyes. "But that's easier said than done. You act like she is the only one I have to worry about. What happens when I'm back on campus next week?"

"Look, all we can do is take it one day at a time. Everything will be all right. You have to trust me."

I sigh. "I know. This is just too much right now. Too much so soon."

"You sound like you're having doubts."

"Doubts? Doubts about what?"

He grabs my hand. "Us."

Our eyes meet. What *is* "us" exactly? I have never had the nerve to ask. Maybe this is the perfect time. The time to look into those blue-grays and hear how he defines us.

"And we are …?"

He looks down in my lap and starts to play with my fingers. It's taking him a minute. *Does he have an answer for what we are?* Maybe he is just struggling to put it in the right words. He looks up and into my eyes. "To me, we are two people who are falling harder for each other every day. If you want to put a label on *us* then I would say we are a couple, and that I would be extremely proud to admit it to the world. At least that's my opinion and how I feel."

He rests his hand over his chest.

I smile. He has basically just given me the title *girlfriend*. It may sound elementary in a way, but to me it is the biggest and boldest word when it comes to Chase Hartford. Well, maybe one of them anyway. "I couldn't have said it better myself."

I lean down and give him a soft, tender kiss. We pull away slowly and smile. There is so much I want to say to him. But even though we are getting closer day by day I still feel it is too soon to use the big *L*-word. I definitely feel it, but I'm not ready just yet to verbalize it.

The College of Charleston campus is swarming with students. I carefully look around as I walk to the science building. I'm a senior. I can't believe this is my final year here before moving on. A rush of excitement runs through me. My cell phone starts to ring, so I hurry to the closest bench to grab it from my book bag.

"Hey, Chase."

"Hey! It's your first day back on campus as a senior. How do you feel?" he asks.

I smile at the excitement for me in his voice. "I'm good. Nervous, but good."

"Don't sweat it. Everything will be fine. I just wanted to tell you to have a great day before you got into class."

"Thanks. I'm going to need it."

I look around at the crowd of girls, guys, and book bags. Geez. Did the student population grow here since last spring?

"Go kick some ass. I want to hear all about your day tonight, okay?"

"Great. I'll fill you in. Good luck on set."

"Thanks. I'll call you later."

"All right. Bye."

I don't want to hang up.

"Later, love."

He's gone. *Wait. What?* He just said "love." That's new. I smile. That big word behind "later" just helped me feel more confident about my day. I'm ready. Ready to rock and roll.

My first class of the day is advanced inorganic chemistry. It's one of my major requirements for graduation, and I am ecstatic. I walk into the class, which resembles a big movie auditorium. There are rows and rows of chairs and a huge projector screen at the front of the room behind a desk, computer, and speech box.

I walk up the stairs carefully and take a seat in one of the chairs in the middle row. I glance down at my watch. It is five to nine. Students are rushing in the door, scoping the room for a seat. Right behind them is my professor, Dr. Wallace. He is a tall, skinny bald-headed man with glasses who looks to be in his fifties. He's holding a stack of papers in his arms. No doubt that is our syllabus for the semester.

The last several students locate a seat and get comfortable. Dr. Wallace messes with a small microphone that is hooked to the top of his shirt. "Good morning."

His voice echoes through the speaker system around the auditorium. "Welcome back. I hope that each of you had a restful summer break, and that you're ready to get busy. I will warn you that this course, along with its lab, is very demanding and time-consuming. I certainly hope that you will give them both your full dedication."

Great. Time to get back in the swing of things with a ton of work. This means less time with Chase. How will I survive?

"Before passing out the syllabus, I am going to check and see who is here and who I need to place on my no-show list. When I call your name, please raise your hand so I can mark you as attending the first day of class."

He calls for attendance in alphabetical order. The class is so large that it seems like forever for him to make it to my name.

"Reagan Calhoun. Leah Childers. Joshua Chisholm. Joanna Dawson."

I raise my hand. To my right, I notice that there are a few girls whispering. I look over at them and see that they are giggling. *What are they talking about? What little secret are they sharing?* God, I hope it's not what I think. I know for a fact that I can't handle hundreds or thousands of students recognizing me. I curse the magazine, and I already want to curse Stacey Phillips for being so sneaky at the grocery store. *Damn that woman!* I slump down in my seat, hoping to keep from drawing any attention.

I turn my focus back to Dr. Wallace. He is still calling out names from the attendance list. The door swings open, and a tall, built guy with blond hair enters. He has his book bag draped across his shoulder and a look of embarrassment for being late on the first day of class.

Dr. Wallace says, "Well, it's nice of you to join us, Mister ..."

The guy stops dead in his tracks and clears his throat. "Johnson. Matthew Johnson."

Dr. Wallace looks down and checks his name off. "Please take a seat."

He climbs the stairs, examining the empty chairs that remain. There are a few on each side of me. I pray in my head that he passes by my row. I'm not so lucky. He stops, gives me a smile, and decides to sit one chair down from me.

"Hi," he says as he sets his book bag down in front of him.

"Hi." I give a small smile in return and face front.

Dr. Wallace continues calling out names. He is now working on the P's.

The guy, Matthew, leans over and whispers. "You know, I hope this guy isn't going to be a total asshole. He already seems the type."

I smirk trying to avoid any conversation.

Dr. Wallace finally finishes and picks up the big stack of papers that he had set down on his desk. He divides them into three and walks to the front row on all three sides of the room. He hands a set to three different students.

"This is your syllabus. Please take one and pass it around your section. We will go over this briefly. It is your responsibility to read it in its entirety. There are specific guidelines and assignments that must be followed in order for you to be successful in this course. I will take questions as soon as we are finished covering what I feel is important to address as a whole class."

I am amazed at how thick and detailed the syllabus is once I am handed a copy. Oh, the long nights I have ahead of me. As I flip through the nine pages, I go ahead and tell myself that it will be advanced inorganic chemistry I will have a relationship with and not Chase.

An hour later, Dr. Wallace is wrapping up his introduction to the class.

"You need to report to your assigned lab tomorrow at the assigned time on your schedule. I will see you again on Wednesday. Come prepared to work and work hard."

I grab my book bag and stand to leave for my next class.

I follow Matthew out of the row. He turns and faces me with his hand stretched out for a shake. "Hi. I'm Matt."

I hesitate for a minute and then extend my hand to quickly shake his. "Jo."

"Nice to meet you, Jo. I just transferred from Virginia State, so I don't know many people around here."

I nod. "Well, I've been here three years, and there is definitely plenty of people to meet."

He smiles. "And I'm glad you're one of the first."

Red alert! I put on a fake smile. "Thanks. I'm sorry, but I really need to get to my next class."

"Where you headed?" he asks.

Do I tell him or should I lie? "Um ... I'm going to Calculus III."

Damn. I told the truth. Lying is something I have never been good at.

"That's odd. Me too. Do you mind if I walk with you?"

Yes. Yes, I do mind. Oh, hell, just let the poor guy walk with you. He's new and doesn't know anyone.

"No not at all." I push myself to say.

"Great."

We make our way out the door with the crowd and walk down the hall.

"You from around here?"

Here we go. Just as I expected. He wants to get to know me.

"I live at Folly Beach."

"I've heard of Folly. You like it?"

"Yeah. It's been my home for ten years."

"I'm from Roanoke," he says.

"Really? So what brought you to Charleston?" I act like I'm interested, even though I could really care less.

"I've always wanted to live in Charleston, so I decided to move here and finish out my senior year before heading up to New York."

"What's in New York?" I ask.

Girlfriend maybe? I hope.

"Everything. It's the city that never sleeps."

I nod. "Ah, I see. The party life, huh?"

He smiles. "I guess you could say that. Besides wanting to see it all for myself, I also want to enroll at Columbia University. I want to further my education there in molecular biophysics."

Wow! I'm actually impressed! This dude must be pretty smart to have such an ambition.

"Well, I wish you luck with that."

"What about you? What is your goal?"

I can tell that he is very curious.

"I'm majoring in biochem. I want to be an oncologist."

He raises his eyebrows as we push through the crowded hall. "A cancer doctor. Impressive I must say. Any particular reason?"

"I guess you could say cancer doctor, but I really want to do research on finding a cure for cancer. I lost a couple of family members to it, so it's something I've always been interested in."

He nods. "Oh, I see. I'm sorry to hear that."

I shrug in hopes that he will recognize that it is something I would rather not discuss further. "It's in the past now."

I scope the numbers by the doors to locate the correct classroom.

"Well, here we are," I say.

We enter the much smaller-sized room that is equipped with desks. I, being the nerd that most people know I am, pick a seat up in the very front. I do this in hopes that Mr. Johnson will be in favor of the back. Again, I am not so lucky. He decides to sit in the empty one right next to me. I sigh. *Now what in the hell am I going to do about this?*

Chapter Twelve

There is a knock on my apartment door. When I swing it open, there stands Chase in all his godliness. *Thank God! I have been dying to see him.*

"Hey, love," he says with a big smile.

I grab his hand and pull him in the door. He said that word again. It does something to me that I can't explain. I shut the door and kiss him. It is sweet yet passionate. I pull away slowly, wanting a look into his blue-grays.

"I missed you too," he says with a big smile.

"You have no idea how crazy today has been. School is going to kick my ass this semester. Literally."

I turn and walk toward the kitchen with him following close behind.

"It can't be that bad. What classes did you say you were taking?"

"Advanced inorganic chemistry, the lab, calculus three, and an English course."

He has a confused look on his face.

"English? Why English now? I thought that was a core class."

"Well, there are English core classes, but this is a more advanced class. I had to pick something to where I had a little over nine hours this semester."

"Damn. That is a lot."

"I know. I'm going to be swamped. On top of all that, I still have work and you."

I grab a couple of glasses out of the cabinet to pour us some sweet tea.

"Look, I'm not going to interfere with what you need to get done for school. I'll completely understand if there are nights when we can't see each other."

I turn to face him and wrap my arms around his perfect waist. I stare up into his eyes. Those few strands of dark hair are touching the top of his right eyebrow again. *Melt!*

"How about on those nights that I have tons of work to do, you can be my assistant," I say in a tone that is somewhat sexy and playful. I have *never* used it before. I'm proud of myself.

"With what? Advanced biochem and cal? I wasn't exactly the valedictorian at my high school graduation, Jo."

I giggle. "Well, you can stay with me and make sure I get all my work done."

He gives me a sexy smile while wrapping his arms around my waist. "I would fail miserably. I am 100 percent positive that I would be a major distraction and keep you from getting all your work done."

I can't argue with that. I like the sound of it, actually. I would much rather study him. *Okay, behave, Jo. Push those dirty little thoughts out of your mind. Hell no, I won't! I like having these thoughts!*

"Well, I must admit I would much rather study you."

Holy shit! I just said that out loud!

His smile gets even sexier. "The feeling is mutual."

We kiss, tongue-tied and all. My hands move up and down his back. His left hand explores mine as he holds the back of my head with his right hand, pushing me closer to him. Our kiss is deep and long-lasting.

We finally pull away slowly, but still stand close. I can feel his breath on my face.

"Don't you have Labor Day off from school?" he asks.

I nod. "Yeah, why?"

"Do you think you can take that whole weekend off from work?"

I shrug, wondering what he has in mind.

"I might be able to. I'll have to talk to Ramona. Why? What's going through your mind?"

"Well, I know that school is going to get intense for you in several weeks, so I thought about taking you somewhere."

"Really? And where is that?" I ask, full of curiosity.

"My home in Key West."

Key West! I try to control the excitement that is building inside of me.

He continues, "Labor Day is a couple of weeks away. We can fly out that Friday when you get out of class and come back sometime early Monday. You can take any school work that you need to do, and we can find time to relax while we're there."

"That sounds wonderful. I'd love for us to go."

He smiles. "Awesome. And while we're there, you can take some time away from studying school, and we can study each other a little bit."

A chill runs down my spine. I *love* the sound of that!

I smile back at him.

"That makes the trip sound even better."

"Do you want me to go and talk to Ramona myself? I'll get down on my hands and knees and beg for her to give you the weekend off if I have to."

I laugh at him. He is desperate for this little getaway. I begin to wonder what ideas he has up his sleeves for the trip.

"That won't be necessary. I can handle it. I'm sure she'll let me go. She is very understanding and knows this year is going to be tough for me at school."

"All right. If you change your mind and want me to, then let me know. I'm game."

"Thanks."

I think about mentioning the guy, Matt, from class, and then realize that it's not something so important or unnerving that I have to do it now. At the moment, all I can think about is hopping on a plane with Chase and flying to Key West for the weekend. The next couple of weeks can't go by fast enough.

I look over my advanced inorganic chemistry lab syllabus and can already tell that it is going to kill me. I will be returning many nights to work on experiments that are lengthy and delicate. I'm the type that refuses to let hard work falter, and I certainly don't take grades less than an *A plus*. The trip to Key West is going to be the perfect jump-start for me. I will relax and prepare myself for the long road ahead of those sleepless nights.

Unfortunately, Matt is in this class with me as well. And since he decided that sitting next to me was on his priority list, he is now my lab partner. *Thanks, Matt. And thanks, Dr. Davis, for assigning us this most inconvenient partnership.*

"Man, this lab is going to kick our ass!" he says as he looks over the syllabus as well.

"Speak for yourself. I refuse to let any class kick my ass."

"Well, with that type of attitude, I'm glad you're my partner." He smiles at me.

I wish I could say the same. I smirk.

"You know, Jo, I hope you don't find me too straightforward, but would you like to grab a drink tonight?"

Oh shit! I knew this was going to happen.

"Um ... I'm sorry, Matt, but I'm dating someone."

His eyes widen and he begins to stutter. "O-Oh. I'm sorry. I didn't realize."

"It's all right. No big deal."

He looks heartbroken. I hope I haven't hurt his feelings too bad. I feel terrible now.

"Well, um ... maybe one day we can grab a bite to eat on our break from class as friends."

I smile. I guess it's the least I could do. Hopefully, Chase won't mind. I wouldn't be committing a crime or anything. A girl can still have friends. Even if that friend is a guy.

"Yeah, we can probably do that."

The disappointment in his face is replaced with a smile. "Great. I look forward to it."

It's Tuesday and week number two back on campus. So far I am surviving. I haven't had too much work yet, and I'm still lucky that I haven't been identified or bombarded with questions from people I don't know. I wonder how long it can stay like this. Forever maybe? I doubt it.

Dr. Davis is getting ready to dismiss us as she points to the big projector screen at the front of the lab. "The last thing you need to remember is that once you are finished with your lab on Thursday, you clean up your area and put away all your materials. The building will be open this holiday weekend, if some of you do not have plans and would like to check on your samples. If not, then you can check on Monday or wait until we meet again on Tuesday. Any questions?"

Dr. Davis scopes the room for hands, but there are none. "Alrighty. I take it that everyone understands what they are supposed to get started with on Thursday. I will see you all then."

I jump from my seat and grab my book bag. It is time for my last class of the day, English 101. I am learning about the major British writers of history and their spectacular works.

"Are you planning to come by this weekend and check on our samples from the lab?" Matt asks as we head out the door.

I shake my head. "No, I'm going out of town this holiday weekend."

"Oh. With your boyfriend?"

I turn and look at him. "Yes. Why? Were you planning on coming by?"

He nods. "Yeah. I just want to make sure that everything is on track."

"Okay, well, if you're sure you want to do that."

"I do. I'll just catch you up on the progress in class Tuesday."

I nod. "Sounds good."

We are walking down the hall when three girls come up to us. I have no clue who they are.

"Hi! We just had to come and speak to you ourselves," says one of them, all giddy.

I'm sure she notices the confused look on my face. "I'm sorry, but do I know you?"

She shakes her head with a huge smile on her face. "No. I'm Katherine, and these are my friends, Carter and Whitney. We've wanted to say hi to you the last several times we have seen you on campus but didn't have the nerve."

I try to act cool. "Why in the world would you not have the nerve to speak to me?" I ask.

Katherine replies, "Well, we saw the first cover of *Star Gaze* magazine about Chase Hartford and his mystery girl. We thought it was you, but didn't know for sure until this one came out earlier today."

She holds up a new *Star Gaze*, and I am speechless. On the cover is a picture of me on campus and then an inset picture of Chase and me holding hands while leaving the set of *The Crane Files* on the morning we had breakfast with the cast and crew.

Holy shit are nice words compared to the one that is actually in my head that I really want to scream out loud right now.

The girl named Carter speaks up. "Now we know for a fact it's you. You are *the* Joanna Dawson. The mystery girl that girls everywhere have been dying to find out about. You are so lucky! We must hang out sometime!"

Yes, I am Joanna Dawson, I do not care who has been dying to find out about me, and no, we are not going to hang out just because you have the hots for my famous movie-star boyfriend!

Matt looks over at me. "You mean you're dating Chase Hartford? *The* Chase Hartford? He's your boyfriend?"

I try to swallow a large lump that has formed in my throat. It has put up more of a fight going down than the ones I've had before.

I put up my hand with a frustrating look on my face.

"Look, this is all very new to me, so if you'll excuse me I have to get to class."

With that, I walk away and don't look back.

As I sit down in English, I pull my Galaxy out of one of my book-bag pockets. I pull Chase's name up and press the new message button.

"Hey. I REALLY need to talk to you. Can I see you tonight?"

A few seconds pass, and there is the ding of a new message in my inbox.

"Of course. R u alright?"

"I'm not sure. Overwhelmed."

"Where and what time?"

"Ur place and as soon as u can."

"My place ... great idea ... time ... six?"

"That works. Okay about to start class. I'll see u later tonight."

"Can't wait. And whatever it is ... it's going to be alright ;)"

"Let's hope so :/"

"??? Can I at least get a :)"

"Sorry. :)"

I don't want to act like a basket case, but all of this is really starting to get to me. Hopefully he can make it better, just like he does with everything else.

I take the new copy of *Star Gaze* magazine out of my book bag that I purchased on the way to Chase's and show him the cover.

"This is what I'm overwhelmed about. Look at this! I read the whole article. They know who I am! They know where I go to school and work! They know about my family! They got what they wanted! Damn that Stacey Phillips!"

"Hey, hey. It's okay. Take a breather," he says, all calm.

I give him a shocked look. "What? 'It's okay? Take a breather?' Do you have any idea what you just said to me?"

He nods. "Yes, I know exactly what I just said, and you need to do that. Breathe."

"You've obviously already seen this cover because you are not acting near as shocked as I thought you would."

He laughs. "Yes, I have already seen the cover. I saw it earlier this morning when it hit the stands."

"How do you do that?" I'm getting angry and frustrated that he doesn't take this as seriously as I do.

"Jo, my career is what these people write about. I told you; I'm used to this. All of this."

I throw the magazine down on the floor and put my hands on my hips.

"Oh, yeah? Well, let me tell you one thing you're not used to. You are not used to dating a normal, small-town girl that is having a hard time dealing with the fact that her name and face is planted on the cover of a national magazine. And God knows what else that she hasn't seen!"

I walk over to the couch and sit down with my arms folded across my chest. I am losing it! I am hot right now!

Chase walks over and sits beside me. "Wow. You're really angry right now, aren't you?"

I don't think he wants me to respond to that question. It's pretty obvious that I am pissed off.

I look over at him. "You don't miss a thing."

"Okay, look. I want to talk to you about this, but I can't when you're so upset."

I sigh. "You know what? You're right. I think it's best that I have some time to cool off. I'll talk to you later."

I quickly get up, grab my book bag, and head out the door to my car.

I'm lying in bed, hugging one of my pillows with thoughts of Chase and me running through my head. I feel terrible for the way I acted, but it was a display of how I really feel. I don't want to have such a hard time handling all this, but I just don't know how to face it the right way. Chase knows because it has been a part of his life for so long. I, on the other hand, never once imagined that I would be in his shoes.

I look down at my faith bracelet. It's wrapped securely around my wrist just like Chase's love around my heart. *Faith* and *strength*. I need to have faith in this, and he's trying so hard to be my strength through it all. To help me find the strength of my own. *What am I doing? This is ridiculous! I'm going to push him away by doing this. I can't lose him over something this stupid!*

I need to talk to him. I need to apologize for how I acted and let him know that everything is going to be okay. I'm going to try to deal with this. *Shit! I walked out on him!* How is he going to react? What if he doesn't care anymore? *No! That's not true. I can't think this way.*

I look around my bed for my shoes. The next thing I know, there is a knock on my bedroom door. I have no time to answer before it swings open. Chase is standing there with a look on his face. I'm not sure how to read it. Is he angry? Hurt? So over it?

He shuts the door behind him and walks over to my bed. He doesn't say a word. He just looks down at me with his sexy eyes and his hair doing that thing it always does. He gently pushes me back on the bed and lies on top of me.

"I'm sorry, Jo," he says as he pushes a thick strand of my brown hair out of my face and behind my ear.

"No, this is my fault. I shouldn't have gotten so upset."

"Yeah, but I need to be more understanding about how you feel in these types of situations. You were right when you said I'm not used to being with a normal, small-town girl who has a hard time dealing with all this. It really does hurt me to see you upset."

"But I shouldn't have walked out on you like that. It was wrong. I'm sorry."

He kisses me and then rubs his lips across my cheek. "It's fine. You said you needed some time, and I was going to give you that. I couldn't wait any longer though. I had to come see you."

I wrap my arms around him. "I'm so glad you're here."

He looks down at me and then grabs my right hand to hold my wrist up. "Remember ... 'faith' and 'strength.'"

He holds his up too and points to both of our bracelets. "You have to hold it together, baby. You have to have faith in me and all of this. Most importantly you must have faith in yourself. My strength will be yours. I am not going to let you fight this alone."

He just called me baby. I want him to say it again. I want him to call me all kinds of wonderful, sweet names.

"I know you won't. I'm ready to get away with you this weekend. I need time with you more than you could ever know."

He smiles. "Me too. I'm excited about having you all to myself for three whole days."

"I'm ready for you to have me all to yourself," I say with a serious look on my face.

His smile fades as he stares down into my eyes. He kisses me hard and long. It's intense. There is so much I want to do right here, right now in my room with him. But we can't. It's not the right place or the right time.

My hands explore his back, and then I move them down to his jeans. I feel his hands on my body and want them to do things to me. Things that I've never experienced, but have wanted with him for what seems like forever. Yet it really hasn't been that long. My courage continues to build with every kiss and every touch that we share. I can tell that his is too.

It's Friday afternoon, and I'm giving my bag for Key West one last look-over. Bathroom supplies? Check. Cute tops and shorts? Check. Sundress? Check. Bathing suits? Check. Comfy PJs? Check. Sexy Victoria Secret bras and panties? Double-check. I'm ready. Ready for my weekend getaway with the sexiest guy in the world.

I walk out of my bedroom and down the hall into the living room. Aimee is walking in the front door.

"Hey, girl," she says as she sets down her purse and keys.

"Hey."

She smiles. "Well, you look all packed and ready to go."

I nod. "Definitely. I'm very ready for this."

"It's going to happen this time isn't it?" she asks as her smile spreads.

I shrug my shoulders. "I don't know. I guess we'll see. If it's right, it's right. If not, then there's always next time."

She shakes her head. "No. This is it. The two of you are going to be completely alone for three whole nights at his beach house. You can't possibly tell me that sex isn't part of this plan."

"It's not. I don't like to plan things. I'd rather them just happen."

"Come on, Jo; just screw the guy already. I mean, that's obviously what he wants. This whole trip was his idea, you know."

I roll my eyes. "But that's not the reason. And if we were to *be* together this weekend, it certainly wouldn't be that way."

"Then what other way is there?" she asks.

I sigh. "Obviously one you are not familiar with. I've got to go. Chase and I are supposed to head to the airport in an hour, and I want to stop by and see Grandpa."

"Okay, well have fun, be careful, and wear protection."

I turn from the door to look at her with a look of frustration.

She throws her hands up. "I was talking about sunscreen. Geez."

It's now my turn to roll my eyes. She walks over and gives me a squeeze. "Seriously, be careful and have fun. I'll miss you."

I hug her back.

"Thanks. I'll miss you too. You and Kevin, please try and keep the apartment in one piece."

"Okay, but I'm not making any promises about my bedroom."

She winks.

"Bye, Aimee."

Grandpa is standing on the porch when I pull into the driveway. He's wearing his yard overalls and old straw hat. He's been working in the garden. Bless him. He smiles as I jump out of my BMW, leaving the ignition running.

He takes a sip of his iced lemonade and sets it down on the porch table as I climb the steps.

"Hey, Jo."

"Hey, Grandpa."

We give each other a hug.

"You packed and ready to go?" he asks.

I nod. "Ready as I ever will be I guess."

"Are you nervous?"

My eyes widen as I look up at him. "Nervous about what?"

"Flying?"

I shrug my shoulders. "No, I think I'm okay. I should be able to handle it fine."

"Well, if you have any trouble, Chase will see that you make it through."

It makes my heart melt how he talks about Chase. He really thinks the world of him. In a way, I'm surprised that he isn't lecturing me about flying to another state with him, and then, in another way, I'm not.

"Yeah, you're right about that. He's real good at making me feel better about things."

He nods. "I've noticed. I just want you two kids to be careful and have a great time."

I smile. "Thanks. I'm sure we will. What about you? What are you going to do this weekend?"

"Margaret and I are going out to dinner tonight, and then tomorrow night we're going to play bingo."

I laugh. "That's great. I'm glad you and Ms. Margaret are enjoying each other's company. It makes me happy to see you happy."

He smiles. "Yeah, she's a fine lady."

I look down at my watch and notice that it's two thirty.

"All right, dear. I know you need to go. Like I said, y'all have fun and be careful."

I throw my arms around his waist. "We will. Thanks. I just wanted to tell you goodbye. I'll see you when we get back."

He nods with a smile. "Okay. Love you, Jo."

"Love you too, Grandpa. Tell Ms. Margaret I said hello."

"Okay, I will."

I walk out to my car and jump in. As I pull out of the driveway to head up the dirt road to Chase's, I stick my hand out the window and give my grandpa a big wave.

Chapter Thirteen

Chase and I are standing by the window, waiting for our boarding call. I'm looking out at the huge planes and the workers scurrying around on their airport carts. Luggage going here, luggage going there. Airport traffic controllers directing planes to and from the runway. These are the same exact things my parents watched as they waited to board their anniversary flight to the Bahamas.

Chase grabs my hand as he watches me stare out the window.

"Are you all right?" he asks.

I nod and turn to smile at him. "Yeah, I'm fine."

"You're thinking about them, aren't you?"

I didn't want him to notice. I didn't want him to ask. I just wanted to try and get through the thoughts of my parents quickly.

"Yeah. I remember when Sam and I went with them and Grandma and Grandpa to the airport. My mom and dad were so excited about getting away together for a few days to celebrate their ten years together. They walked down the terminal, hand-in-hand, with these big smiles. They were so in love. They had no clue what tragedy was before them."

Chase squeezes my hand. "No one ever does, Jo."

We look at each other.

"Okay, enough talk about this. We are going to board this plane and we are going to have a great time together."

He nods and smiles. "Yes, we are. No worries. I'm here. You'll be just fine."

I smile back at him. He's right. I will. I'm going to sit right there beside him and fly to Key West. I might even gather up the nerve to look out the window.

A lady comes over the airport intercom and makes her announcement. "Attention, Delta customers for Flight 1020 to Atlanta, Georgia. We are now ready to board all first-class passengers."

Chase looks over at me. "Well, that's us. You ready to go?"

"Very."

His smile gets bigger.

"Well, let's go."

We stop at the lady standing behind the ticket booth by the terminal.

She checks our tickets and says, "Mr. Hartford. Miss Dawson. Thanks for choosing Delta airlines. Enjoy your flight."

Nice choice of words, lady. At this point I'm just glad she didn't say, "Have a safe flight." Those words would have freaked me out.

As we approach the long terminal to our plane, Chase stops and turns to me. "Wait, you've never flown before, have you?"

I shake my head.

"Shit. Why didn't I ask you that before I booked this flight?" He has a look of concern.

I hold up my right wrist with my faith bracelet. He looks right at the word, so perfectly engraved.

"I have faith in your strength. Your strength shall help me with my own."

He smiles and nods. "Good."

He winks and continues leading me down to the plane.

The pilot and co-pilot, along with the two first-class stewardesses, are standing at the door of the Boeing 737.

The pilot extends his hand.

"Welcome aboard. I'm Captain Brantford, and this is Second Officer Kipling. It is our main priority that you have a safe and enjoyable flight to Hartsfield-Jackson Atlanta International Airport."

Chase and I smile at them both.

Chase says, "Thanks."

Captain Brantford continues, "These fine young ladies, Jasmine and Holly, will make sure that you are comfortable and have everything you need."

They both smile at us.

Jasmine points to the curtain that hangs in the doorway, giving privacy to the first-class passengers from those in coach.

"Right this way, please. I'll take you to your seats."

We follow her through the curtain and into first class. I have never been on a plane and never imagined that my first time on one would be experiencing the luxury of first class.

The seats recline and are made of leather. There are individual workstations and private TVs. Wow. I'm amazed.

Jasmine shows us to our seat and offers to take Chase's carry-on bag to put in the stowaway compartment. He hands it to her.

"Miss Dawson, would you like for me to take that for you?"

She points to my Kavu keeper bag.

I shake my head. "No, thanks. I'd like to keep it with me."

She smiles.

"Very well. Can I get the two of you a beverage?"

Chase and I sit down in the leather chairs and look at each other.

"What would you like, Jo? We will be arriving in Atlanta in a little over an hour."

"I'll take a glass of wine."

He smiles and turns to Jasmine. "We'll both take a glass of the best on the plane."

She nods. "Yes sir."

Chase turns back to me. "Are you going to be okay by the window?"

I give him a don't-you-remember-what-I-just-told-you look.

He chuckles. "Right. I forgot. Faith and strength."

I grin at him.

"So are you comfortable?"

I nod. "Yeah, this chair is awesome. It makes me want to go to sleep."

"Great first experience, huh?"

"So far," I reply.

Jasmine returns with our glasses of wine. I take a sip, and it is delicious. My eyes light up from the crisp taste.

"Excuse me, Jasmine, but what is the name of this?" I ask, holding up my glass.

"It's 2008 Groom Sauvignon Blanc. Do you like it?"

"Oh, it's amazing. Thanks."

Chase watches as I take another sip. "I guess it's safe to say you will not be enjoying more than one glass of that."

I wink at him. "Why, Mr. Hartford? Would you be embarrassed if I were to get drunk in the air?"

"Not at all. I'd find it entertaining." He winks back.

"Let's leave the entertaining for the beach house."

His eyes widen at what I have just said. *Joanna Lane Dawson! Control your thoughts! They are escaping through your mouth!*

His expression changes to another smile, yet this one has sexy all over it. "You got a deal."

I blush. I'm not embarrassed or regretful for what I have just said, even though my mind finds it necessary to scold me.

He takes a sip of his wine and sets down his glass. "We have a short layover in Atlanta. We should be there about an hour, and then board our next plane to Key West. That flight should take about two hours."

He looks down at his watch. "It's almost four. That means we should be arriving in Key West around eight thirty tonight."

"Exciting. How will we get to your place?"

"We'll take a cab. I never leave my cars at the airport unless I'm taking a short trip somewhere, and I feel they are safe."

"Gotcha."

Captain Brantford comes over the intercom and announces, "Ladies and gentlemen, welcome aboard Delta Airlines Flight 1020 to Atlanta. We are looking at beautiful skies with a few clouds on this Friday afternoon. We will be ready for takeoff shortly. Please make sure that all luggage is stowed away safely, all electronic devices are off, and that all seating compartments and trays are securely fastened. We will be flying at thirty-four thousand feet, and our estimated arrival in Atlanta is five twenty."

Chase reaches over and grabs my hand. "Are you ready for takeoff?"

I feel a lump start to form in my throat. I can't hide the fact that I'm nervous. I'm about to climb thirty-four thousand feet into the clouds. The world will be below me. The wine will help calm my nerves.

I nod.

"Everything is going to be fine," he says softly.

Captain Brantford comes back on. "All right, fellow passengers the doors have been tightly secured, and we are ready for takeoff. Please make sure you follow the proper guidelines for takeoff and double-check to make sure that your seatbelt is securely fastened. Remember that you should remain seated until given further notice. Also, please remember this is a smoke-free flight."

The Boeing 737 starts to move. The wheels are rolling slowly beneath us toward the runway. I can feel the lump growing in my throat, and my stomach start to turn. This is it. We're about to be off the ground and in the air. I take a deep breath and close my eyes. I can do this. There is nothing to be afraid of.

Chase gives my hand one last squeeze as our plane reaches the runway and comes to a stop. "All right. Here we go. Just squeeze my hand or put your head on my shoulder if you need to. It's going to be fine. I promise."

Suddenly I feel the wheels rolling beneath us again. The plane starts to increase its speed as it heads down the long strip. It brings my head back to the seat. I close my eyes once again and take another breath. My heart is racing. Then it happens. The plane soars into the sky, leaving the ground below us. The feeling is intense. I lean over and bury my head in Chase's shoulder. He giggles at me. My eyes are tightly closed.

"It's okay. We're in the air now. Come on and open your eyes."

I slowly pull away from him.

"You did it. See that wasn't so bad."

I smile. *I did it. I'm in the air.* The lump in my throat is gone, my stomach is no longer turning, and I'm eager to look out the window. Still holding on to Chase's hand, I turn and look down at the world below us. It is so fascinating! I still can't believe that I am soaring in the air with Chase! The plane is still climbing. I watch as the buildings, trees, streets, and bodies of water get smaller. We are on our way. Next stop, Atlanta, Georgia, and then Key West, where I will spend three amazing days with the guy of my dreams.

The taxi makes a right onto Key Haven Road. Palm trees are spaced perfectly on each side of the road, and lantern-style street lamps light the way. The homes in the neighborhood are breathtaking with their architecture and beauty. I have never seen anything like it in my life.

"Here we are," Chase says as the taxi driver pulls up to the security gate of a home on the left.

We get out, and the driver assists us with getting our luggage out of the trunk. Chase hands him some cash and tells him thanks. The driver nods with a smile and expresses much thanks to Chase in return. No doubt there was a little extra cash involved. He then gets in his cab and drives off.

Chase enters the code in the access box, and the gate slowly swings open. He grabs my hand as we walk toward his huge, contemporary-style home, and the gate closes behind us.

"Chase, it's absolutely amazing," I comment as we arrive at the front door.

He takes a key out of his pocket and smiles. "Thanks. I'm glad you like it."

He unlocks the door and pushes it open. He holds his hand out for me to go first. I smile and step inside. Wow! I am overwhelmed by the sight. Chase and I set down our bags as I look around.

"Let me take you on a tour," he says with his hand outstretched.

I take it as he leads me through the house. There is everything remarkable about his six-thousand-square-foot home. Its cathedral ceilings are made from tongue-and-groove, the walls are cypress, and there is an elegant marble fireplace in the living room. The kitchen is gourmet with custom-made cabinetry. Upstairs is a game room equipped with a pool table, poker table, huge movie-theater screen, theater chairs, and a wet bar. Outside are a gourmet kitchen and a large infinity pool next to his private access to the beach. Connected to the infinity pool is a natural stone grotto and spa with a waterfall.

We are standing outside by the pool.

"It is all absolutely breathtaking. I have never seen anything like it. Well, not in person at least. Only on *MTV Cribs*."

He laughs and then turns to face me. He's still holding my right hand and takes his right to rub my cheek.

"I want us to enjoy being here together. I can't imagine not having everything perfect for you."

I look into his eyes. "You are perfect for me."

We stand for a moment lost in each other's eyes.

"I only want to be here with you. No one else. Ever."

Shit. Another lump. Swallow it down, Jo, and breathe.

He leans in and gives me a single soft kiss. I savor the innocence and sweetness of it. As he pulls away, the hazel and blue-gray of our eyes meet.

"Let's go in and unpack."

He leads the way again as we enter the house to get settled for our first night.

We walk down the long hall to Chase's master suite that waits at the end behind massive wooden double doors.

He stops before reaching for the handle.

"Now, as they say on *MTV Cribs*, I'm about to show you where all the magic happens."

After a second, we both break out into laughter. Then the thought crosses my mind. Has he worked his magic in his bedroom with any of the other girls he considered serious in his life? Maybe some of his past famous girlfriends? The thought haunts me and is a little unsettling.

He holds his hand up. "I was only kidding. I swear."

We laugh a little more. It takes us a minute to pull ourselves together.

"Okay, so let's get serious. I need to know something," he says.

"What is it?" I ask.

"I didn't bring you here with the expectation of you sleeping with me."

I give him a weird, confused look.

"I mean not in *that* way. What I'm trying to say is that if you would feel more comfortable sleeping in another room, I will completely understand. I just wanted to get you away from work, school, and all the other craziness you have to deal with right now."

I step in closer to him. "I don't want to be away from you for one minute."

He smiles and closes his eyes while standing in front of me. "I was hoping you'd say that because I can't bear the thought of you not sleeping in my arms."

Oh, and how I want to be in those arms!

He opens his eyes, looking down at me. He plants another kiss on my lips just like the one before out by the pool. I love the gentle touch of his lips, yet I'm yearning deep inside for his hard and passionate kisses. I desire so much more. Here. All alone. Together.

He turns the doorknob and swings open the double doors. It is by far the most beautiful room in the house. The hardwood floors are made of cypress, and the wall-paint color is a very light shade of blue with a soft cream color on the crown molding. There is a magnificent antique king-sized four-post corner bed with blue-and-cream colored patchwork quilts and large, decorative pillows. There is a sitting area with two chairs and a table by a huge bay window overlooking the ocean. A stone fireplace and large wall-mounted flat-screen TV are nestled to the right of the bedroom entrance in front of the bed. It is just as I had imagined it. It's everything warm, calming, and romantic. This I love! There is no leather or animal print suffocating the room, giving the impressions of a sex-crazed bad boy.

"Do you like it?" he asks, glancing over at me.

"It's just as I pictured."

He cocks an eyebrow. "You've imagined what my bedroom looks like?"

I blush. "Well … yes."

He smiles, no doubt at the redness of my cheeks. "My mother did all this. She's quite the decorator. I guess you could say she knows me well."

"It's very warm and romantic in here." I glance back at him.

"Let me show you my master bath."

He leads me to another set of double doors that are between the sitting area and fireplace. Inside is a large marble and glass walk-in shower with double shower heads. An oversized cast-iron claw-foot tub with oil-rubbed bronze fixtures is perfectly placed next to a small fireplace that's been built into the wall. There are double vanities, a small, flat-screen TV, and private toilet. It's my dream bath.

"Very nice. That tub is definitely a place I would like to relax."

"Well, please. I insist. Use it as much as you'd like. And yes, I have bubbles and oils."

I look at him quickly. I'm red again. We smile.

"Well, now that you've seen everything, let's get unpacked."

After we get everything put away in his room, and he stores our bags in the closet, he asks, "You ready to try out that tub?"

My eyes widen, and my heart races. *Does he mean together? Oh shit!*

"I have everything you need in there. I'll go use the guest bathroom, and then we can relax with a glass of wine."

Damn. Why am I so disappointed right now? He grabs his clothes and starts to head out of the bedroom but stops. He gives me another kiss. *Why is he doing this to me? Every little kiss makes me want him more and more.*

He smiles. "I'll see you when you're done."

I nod and return the smile. He leaves, and I grab something comfortable of my own to slip on and head for the master bath.

I walk out of Chase's grand master suite and head down the hall to the living room. I'm wearing a matching Victoria Secret cream-color sports-bra-and-panty set with a forest-green tank top and cream-color pajama pants with palm trees. I guess you could say I'm in the Key West spirit.

As I enter the living room, I notice that Chase is standing in the kitchen, pouring us both a glass of wine. He has on a light-blue sleep tank and gray sweat shorts. *Hot flash!* The sight of his tan body and muscles makes me quiver. He looks over his shoulder and smiles. The blue-gray of his eyes goes together perfectly with his clothes. *Major hot flash!*

"Cute PJs."

I smile. "Thanks. I thought they fit the occasion."

I walk over, and he hands me my glass.

"Yeah, I'd say so."

We both take a sip. It's just as good as the wine I had on the plane.

"So I must ask, what is on our agenda this long holiday weekend?" I ask.

"Well, I do have several things in mind."

"Can you share what you have planned?"

He shakes his head. "Nah. You have to wait and see."

I cock an eyebrow at him. "Really?"

"Yes, really. It all starts in the morning."

"I can't wait."

"As soon as we finish this wine, we need to get to bed. We have an early start."

"How early exactly?"

"Don't worry about that. I'll wake you." He smiles.

"I'm counting on it." I smile back.

I take a seat on one of the stools at the island. Chase leans, propping himself against it with his elbow resting on the smooth granite.

"I'm excited about you seeing the ocean water here. It is amazing how clear and blue it is."

"I'm excited about seeing a lot of things."

"Well, I'll get you out tomorrow to enjoy a few sights, and then Sunday we will relax around here for the most part. Does that sound good to you?"

I nod. "Wonderful. I have a feeling I'm not going to want to return to the real world on Monday."

He shakes his head. "Most likely not, and I promise you won't be the only one. The next place we need to go is Denver."

I grin.

"Oh, so you're planning on taking me somewhere else?"

He nods. "Maybe in the fall for Thanksgiving or Christmas might even be better."

I'd go anywhere with him anytime. At the moment, I just want to enjoy being with him here. Right now. "That sounds awesome."

I take the final sip of my wine as he reaches for my glass. He takes it gently and sets it down.

"But right now I want to take you to bed and hold you in my arms."

Yes! Please! Please take me to bed! A sensation runs through my entire body.

I stare at him, watching his every move. He walks around the island and reaches for my hand as I stand from the stool. There is no embrace. No kiss. Just silence as he turns out the light, and I follow him to his suite.

I'm in the master bath. As I finish brushing my teeth I stare at myself in the large mirror. Is this it? Is *it* about to happen? I don't know what to expect. He's already told me that he didn't invite me here to sleep with me in *that* way. *That* is not his intention. I personally couldn't have picked a better place for *it* to happen. If there is one thing I know for sure, it is that I want him, and I will not stop him because of how badly I want him. How badly I need him. I take a deep breath and walk out of the bathroom.

Chase is already standing next to the bed. He pulls off his sleep tank and sweat shorts. My heart pounds against my chest. Armani boxer briefs again! Gray this time. *Damn!* There's just something about seeing that name wrapped around his tan, sexy waist that does something to me. Is he just getting comfortable? After all, we are going to sleep. Aren't we?

"Don't be afraid to get comfortable," he says, looking across the huge bed at me.

"I'm not afraid," I say in confidence. I then pull off my pajama pants and throw them at him in a playful way. He catches them and smiles. He then proceeds to throw them over on the chair next to his sweat shorts. He reaches over and turns off the nightstand lamp. I climb into the bed, waiting for him to do the same.

"Oh, wait," he says.

He then turns and walks over to the huge bay window. He unlocks the windows and slides them up. The sound of the waves hitting the shore fills the room through the screens. It is so soothing. He then takes a minute to switch on the ceiling fan above the bed.

"I thought we could fall asleep to the sound of the waves."

Next, he walks over to a large, built-in wall cabinet and opens it to expose a surround-sound stereo system.

"And some music maybe?"

"What kind of music?" I ask.

"A variety. Some of my favorite songs are on here."

"I actually love falling asleep to music."

"Awesome."

The first song that plays I recognize. It is "Broken" by Lifehouse. There is just something about Jason Wade's voice that is so soothing.

I smile at Chase as he climbs into the bed next to me. The sheets and thin quilts are pushed down to the foot of the bed. I am lying flat on my back with my right leg propped up, bending at the knee. He lies on his right side, keeping himself up with his right elbow. He slides his left hand up under the bottom of my tank and gently caresses my stomach. My heart rate escalates just a little. Is he ready to make the trip north? South? Am I ready for it? I'm trying to have faith. Trying to have faith in his strength. In the strength that he is giving me to let him lead.

"Jo, I am so intrigued by you. There is so much I want us to experience together. You're like my obsession."

I let out a small giggle.

"Well, I must say that I love being your obsession. Hearing you say that means it's safe to admit that you are mine."

The touch of his hand on my stomach feels so good. I don't want him to stop. He carefully massages my side as he smiles down at me. A few strands of his dark hair brush the top of his right eyebrow.

"We still need more time," he says.

That wasn't what I expected him to say. You would think that, being here alone together all weekend, he would jump at the chance for us to be together. You would think that this would be the perfect place and the right time.

"I hope you're not disappointed with me saying that," he adds.

I shake my head.

"No, it's not that I'm disappointed. I'm just confused."

He reaches over and grabs my hand. Our fingers tangle together.

"What do you mean confused?" he asks.

I give a slight shrug of my shoulders. "I don't know. I mean, how do you know when the time is right? How do you know when it's perfect? Does that even exist when it comes to something like this?"

He nods and replies, "I believe it does. I will say that I have honestly never experienced it. I just believe it exists because I want it so badly with you. I want the right, perfect time with you. To me, the right and perfect time is when we both know it's arrived. I'm getting closer, and so are you, but I still feel that there is a part of your heart that isn't quite ready yet. There's a part of mine that feels that way too."

I give a small sigh. "If there's one thing I have tried so hard to do with you, Chase, it is to stay guarded, but instead I feel like I have been nothing but an open book. I have shared so much about my personal life with you in such a short period of time. I have been broken and broken-hearted with the deaths I have endured, my break-up with Jake, and the rape."

"Exactly. That is why I feel that we still have a little while yet before we can make such a big decision. If there is one thing I will promise you, it is that we will be together when we just can't stop because we know that it is meant to be."

I smile at him. What am I doing? Shouldn't I be thankful for how he sees and wants things? Shouldn't I be thankful that he cares so much about how I feel, and if I am truly ready for such a huge step in my life? This is what girls dream about in their perfect guy.

"Thank you so much."

"For what?"

"For being so wonderful."

He smiles down at me and gently strokes my cheek. "No, you are wonderful. You deserve so many amazing things in your life. I want to be the one to give them all to you. I'm going to do the very best I can as I learn along the way."

I close my eyes as his fingers continue to softly rub my cheek.

"I still find myself wondering when I'm going to wake up. I'm still trying to convince myself that this really isn't a dream."

He lets out a small laugh.

"No, baby, it's very real. I'm real. This is real."

I open my eyes and gaze into his. I reach up and push a small strand of hair from his brow.

"Kiss me," I say in a whisper.

He gives me another smile and says, "With pleasure."

Chapter Fourteen

I open my eyes to the touch of soft lips on my cheek. It is Chase, and the bedroom is still dark.

"Good morning beautiful," he says to me with a smile.

I smile back.

"Good morning. What time is it?"

"Six a.m." he replies.

What the hell? It hasn't been that long ago that I fell asleep in his arms.

"Why are we up so early?" I ask.

"Well, I have something planned for us, but I also made you breakfast in bed."

I sit up and see a tray resting at the foot of the bed with a plate of eggs, grits, bacon, and toast. He's even made me coffee and added a glass of OJ.

He picks up the tray and sets it gently in my lap. He is dressed comfortably again in his sleep tank and sweat shorts from last night. Armani peeks just a little bit over the waistband of his sweat shorts.

"I made your coffee just the way you like it; milk and three sugars." He winks at me.

I smile again. "Thanks. I didn't expect this."

He sits down next to me. I give him a confused look.

"Aren't you going to eat too?"

He shakes his head. "I already did. I nibbled while I cooked."

I giggle. "I have had that same problem on the few times I have actually cooked."

"So you can cook?" he asks with a smirk.

I nod. "Yeah, I can, but not like you or my grandma."

I take a bite of my toast and ask, "So what are we doing first on this early Saturday morning?"

"I can't tell you."

"Is there anything in particular I need to wear?"

"Nope. Your tank and pajama bottoms will work just fine."

"What?"

I give him an even more confused look than the one before.

"Just trust me," he says with a smile.

We talk and laugh as I quickly down my breakfast and coffee. Chase takes the tray from my lap and says, "I'm going to put the dishes up. I'll be waiting for you in the kitchen."

He leans down and gives me a soft, quick kiss on the lips. I don't want to go anywhere.

I would much rather relive the events of last night. Being able to lie in bed and talk about anything and everything with him. I truly believe that Chase wants me to be able to confide in him about all things. He wants me to see that I am strong enough to let him. However, he is very cautious about what he does and what he says.

I jump out of his huge bed, freshen up, slip on my pair of Rainbow flip-flops, and head out of Chase's master suite. When I reach the kitchen, Chase is standing by the island with a thin blanket.

"You ready?" he asks.

I nod. "I'm just trying to figure out where we could be heading at six thirty in the morning. And in our pajamas at that."

He reaches his hand out for me to take. "Like I said, trust me. You will see."

I take his hand.

"Oh, and you really don't need to wear your flip-flops. Bare feet are completely acceptable and necessary."

I quickly kick them off. I crack a small smile at him, and he leads me out the back door.

The sound of the water falling over the rocks of the grotto and the waves crashing against the shore are calming. I am somewhat nervous about what he is up to.

We walk past the grotto and pool toward his private access path to the beach. The sand feels exquisite between my toes. Its texture is very different from the sand I am used to at Folly. Refined. Cool to the touch. There is a soft breeze with a small hint of salt in the air.

Chase stops not too far from the path and turns to me.

"Would you like to have a seat?" he asks as he points to the sand beneath us.

"I would."

He sits and pats the sand in between his legs. I smile and gladly take the seat he offers. He takes a corner of the blanket with his left hand and then another with his right and reaches around us. He pulls me in close to him. I lay back into him with my back against his chest. He plants a small kiss on the top of my head as he wraps the blanket around our bodies.

"It's a little breezy this morning. Not too bad, but I didn't want you to get cool out here."

"It's so relaxing. The waves sound amazing."

I notice that light shades of orange and yellow are beginning to caress the ocean.

"It's almost time. It won't be much longer now. There is nothing like a Key West sunrise."

"I have never seen a sunrise this way before," I say as I continue to gaze out at the water.

"Wonderful," he says.

I snuggle in as he pulls me even closer to him. Nothing can compare to the feeling of being in his arms. What I have always dreamed is becoming my reality more and more each day.

Slowly but suddenly, a small portion of the sun begins to peek over the ocean. It seems to dance as the sky brightens and the water glistens. Chase and I are silent as we watch it continue to rise. I close my eyes as its rays warm my cheeks.

"You have no idea how happy it makes me to have you here. I can't imagine doing this with anyone else."

I keep my eyes closed at the sound of his voice and the tender words that have escaped his lips. I open my eyes. The sun has almost completely risen. It seems to be letting go of the ocean. They are disconnecting. It is freeing itself higher into the sky. I turn to face Chase. He gives me a simple smile and pulls me in for a kiss. A sweet kiss. We look into each other's eyes for a moment and then find ourselves trapped in a long, passionate kiss.

I'm a Southern girl at heart and proud to show it. For our day out, I have paired a simple flower printed sundress with smocking at the chest with a comfortable pair of brown slides. It's a great choice, since it highlights my golden tan perfectly. I throw my hair up into a loose bun and slide a cream-colored pair of pearls into my ears. A few strands of hair brush the sides of my face.

I am sitting in the living room looking through a huge photo album of Chase's family. Every photo is the portrait of the perfect family. The family that every child or even everyone dreams of. Each photo speaks. Speaks many things. Happiness. Love. Joy. Togetherness. With the turn of each page I recall how long ago I felt all of those things. I remember my family. My mother, father, and Sam. The memories of our times together come back as I glance upon vacation and holiday photos of the Hartford family.

Why? Why did they all have to be taken away from me so soon? So young? They were cheated. Cheated out of the life that we were all supposed to share and experience together.

Chase walks into the living room with his keys in his hand.

"Ah ... the famous family photo album. It's very rare to come across a home that doesn't have one as the highlight of the living room."

I give a brief nod as I look over at him. The expression on his face is one of regret.

"Damn it. I'm so sorry, Jo. I really need to think about things before I say them."

I wave my hand in a don't-worry-just-forget-about-it gesture. "It's fine. I try to think about the future and how I hope to have a family of my own to replace the one I have lost."

Chase smiles. "You will. I promise. It will happen."

I put the album back on the large wooden coffee table and stand.

"Shall we go have some fun?" he asks with his hand outstretched. I can tell that he wants to move past the moment very quickly and focus on the good moments that lie ahead.

I nod and give him a big smile. "Yes, please."

I grab his hand, and we head for the garage.

The five-car garage is huge. His silver Mercedes SL93 coupe is parked next to a navy-blue Kawasaki Ninja ZX 10R motorcycle.

"That bike is kick ass!" I say as we walk toward the Mercedes.

"Yeah, it's pretty fast. I'll have to take you for a ride before we leave on Monday."

I picture us riding along the coast of Key West at high speeds. The thought makes me feel wild and dangerous. I crack a mischievous grin. "Sounds exciting."

He opens the passenger door for me, and I slide in. The interior is miraculously clean, with gray leather seats and wood-grain trimming. Within a few seconds, he is seated next to me and inserting the key into the ignition.

"Am I allowed to know where we are going?" I ask.

He looks over at me with a pouty lip.

"Can it be another surprise? Please?"

I chuckle at the sight of him and nod.

"Great!"

He leans over and gives me a short French kiss. I can feel the chill bumps rise on my skin. Before I know it we are traveling down Key Haven Road.

It was a day like I had never experienced. It was almost as if it came right out of a dream. We took a two-hour drive to Key Largo, where Chase had booked us a private session to swim with bottlenose dolphins. After spending a couple of hours swimming, feeding, and playing, we changed out of our wetsuits, thanked the trainers, and went for lunch. He took me to Tower of Pizza. A good friend of his owns the restaurant and provided us with a private table and all the pizza we wanted. Chase insisted that I try some of the unusual types that were renowned in Key Largo as some of the best your mouth ever tasted. Over salad, the variety of sliced pizza, and a glass of wine, we joked and laughed. After eating, we decided to take the trip back to Chase's and spend the rest of the afternoon and evening relaxing.

I could definitely get used to breakfast in bed. It's Sunday morning, and Chase has served me yet again. This time I enjoyed French toast with maple syrup, scrambled eggs, and honey sausage. My coffee was made just the way I like it. I wouldn't necessarily say I'm spoiled, but I'm getting pretty close.

"How do you feel about relaxing around here today?" Chase asks.

I reply, "I think that sounds like a wonderful idea."

He smiles. "We can go for a swim and watch a couple of movies. I thought that tonight I could grill us up something good."

Whatever he wants to do will be done. Returning to the real world tomorrow is definitely going to be tough. I already wish I could go back to Friday night and relive every event that we have already shared together. But you know what they say … all good things must come to an end. But can't all of this be an exception?

The day has gone by quickly. However, it has been wonderful. Chase and I went for a morning swim and spent some time catching a few rays by the pool. We went inside and had a sandwich for lunch and then tried to take a nap. We weren't very successful. We had a hard time keeping our hands and mouths off of each other. I guess we realized that the sun didn't make us quite as tired as we thought. We did fit in the time afterwards to attempt to watch a couple of movies while snuggling on the couch. We started off with *The Notebook* and then finally fell asleep while watching *People Like Us*. I figured I needed to get a little rest in because with it being our last night in Key West, I wasn't sure what might happen.

Chase lifts the lid of the grill in his outdoor kitchen. He brushes butter over the shrimp-and-veggie kabobs before squirting a little more lemon juice over the salmon filets. The rice is cooking on the nearby stovetop, and the garlic-cheese biscuits haven't been in the oven long. It all smells mouthwatering. I am sitting on the nicely cushioned couch, sipping on a glass of wine.

"It looks like it's close to being ready. I suppose we could go ahead and start preparing the salads," he says as he gently closes the grill lid.

"Okay."

I set my glass down on the patio table and walk over next to him. He grabs the salad mixture and toppings from the patio fridge while I grab the salad bowls.

As we begin to get them ready, I ask, "Do we really have to go back tomorrow?"

He lets out a small chuckle. "I would love to say no, but you know it would be a lie."

I shrug my shoulders. "So lie to me then."

He looks over at me standing next to him as I sprinkle cheese over our salads. "Never."

I notice that his look is one of seriousness. "Okay, then don't."

That was strange. What just happened there?

"Jo, I just want you to know that I will always be honest and straightforward with you. I will never give you any reason not to trust me."

I nod, feeling very grateful that he feels this way.

"I appreciate that and I hope you know the same goes for me. I'm a firm believer that honesty is the best policy."

He nods back. "Most definitely. Will you promise me something?" he asks.

"Anything."

"No matter what you see, read, or hear about things I have done or things I will do, will you please come and talk to me about it first before you believe anything or pass judgment?"

"Of course I will. I promise."

"There are so many people of my past, including the aggravating-ass paparazzi, that will make up all this crazy shit and make it seem so believable. I just don't want you getting your information from the wrong source and then finding out that it was all just a way for them to stir up trouble."

He grabs our salad bowls and walks over to the patio table to set them down. He's right. There really is no telling how many people out there would love to ruin things for him and for those he loves. I start to think back to an article that was published in a magazine a few years ago about his family. A writer had put some false information about his father having an affair and his sister being seriously involved with a drug dealer who got arrested. None of it was true.

"This kind of stuff really gets you worked up doesn't it?"

"It does. I'm sorry, I don't mean to sound so angry when I talk about it, but things like that are a real threat to the ones that are so important to me. I mean, I can't tell you how many of the paparazzi I have spotted since we arrived Friday night."

I raise my right eyebrow. "Really? You've seen them? I never noticed."

"Yes, I have, and you really wouldn't would you? I know exactly who and what to look for. Don't worry. It won't be much longer, and you'll get the gift. You'll be able to spot them a mile away."

I sigh. This is all so crazy. Why does there have to be so many complicated things that surround us and what we have? Girls, paparazzi, reporters, tabloids, and I'm sure other problems that I haven't even thought about. This is so hard. I have to remember what Dr. Black said when I first met Chase. The bad must come with the good. He's not good, he's great, and he's worth every bad thing that comes my way.

Chase wraps his arms around my waist and looks down into my eyes. "Jo, I don't want to lose you over something stupid. I am going to try everything in my power to protect you and teach you everything I have learned about the dread that comes with my career. I refuse for any of the negative things or people to make you run. I want you."

I smile up at him as I throw my arms around his neck. "I'm not going anywhere, and I'm all yours."

He smiles back and leans down to give me a gentle kiss. He pulls away slowly and asks, "You ready to eat?"

"I'm starving."

The water in the grotto is a lukewarm temperature that is just perfect for a little relaxing. I saved my favorite two-piece from Victoria's Secret, which also happens to be my sexiest, for a night like tonight. It's a perfect shade of baby blue with tan–and–pink pin stripes. The triangle top holds my boobs up nicely, and the bikini bottoms hug low on my waist. Chase has on a pair of tan Gucci swimming trunks that fall a little above the knee.

We are sitting on a rock slab bench, propped up against some rocks with the water up to our chest.

"When will you have your next official break from class?" Chase asks.

"It will be the week of Thanksgiving. Why?"

"I really want my family to meet you. We usually spend Thanksgiving together at my home in LA and then Christmas in Denver. I am trying to plan the best time for us to get together with them. I would rather you meet them before then, but I don't know how we would work it. The only thing I can think of is going for a quick weekend getaway to LA before the holidays get here."

The thought of meeting his family makes me excited and very nervous. I love how he wants me to meet them as soon as possible. It definitely makes me feel special. Special to him. Wow. I still can't believe this is real. This is *really* happening.

"I'm nervous," I say to him.

"Nervous about what? Meeting my parents?"

I nod.

"Don't be. They are going to love you. So will Mary and Cameron. There's just something about bringing home a beautiful, small-town girl. The family always loves her."

He gives me a wink. "Oh, so you've done that before?"

He shakes his head. "No. This will be my first time."

I smile.

He smiles back and reaches over, pulling me in close to him. We connect with a deep kiss. Our tongues are playing again. They have been doing that quite often this weekend. They can play all they want. I need it. I want it. I love it. Like I never thought I would. He moves his lips to my left cheek and then down to my neck. I allow my head to fall back slowly as I savor each touch, each kiss. His hands run from my waist up my back to the nape of my neck as he moves his lips back to mine. I can feel his fingers as they play with the tie that holds my bikini top up. *Oh shit! Is he going to take my top off?* He stops himself. Instead he wraps his strong arms around me and pulls me in even closer to him. Our kiss is getting harder and even more passionate. We slowly turn in the water, still embraced and tongue-tied. He lies me down on a flat, smooth surface, and it is there that we continue with deep, erotic kisses, but with gentle, innocent touches.

Chapter Fifteen

It's Tuesday, and I am back on campus. Yep. Back to the real world. You know the one I didn't want to return to. Well, that's where I am, and that's where he is. We have arrived.

I have just taken my seat at the lab table in my advanced inorganic chemistry class. Just as I get settled with my materials, Matt comes walking in. *Great. Here we go.*

"Hey, Jo," he says with a big smile on his face.

I smile back in return. *Okay, Jo, now you have to be nice. Don't be a bitch. He's done nothing to you.*

"Hey, Matt."

He sets his book bag down and sits beside me.

"How was your holiday weekend? Did you and Chase have fun?" he asks.

I nod and reply. "It was great, and yes, we did."

Now all I can do is think about all the wonderful moments we shared while we were there alone. All the things we talked about. All the things we did. How he made me feel. *Thanks, Matt. Now how in the hell am I supposed to concentrate on the results of our lab when you just had to go and mention my fantastic, romantic weekend? Geez!*

"So what about you, Matt? Did you have a good, long weekend?"

"Yeah, I did. I hit up a couple of parties. I had a great time. There are a lot of fine women around here."

Really? So I guess that's all that matters in a girl. Her looks. Guys just have no clue. Well, at least some of them don't. I know I can't speak for all of them.

"Did you meet anyone special?" I'll admit I'm curious. It would be wonderful actually if he did. It would totally help my situation with feeling that he has an interest in me.

He shakes his head. "Nah. I'm really not looking right now. I just want to have some fun."

I shrug my shoulders. "There's nothing wrong with that."

He reaches down into his book bag and pulls out his binder for the lab. I already have mine out. I'm always prepared and ahead of the game.

"I was able to come by Saturday and yesterday to check on our samples. Everything looks good with them. Today we are supposed to collect an IR spectrum and prepare a solution for conductance UV-Vis measurements. After we do that, we need to measure the conductance of the deionized water and the compound to calculate the molar conductivity."

"Simple enough. I guess we will just wait for Dr. Davis to get here and give us the go-ahead to get started."

At that very moment, Dr. Davis walks in, carrying her briefcase.

"Please pardon me, class, for running a little late. I'm going to assume that all of you are aware of what today's lab entails. Most of you stopped by over the holiday weekend and checked on your samples. If you feel comfortable with the printed instructions that have previously been placed at your lab tables, then you may begin. Don't forget to calculate the molar conductivity and turn in your final results by the end of class. If you have any questions or concerns, please let me know."

Matt and I look at each other.

"All right then, let's get started," he says.

We remember to follow the tips and rules to lab safety and work through our assignment.

That night I'm at the cafe, helping Zach clear off a few tables. I am so tired. You would think that after having a long, relaxing weekend with Chase that I would be geared up and ready to go this week. I guess I had a little too much fun. If the feeling of exhaustion is the after-effect from spending time with him, then I'm ready to handle it anytime. I got this.

The bells over the cafe doors ring, and I turn to see who is walking in. It's Aimee. My exhaustion rate just skyrocketed. I really don't know if I can handle her right now, no matter how much I love her.

She walks over to the table with this big grin on her face. She is up to something. "Well, good evening, my most wonderful, best good friend."

Yep, I was right. She *is* up to something.

"What do you want, Aimee?" I ask as I turn to face her.

She throws her hand up to her chest in that oh-how-dare-you-think-I'm-here-just-because-I-want-something gesture.

"What? No 'Hello' or 'Hi, Aimee, how are you?'" she asks with a pouty look on her face.

I put down the wet rag that I had been cleaning with and sigh.

"Okay, let me try that again. Hi, Aimee. How are you, and what do you want?"

She lets out a small giggle. "I just love how well you know me, Jo. I'm good, and guess what?"

"What?" I am trying so hard right now to sound and act interested.

"Zeta Tau Alpha is going to host an eighties party Halloween weekend in the field house to raise money for the Susan G. Komen Foundation."

I am totally interested now. "That's awesome. I'm sure this was your idea."

She nods with a look of excitement. "Yes, it was, and I have to ask you a huge favor."

"See, I knew you wanted something." I shake my head at her.

"Oh, please, Jo? It's very important to the success of our fundraiser."

"What is it?"

Lord, there's no telling what she is about to ask me. I have a strong feeling that it is going to pertain to someone very important. That someone being Chase.

"Well, the girls and I were hoping that you could talk with Chase about showing up and signing autographs and taking pictures with our guests. We could have a photo booth and a table set up for him to sign pictures. It would be an awesome way to raise money for the cause! We can charge a five-dollar admission fee. For autographs or photos, we could charge thirty dollars, and to do both we could charge say fifty dollars."

My eyes widen. Does she really think that would work? "Aimee, are you kidding me? The majority of college students around here are broke. They can't afford to spend that kind of money on autographs and photos, or even both."

She rolls her eyes at me. Like I've said before, she is so famous for that. And don't forget, a veteran. Yeah, a veteran eye roller. Ha.

"Jo, really? You can't be serious? That is a great price! I promise you that parents all over Charleston and Folly Beach will be handing over that money. What Mom or Dad wouldn't want their daughter to experience that type of opportunity?"

"So, basically you're just thinking about the female population here?"

She nods. "Well, mostly, yes. I mean, I'm sure there will be some guys that may have a little interest in an autograph. Photos, not so much."

I place my hands on my hips as I look at her, thinking about how it could all work. Would Chase be willing to do something like this? I mean, he gives out autographs for free. If he does charge, he donates the money to one of his favorite charity organizations, which means this would typically qualify as such.

Aimee starts to jump up and down in front of me like a little kid at the toy store begging to take something home. She folds her hands prayer style. "Please, Jo? Please don't make me stand here and continue to beg? You know he would do it for you. Especially with the way you feel about cancer and organizations that raise money to research it."

I sigh again, except this time much deeper. "Okay, okay. I will talk to him about it. I'll let you know just as soon as I can."

"Yes!" she screams out loud.

People turn and stare at us.

"You are the absolute best! Thank you so much!"

I shoot her a smile. "All right. Calm down. Our customers are trying to enjoy their meals."

She grabs me and gives me a big squeeze.

She pulls away and says, "I'm going to the sorority house to tell the girls. I'll chat with you later. Bye."

With that she turns and heads for the door.

"Bye."

I'm sitting on my bed, reading over a chapter in my literature textbook when my Galaxy dings. I glance at it right beside me and smile at the sight of Chase's name. Surprise messages are the best! I miss him so much right now.

"Hey love! What r u up to?"

I absolutely love it when he calls me that!

"Hey! Just doing some homework. U?"

"Thinking abt u as always! Do u have plans tomorrow?"

"Nothing major. Just class and my session with Dr. Black."

"What abt work?"

"I'm off tomorrow. I have to work the rest of the week tho ☹"

"Well I am going to be finished on set early tomorrow. Can I take u out for dinner?"

Why must he ask? He already knows the answer.

"Most definitely! I can't wait 2 c u! I have missed u so much today!"

"Awesome! I have missed u too! Will 6:30 work for u? We r going into Charleston."

"Of course! Charleston again, huh? Can u tell me where u r taking me this time? ☺"

"I'm taking u to a new 5 star restaurant called Husk."

"Five star? Sounds wonderful! How should I dress?"

I am totally panicking right now. I don't want him to know it though.

"Don't panic. U can wear a nice, simple dress like when we went to Magnolias. Don't worry abt getting fancy."

How did he know? Damn he's good.

"Alright sounds gr8! I'll be ready ☺"

"Ok love. I'll let u get ur work done. I can't wait 2 c u! Let me know if u need anything!"

I blush. He's just so sweet.

"Ok. I will. Tomorrow can't get here fast enough! C u then!"

"Agreed ;)"

"☺"

I wonder exactly how detailed Dr. Black is going to get with her questions about my trip to Key West with Chase during my session this afternoon? I'm quite nervous. I can't seem to focus for a long period of time on any of the magazines in the waiting room. I glance down at my watch. It's three thirty. She should be coming out any minute. Hopefully I'll be done within forty-five minutes and then head home to get ready for dinner with Chase.

The secretary at the desk is clicking away on her computer mouse with a look of frustration on her face. I won't be bothering her anytime soon. Normally Dr. Black is right on time. I'm trying hard not to get impatient because it's just not my personality, but today I'm struggling with the concept.

Finally the door swings open, and there she stands, not letting go of the knob. "Please come on in, Joanna."

She displays a small smile as I rise from the waiting room couch and head in her direction. She closes the door behind us. We both take a seat, and I take a deep breath.

"So, how is everything going, Joanna?" she asks

I swallow the somewhat small lump that has formed in my throat so I can speak. I'm hoping she doesn't take notice. "It's been great."

There goes her pen. As usual. It gracefully moves across her big legal pad. "All right so tell me what has been great. Work? School? Chase? What about your nightmares?"

She looks up at me, patiently waiting for a response.

"All of it actually, and my nightmares have gotten so much better. I hardly have them anymore," I answer.

"Well, that is absolutely wonderful, Joanna. Now explain to me how each one is great."

Okay, that is simple enough. I can do that. "Well, work is steady. I'm still trying to work at least five days a week, even with school. All of my classes are great. Time-consuming, but great. As for Chase, I don't know if I have the time to describe how great he is."

"Well, you have a little under an hour. Do you think that's sufficient?" she asks with a grin on her face.

I really don't know how to take her tone and her facial expression. Is she being sarcastic? Serious? I sit there quiet for a moment.

"Go ahead." She motions for me to speak with her hand.

"No, an hour is not sufficient, but I'll do the best I can with the time I have."

She lets out a small laugh. "Joanna, I was only trying to be funny. I apologize if I gave you the wrong impression."

I'm so relieved. I was beginning to wonder how I would handle talking to her the rest of the session if she was going to act like that.

"What I can say is that Chase is beyond everything I had ever imagined. He is caring, loving, funny, and makes me feel like I can do things I never thought I could."

"Things like what?"

Oh, shit. How do I answer that question? "Well, I can talk about things, go places, have fun, but most importantly, I am able to trust."

She writes some more. "Wow. Being able to trust again is a pretty big deal. I'm proud that this has happened for you, and I am thankful to him in helping you find the courage to do so. That is fantastic, Joanna. Now you know I have to ask about your trip. You know that you don't have to share anything with me that might make you uncomfortable. Just know that I am here to listen and give advice, but never to judge."

This is true. That is exactly what I'm paying her for.

"I had an amazing time. He took me swimming with bottlenose dolphins, out for pizza and wine, we watched the sunrise on the beach. He cooked several meals for me. Needless to say, I dreaded coming back here."

There's silence for a brief moment as she finishes writing. "It sounds like you had an amazing time indeed."

I look down and start to play with my fingers. "I did. There have been a few moments before and during our trip that things between us have gotten a little intense."

"Intense?" she repeats.

I nod.

"Intense how?"

"Intense in a way that we have had to stop ourselves from going a little too far."

"I'll be honest with you, Joanna, I was wondering when that would happen between the two of you. So you haven't gone all the way then?"

I shake my head. "No, not at all. I must admit that a big part of me wants to. However, I find that a part of me is angry for having this feeling. Chase has been so respectful about the whole thing. I know it may be hard to believe, but Chase is the one that has kept us from getting to that point."

She raises her right eyebrow. "He has?"

Yep, she's obviously surprised. Yes, Dr. Black, I'm afraid there are guys in this world that hold respect for girls.

"Yes. He told me that he couldn't do it. It wasn't the right time or the right place. He said that we need a little more time, and when it is right, we will know. We will both know."

She smiles. She has a look of satisfaction on her face.

"I know that he is right. With the traumatic experience I had with the rape, I know deep down that I want my very first time to be special. I want it to have meaning."

"And you believe that is what is going to happen? That will be the outcome? It will be special and have meaning?"

"Most definitely," I say it with so much confidence.

She lets out a small sigh with another smile. "Joanna, I wasn't sure I would say this before, but I have a lot of respect for Chase right now. I am a little surprised that this has turned out the way it has. However, I am still a little worried just because of who he is and what all his career life involves. My advice to you is to still be careful. I'm glad you're letting your guard down, but I just think that, since it is still early in the relationship, you need to watch yourself. Now, Chase, I'm not real concerned about him doing something to hurt you. It's other people out there. There has been a lot of publicity going on about your relationship and who you are. I wouldn't doubt there are many jealous girls out there that would love nothing more than to get you in some way. The main reason I say this is because you are just a sweet, attractive, small-town girl. To put it bluntly, you are the last person most people would think he would end up with."

She is right. I wouldn't disagree with her in a second.

"I completely understand and realize that, Dr. Black. At times I feel like I need to pinch myself and wake up. Yet it's all so real. I'm trying so hard to be careful and to make sure I am making the right decisions. The main thing about it is, I am the person I have always wanted to be. He is breathing life into my life. With him I feel like I am no longer a prisoner to myself or anyone else."

"So what it all comes down to is he has given you a sense of freedom."

I nod with a huge smile on my face. "Yes, he is setting me free."

Chase and I are sitting in the main dining room of Husk. The design and details of the modern décor are breathtaking. Reclaimed floors, original windows, and exposed brick surround us, along with the open kitchen that features a wood-burning oven. Soft, classical music plays over the speaker system above.

We just finished up our appetizer, or "first," as they call it on the menu. I enjoyed a Bibb salad that was covered with fried oysters, heirloom tomatoes, shaved onion, Derby cheddar, and buttermilk ranch. Delish. Chase, on the other hand, ordered chilled sweet-corn soup that had grilled shrimp with ricotta and a relish of early chanterelles and roasted red peppers. It looked quite tasty.

"How was your appetizer?" Chase asks.

"It was very delicious. And yours?"

"It was pretty good. I may have to try the salad next time. Those oysters looked fantastic."

I nod. "They were. So I was going to tell you that Aimee came into the cafe last night to see me."

"Oh yeah? Was she up to something?"

I smile. It amazes me how well he learns people.

"Do you have to ask?"

We both let out a small laugh.

"What huge favor did she ask of you?"

"Well, her sorority, Zeta Tau Alpha, is having an eighties party for Halloween in the campus field house. They are partnered with the Susan G. Komen Foundation and hold events to raise money for the organization. So Aimee wanted me to talk with you about the possibility of taking part in the event by signing autographs and taking photographs with our guests. She said that they would charge a general admission of five dollars to get in the door, and then she was thinking about giving guests three options to choose from. They could pay thirty dollars for an autograph, thirty dollars for a photograph with you, or pay fifty dollars to get both. All of the money made goes to the foundation. What do you think?"

"And this is on Halloween weekend?"

I nod.

"Honestly I think it sounds like a wonderful idea. I'd be glad to come and help."

I smile. "Really?"

He nods back. "Aimee will be so thankful that you are doing this for her."

"I'm not doing it for her, Jo. I'm doing it for you. I know how you feel about a terminal illness like cancer. I would be honored to do something like this."

My smile widens. "Thank you so much. It means a lot."

He smiles. "That's exactly why I'm going to do it."

"I know it is going to be insane, though. There will be girls everywhere. I hope we will be able to keep the madness under control."

"Well, I'll have the guys with me. I never do any type of charity or fundraising event without them. Especially when it comes down to me signing autographs and taking pics. Some girls get a little crazy."

"Yeah, I can see that."

Stephen, our waiter, arrives at our table with our main dishes. In front of me he places my order of the South Carolina coastal grouper with grilled fields farm green beans, embered fennel and mizuna, and mushroom tea with lemongrass. Next he sets down Chase's order of American Red Snapper, summer squash and zucchini, spinach with sweet onion, and shrimp bisque.

"Do we require anything else at the moment?" Stephen asks.

Chase and I both shake our heads.

"We are good, Stephen. Thanks," Chase replies.

"Splendid. I shall return to check on you both."

We nod as he walks away.

"I was going to tell you that I have to go next weekend to LA to guest star on the *Ellen DeGeneres Show*. It's just another way that I will be promoting *The Crane Files*."

"When will you leave?" I ask with great curiosity.

"Well, I would like to say we will leave next Friday night if that is something you would like to do."

"What?"

"I'd like for you to go with me to LA. Do you think you can pull that off?"

Los Angeles? Wow! Think, Jo, think. Is this doable?

He speaks up. "If you can't, I completely understand. I just don't know if I can go a whole weekend without seeing you."

I am blushing, and I'm sure it is greatly noticed.

"Actually, Ramona just put up the schedule for next week, and I am off next weekend."

"Are you serious?" he asks with a smile.

"Yep, and according to my lab syllabus, we have another lab, but we won't work on the results until the week after we get back."

"Awesome. While we're there, I want you to meet my family."

My heart starts to pound against my chest. My ears are throbbing from the strength it possesses. I shouldn't be nervous. I should be honored. My mother always told me when I was little that when a guy wants you to meet his family, that's a sign of how much he really cares about and loves you. Love? Is that what this is? I keep wondering, but still don't know for sure.

"Do you want to go?"

"I would love to."

We smile at each other.

"Wonderful. Our flight leaves Friday night at 6:45 for Atlanta. Then we will fly out from there to LA. It will almost be eleven p.m. Pacific time when we arrive in LA. You will be exhausted, I'm sure, since we are three hours ahead here on the East Coast."

"It'll be fine. No worries."

"We'll get some rest, and then I have to be on set Saturday morning at ten o'clock with Ellen. After that, we'll grab some lunch, and then you can meet my family. If you're up to it, I'd like to take you to one of my favorite clubs Saturday night. I have a few friends, and their girlfriends that may join us."

"That sounds fun. I'm excited."

Stephen walks up to our table and asks, "May I interest you in one of our fine desserts tonight?"

"I'm not sure. Jo, do you have room?"

I look up at Stephen. "What do you have?"

He hands Chase and me a copy of the dessert menu.

"If you would like any recommendations, I shall say that our lemon pound cake is a guest favorite and has been featured in *Southern Living's* Best Desserts issue."

Chase and I cock an eyebrow at each other, showing interest in the suggested selection.

"I think I would like to try a piece of that."

Chase says, "I, as well. Thanks, Stephen."

He takes the menus from us and nods. "My pleasure."

I walk into the apartment and find Aimee and Kevin on the couch. They are both snuggled up under a blanket, watching a movie. I set my keys and purse down and plop down into the chair next to them.

"Well, how was dinner?" Aimee asks.

Please Lord don't let her have a hundred questions, and if she does, please give me the strength and patience to handle each and every one. Amen.

"It was wonderful. There is no comparison to the food that they serve there, and the atmosphere is so gorgeous and relaxing."

"So, it's school and work for the rest of the week, right?"

I nod. "Yeah. And I've also got to try and get a little ahead in my lit class because I won't be here next weekend. I'm off, and Chase is taking me to LA."

Aimee jumps sitting next to Kevin and gives me a look of shock. Kevin gives her a look and rolls his eyes. Yeah, he possesses the eye-rolling gift too.

"LA? Are you serious right now?" she asks.

"Yes, I'm serious. He is starring on the *Ellen DeGeneres Show* on Saturday. He wants me to meet his family, and we are going out to one of his favorite night clubs with some of his friends and their girlfriends."

"I am so jealous! I bet the friends he's talking about are Brandon Vanderbilt and Shane Moore. You are such a lucky heifer!"

Kevin glances down at Aimee and asks, "How can you be jealous, babe? I mean, you totally have me."

Aimee looks over at him and gives him a slap on the chest. "Oh, shut up, Kevin."

He gives her a cocky grin.

She shakes her head, still holding a look of shock. "I can't believe this. All of this is really happening for you. You realize that, right?"

"Yes, but, Aimee, it's no big deal. It's just a trip to LA."

"It kills me how you say, 'It's no big deal, Aimee, it's just a trip to LA.' Jo, he's taking you to meet his family. That's a pretty big deal."

I nod.

"I realize that. Of course I'm nervous and everything, but it will all be just fine. I'm still trying to process it all."

"Okay, so I have to ask, did you talk with Chase about the party?"

"Yes, I did, and he said he would be happy to help."

Aimee starts to jump up and down in her seat next to Kevin. You can see the look of aggravation on his face.

"Hey would you chill out?" he asks.

"This is so awesome! We are going to raise so much money for the organization. This is insane! The girls are going to just die!"

I smile at her. I do like to see her happy and excited over things like this.

"Thank you so much. It wouldn't happen if it wasn't for you."

My smile widens, and I say, "Oh, I know."

I miss my Grandpa so much. I have hardly seen him since I have been so busy with school, work, and Chase. I feel like so much has happened that I need to tell him about. I park my BMW in the school lot close to my lab class and pick up my Galaxy. It's not too early to call him. He's usually up, having coffee by now.

"Hello?"

"Hi, Grandpa!"

It is so good to hear his voice.

"Jo! How are you, sweetheart? It seems like it's been forever since I've heard your voice."

"I'm good. I know, it has been too long. How are you doing?"

"I'm doing well. I know you are staying busy. Are you about to go to class?" he asks.

"Yes sir. I just pulled up at the school. I have lab at eight o'clock. I just wanted to call and tell you that I miss you."

"I miss you too, sweetheart. How is Chase?"

I smile. "He's doing great. He's staying busy too. I wanted to let you know that I am flying out to LA with him next weekend to meet his parents."

"Wow. It sounds like you have really knocked this guy off his feet. That is wonderful. I'm very happy for you. Are you nervous?"

"Most definitely. It's going to be all right, though. How is Ms. Margaret doing?"

"She is doing real good. We are still going to bingo and eating together every week. She keeps me busy, and she's great company."

It really makes me feel so good that my grandpa has someone to spend time with. I know that the loss of my grandma is getting a little easier for him to bear.

"Why don't you and Chase come by when ya'll get back from LA and have a bite with us? Margaret and I can cook up one of our best dishes."

"That sounds like a great plan. I'll talk to you again before I leave next Friday, and we'll set a date and time. Does that sound okay?"

"It sounds splendid. Well, you go on into class and have a good day and rest of the week. I miss you, and I'll talk to you soon."

"Okay, Grandpa. I miss you and love you."

"I love you too, Joanna. Bye."

"Bye."

Chapter Sixteen

The audience looks so much bigger on set than on TV. I am so nervous, and I'm not even the one going out in front of everyone. It's a piece of cake to Chase, though.

Ellen is sitting in her chair with her coffee mug resting on the table beside her. I notice that she has even had one prepared for Chase. She starts talking and cracking some of her jokes. The audience breaks out in laughter.

Chase turns to face me and says, "All right, so she is about to welcome me on stage. Be prepared for some chaos. Everything will be fine."

He is dressed in a comfortable pair of blue jeans, a tight-fitting gray cotton T-shirt, and a black pair of Converses. Hot! No doubt the crowd will go crazy.

He winks and then plants a small kiss on my lips.

"Now, ladies, and I would say gentlemen, but I don't think there are any out in the audience today, let's all give a big welcome to one of the hottest young actors on the planet, Chase Hartford!"

All the girls rise to their feet and start to scream uncontrollably as Chase walks out onstage to meet Ellen. It is insane. I mean I've seen girls act crazy over Chase, but wow. There are hardly words. My ears are ringing. He waves to the crowd with a big smile on his face and then reaches out to embrace Ellen in a hug. They both take their seats.

"Wow! It's great to have you back on the show, Chase."

He smiles and nods as the girls in the audience try to calm down so they can hear him speak.

"Thanks. It's always a pleasure to be on your show, Ellen."

"So it seems that you have been pretty busy with the new TV series that you're filming, *The Crane Files*."

"Yeah, it's keeping me busy. We, um, try to shoot pretty much every day that we can. We still have a ways to go, but we're moving along pretty good with it."

"Now explain to us what the series is all about."

"Well, I, uh, play the role of Foss Crane. I'm a new cop to the Charleston Police Department, and I was hired to try and solve all these homicide cases that have basically been labeled cold-case files."

Ellen nods. "I see. Pretty intense stuff, huh?" she asks.

"I guess you could say that. I mean there are a lot of action scenes and some graphic situations about the homicides, but I think the show has a lot of potential."

"That's great to hear. Sounds like we have another great crime show on our hands here, ladies," Ellen says as she looks out into the audience.

She continues, "I'm sure a lot of these ladies wouldn't mind you solving their case."

The girls break out into screaming and hollering again. Chase blushes. He is speechless. Ellen laughs.

"Oh, so you do blush?"

Chase nods and says, "Yeah, I do every once in a while. And, Ellen, you are real good about catching me off guard with your spectacular female audience."

More screaming. Geez.

"All right, so you are filming on location in Folly Beach, South Carolina. I hear that's a pretty little place."

"Yeah, it is. I like it a lot. It's quiet, and if I want to get out to grab a bite to eat or hit the clubs, Charleston isn't too far up the road."

"Oh, I love Charleston. And I hope you don't mind me mentioning this, but it seems that you have met a special someone since you have been on location."

Chase has a big smile on his face. "Yeah, I have. She's very special."

The girls scream some more. I was expecting a few boos, but that didn't occur. Thank God. I would be so embarrassed, even though I am tucked away safely out of the sight of the audience.

"Yeah, I met her just a little bit ago, and I can definitely see that. She's a sweet girl. So tell us, how did you two meet?" Ellen asks.

"Uh well she works at a cafe, and I went in my first night to grab some coffee, and she just happened to be the one working and serving me, so without a doubt in my mind, you could say it all started then."

Ellen smiles. They continue to talk about us and any work that he has in the future with the movie industry. She cracks some more of her hilarious jokes and comments. I just continue to stand there and watch and listen, thanking the good Lord that she hasn't called me out on stage. I couldn't handle that. Not now, anyway. If ever. And I think Ellen and Chase both know it too.

Early that evening, Chase and I pull up into the driveway of his parents' small, brick home in Thousand Oaks. The grass is perfectly manicured, and the landscaping of the side garden is immaculate. I take a deep breath in and exhale. I can't even explain how frazzled my nerves are right now. I'm about to meet his family for the first time. This is something, along with everything else, that I never envisioned happening. Chase looks over and can instantly tell how nervous I am. He grabs my hand.

"Jo, everything is going to be fine. They are going to absolutely love you."

I nod and try so hard to let his words calm me. I'm sure he can feel the pulsating beat of my pulse in my wrist.

He gets out of the car and then comes around to open the door for me. I step out. He gently closes the door and then wraps me in his arms. Nothing compares to how they feel. They soothe me in so many ways. After a minute, he pulls away and grabs my hand.

"Let's go," he says with a smile and a nod of his head toward the front door.

I smile and follow, holding his hand tightly in my own.

Before we can make it to the door, it swings open. There to greet us are Bradley and Linda Hartford. Bradley reaches his arms out for Chase. "Chase, my son, it's so good to see you tonight."

They embrace in a father-son hug. I continue to smile as I look on.

"Hey, sweetheart," Mrs. Hartford says as she also gets a hug from her oldest son.

Mr. Hartford looks over at me and says with a smile, "And you must be Jo."

I nod and reply, "Yes sir."

He gives me a quick, welcoming hug. "I'm Bradley. I have heard so many wonderful things about you from Chase. It is nice to finally meet you."

"It's nice to meet you as well."

Mrs. Hartford comes over to give me a hug. "I'm Linda. I'm so glad you could come tonight and have dinner with us."

We all smile at one another.

Mr. Hartford says, "Well, let's go inside."

After meeting Chase's older sister, Mary, and his younger brother, Cameron, and having a tour of the house, we are all seated at the big dining-room table. A part of me feels like I am back in Folly, sitting around the table at Grandma and Grandpa Dawson's for Thanksgiving. Mrs. Hartford has prepared a delicious-looking meal. There is salad, sweet peas, sweet corn on the cob, hash-brown casserole smothered in cheese, green-bean casserole, rice and gravy, black-eyed peas, fried chicken, and a huge baked ham. I wish she wouldn't have gone through so much trouble.

She points to the center of the table, dressed with all the food. "I wasn't sure what you liked, so I decided to cook several things. As you can tell, it is all Southern food. Being that we are originally from Louisiana, it is hard to leave the South behind."

I smile at her.

"It all looks very delicious, Mrs. Hartford. Thanks so much."

She smiles back.

"Let's all join hands and give thanks to the Lord for this fine meal and time together," Mr. Hartford says.

We all do just that. We bow our heads as he gets ready to bless us and the food.

"Our heavenly Father, we want to thank you for all the wonderful blessings in life. We take so much for granted. Thank you for this wonderful meal that Linda and Mary prepared for us. Thank you for the success that Chase has found in his life, and we ask, Father, that you help him stay strong and to keep his head in the right place, and we know that right place is with you. Thank you for all the wonderful things that

Mary and Cameron are doing with their lives and the people they love. We thank you for our wonderful guest, Joanna Dawson. Lord, we see the true blessing she is for our son, and we ask that you watch over them both as they focus on their love for one another and the goals they have in life. Please bless this food and our bodies to your service. It is in your gracious and most glorious name we pray. Amen."

I smile at how Chase sounds just the same when he prays. He obviously had a great teacher.

Mr. Hartford starts to pass food around the table. "So, Jo, Chase tells me that you are going to school to be a doctor," he says.

I nod.

"Yes sir, I hope to be. I want to be an oncologist."

"That's what Chase told us. He said that you want to work with children that have cancer."

"Yes sir. I'm hoping that I will be able to complete my residency at St. Jude in Memphis. I would love to have a job there once I'm done with school."

Mrs. Hartford asks, "And it was your little brother that had leukemia?"

"Yes ma'am. Sam was eleven when he passed. He has inspired me to do this."

Chase speaks up. "Just in case ya'll didn't know, Jo is going to save the world." He smiles over at me and gives me a quick wink.

I shake my head. "Now I wouldn't say that, although I wish I could."

"You are going to help save the lives of children. To me that's like saving the world."

I blush, hoping that it will help hold back the fact that I would really love to cry right now.

Mary wipes her mouth with her napkin and then places it back in her lap. "Jo, I would just like to say that I admire you so much. I can't imagine how hard it has been all these years without your parents and your brother. In my eyes, you are a very strong girl, and you seem to be the type that knows what she wants and goes for it. Nothing stops you. I think that is wonderful, and I have so much respect for you. I'm sorry that you have had to go through so much."

"Thanks, Mary."

Chase speaks up. "I think we've heard enough of the sad stuff. Let's talk about something else tonight. Besides, it is Jo's first time coming to meet all of you, and her first time in LA."

Mrs. Hartford nods in agreement.

"You're right, Chase. Sorry, Jo, if we made you feel uncomfortable."

"I'm fine. It's all okay."

"I'm sure ya'll have big plans tonight since this is your first visit here in Los Angeles," Mrs. Hartford says.

Chase nods. "Yeah, I think we're going out tonight."

"Really? Where are ya'll planning to go?" Cameron asks.

"I want to take Jo to Lure. For her first LA night experience, I thought it would be the perfect place."

"Awesome. Do you mind if I come along?"

Chase glances over at his younger brother and replies, "Not at all. What's Katherine doing tonight? You want to ask her to join us?"

"She's home this weekend from school. She's having dinner with her parents, and then she is supposed to call me. I'll ask her if she wants to go."

"Where does Katherine go to school?" I ask with curiosity.

"She attends the University of San Diego. It's just a couple of hours south of here. Not a bad drive."

"Cool. What is she studying?"

"Design. Her dream is to be the next top interior designer for the stars."

I nod and smile.

"Sounds like a good dream."

I guess my nerves just won't catch a break this weekend. Not only have I just walked into one of the most popular nightclubs in LA, but I am dressed out of my element tonight. I have paired a black spaghetti-strap miniskirt with black high heels and dangling diamond earrings. My hair is down and flowing with big curls. My outfit and jewelry are the result of Chase insisting that he take me shopping on Rodeo Drive before we went to have dinner with his family. I was quite shocked at myself that I favored the dress so much. Normally I shy away from wearing something this sexy, but I feel confident. And I must add that I am getting better at walking in heels.

As I enter the door of Lure with Chase, Cameron, and Katherine, I can tell that my experience here will not compare to the clubs in Charleston. The club is like no other I have ever seen. There are LED walls, a fire-carved image, a chic lounge, glossy dance floor, and a private VIP area. I can see four mosaic bars and a DJ jamming out on a state-of-the-art sound system. People are everywhere. Aimee would die. Thankfully, Chase has brought his protection. There is no doubt that the services will be needed in a place like this. Also with us are Chase's close friends, Brandon and Shane, and their super-hot-model girlfriends, Zoe and Vada. Aimee was right. They are the guys he invited to come along.

Several girls notice that Chase has entered the club and make their way toward us. Boss, Lincoln, Mac, and Zane make a barrier. Chase keeps a firm grip on my hand. Boss holds up his hands in a get-back gesture. "All right, ladies. Let's keep some distance. Give them some space."

"I have never seen this many people in one place, Chase," I say to him as we walk through the crowd.

He nods and leans over to speak. "It gets pretty crazy here. I'm sure you see why I would never come without the guys."

I nod. I can most definitely understand why he wouldn't. The girls here would have him on the ground in a nanosecond flat!

We approach the VIP area and take a seat at a huge booth with a long table. We order our first round of drinks. We have a good view of the dance floor and two of the bars. The protection mafia stands within a safe distance of our table in case Chase needs them.

"You have never been to Lure before, Jo?" asks Vada in her Australian accent. It is to die for.

I shake my head. "No. I have only been to a few clubs in Charleston. This is my first trip to LA."

"Oh, I see. So Charleston is where you live?"

"Actually I live about twenty minutes outside of Charleston on Folly Beach."

She smiles. "Oh, the beach is nice. You should definitely try to go to Venice before you head back east."

Brandon asks, "Yeah, when do you guys fly out?"

Chase takes a sip of his Crown and Coke and replies, "We leave tomorrow at lunch. If we don't make it out there before we go, I am

100-percent positive that Jo will be coming back with me, and I can take her then."

Chase looks over and gives me a small wink. I love it. Melt. Melt. I blush. He's right. I will be back with him. Anytime.

"Man it's so good to get out with you. It's been a while since we've been able to hang," Brandon says to Chase.

Chase nods. "Yeah, it has been. The show has been keeping me busy. It seems like I have had several breaks, but my brain keeps wanting more. I'm ready for Thanksgiving and Christmas to roll around."

Brandon agrees with a smile. "Yeah, man. It also looks like someone else has been keeping you pretty busy too."

Chase smiles back and looks over at me. "Jo can keep me as busy as she wants. No complaints here. Ever."

I can feel the heat on my cheeks. They are red as fire. I wish he wouldn't do that in front of all his friends. It's embarrassing, and I know they notice. I simply smile and look down at my hands in my lap. I try to hide, but it's no use.

Shane decides to join in. "So the show is going good then? You think it's going to do well when it hits in January?"

Chase takes another sip of his beverage and replies, "Yeah, it's going good. I think it will be a hit. I'm excited about it."

"That's good. I'll be ready for it," Shane says.

As I am reaching for my Sex on the Beach, I hear the excited shout of a female voice. "Chase!"

I look over in the direction of the voice and see a tall, gorgeous blonde wearing a pair of blue-jean, boy-cut, hip-hugging shorts with a red-and-midnight-blue low-cut tank. Her well-groomed hair falls near her boobs, and the blue in her eyes shines bright in the low-lit room. I am shocked at who is fast approaching our table.

I can feel Chase's eyes glance over at me. We look at each other. He grabs my arm and points to my faith bracelet and then to his strength. I nod with a small gulp as he quickly turns to respond.

"Claudia. What a surprise. How have you been?" Chase asks her with a small smile on his face.

She puts her hands on her hips as she checks out all the faces around the table. "Well, I've been great, my old love, and how about you?"

Chase grabs a firm hold of my hand and responds, "I can't recall a time that I have ever been better, to be honest."

Ouch. I am a little shocked that he answered that way, but also proud. Chase dated Claudia for nearly two years. They were the hottest young Hollywood couple. Tinseltown went into a big tizzy when they called it quits.

"Oh, well now, Chase, I would have to disagree with you on that. How is everyone tonight?"

Everyone at the table gives her a smile and nod with several "good" and "fine" remarks. I really don't know what to say or how to answer her. My nerves have never been this much on edge. It's like a whole new experience for me. I mean meeting the gorgeous, famous ex of my hot, famous boyfriend is something I haven't really prepared myself for. How did I not think this could and would happen? *Really, Jo?*

Claudia looks right at me and puts on what I believe looks like a fake smile. She reaches her hand out across the table to me. "I'm sorry, but I *know* we have never met. I'm Claudia Williams."

I give her the same type of smile right back and welcome her handshake.

Chase speaks up before I can. "Claudia, it's a pleasure for me to introduce to you my girlfriend, Jo Dawson."

"Oh, yeah, that's right. You're the small-town girl that the magazines are going crazy about. Where is it that you're from?"

I reply, "Folly Beach, South Carolina."

She nods. "It's all like a dream come true isn't it? Meeting the famous, hot movie star and him coming along and sweeping you off your feet. I bet you have a lot of jealous friends back home."

What? Really? I can't believe she is trying to go there. Her voice has somewhat of a bitchy tone to it, and it doesn't sit right with me. *Keep it cool, Jo. Just keep it cool. Have faith. Have faith that you can handle the situation. She's just trying to push your buttons right here in public. Make a scene maybe? Well, she won't get it.*

Chase wraps his right arm around my shoulder and pulls me in close. "Actually, Claudia, you got it all wrong. Jo is *my* dream come true."

Boom! Take that! It's apparent that she is still not over the breakup. She gives a little eye-roll.

"Hey, Vada and Zoe, when you two get ready to hit the dance floor, come find me. We'll own this place."

They nod and smile.

"All right, well, you guys have fun tonight. Later." She gives us a small wink and walks away.

Shane speaks up. "Well, that was intense."

Chase agrees. "Yeah. She's been pretty bitter about things, but she has her good moments. She must not like the fact that I am here with Jo."

I watch her as she stops to talk with some people close to our table. She laughs loudly and seems to want to put on a show. She definitely wants people to notice her.

"She's still got it pretty bad for you, man," Brandon adds.

"Well, she's just going to have to get over all that. I realized a while back that what we had wasn't what I needed, and it put me in a place that I knew I didn't want to be. I feel like myself again."

Chase looks back over at me with a smile and squeezes my left hand with his while his right arm still lingers around my neck and shoulder. I can feel his breath on my face. I want to kiss him so bad. I think about how odd it would feel to do that. Right here in public in front of all these people? Nah, I'll wait.

How did I get so lucky? Why is this happening to me? What did I do to deserve this? All I can do is constantly ask myself these questions while I am gazing into the most gorgeous blue-gray eyes ever created. I never in a million, trillion years thought I would be here with him in this moment or any other moment, for that matter, and I won't allow anything or anyone to take him away from me.

Chapter Seventeen

Star Gaze just released their latest issue of all the juicy star gossip that you've been waiting for. Of course Chase and I are on the cover, *and* who else gets the opportunity to join us? In her own little circle at the bottom right-hand corner … none other than … yep … you guessed it … Claudia Williams!

I have already had to deal with the issue that came out after our Key West trip and our dining experience at Husk in Charleston. It seems that here recently the one and only jam-up writer and photographer, Stacey Phillips, has been on her A-game. She has been keeping tabs and following us everywhere.

I just happened to come upon the issue as it hit the stand this morning at a local gas station before arriving on campus. I am sitting in my car reading over the article and taking in the pics that Stacey took of us while we were at Lure. She made it a point to put in her article how Claudia paid us a little visit at our table. I can't help but smile and find satisfaction in it. Claudia obviously deserves it if she is going to treat me the way she is. I have done nothing to her. I can't help that Chase walked into Ramona's when I was working, and I had the privilege of waiting on him. It was just my lucky night. Her time has come and gone.

I notice that it's almost time for class, so I set the magazine down in the passenger seat. I grab my book bag and get out of my car.

"Good morning, Jo."

I turn to see Matt. First thing this morning. Geez. I haven't even made it to the classroom yet. *You know, Jo, you really need to stop acting like this when you see him. He's just trying to be your friend.*

I put on a smile. "Good morning, Matt. How's it going?" I ask.

He smiles back and holds up his right hand, which is carrying a Starbucks cup. "Great, as long as I have my Pumpkin Spice Latte."

Pumpkin Spice? Really? I would have guessed something else.

"Oh, that's right, they have that flavor back out. It is time isn't it? I can't believe it's already October."

Matt nods. "Yeah, it's crazy. We only have two months left in the semester."

We start walking toward campus. We pass several students that give out a "good morning" or "hello."

"Two months seems so unreal. There is so much going on between now and then that I am trying to figure out how to fit it all in."

"Really? Like what?" Matt asks.

"Well, I have the rest of all these assignments, work at the cafe, dates with Chase, the Zeta party, Thanksgiving, Christmas, finals. The list goes on and on. I need to stop before I get overwhelmed. I really don't have time for that this morning."

"Did you say Zeta party?"

I nod. "I didn't realize you were a Zeta."

"Oh, I'm not. My best friend, Aimee, is the president."

"Cool. What is the party for?"

"It's a fundraiser for the Susan G. Komen Foundation. It's an eighties party. They are having it Halloween weekend in the field house."

"Oh, that sounds awesome. So what are they doing to raise money? Charging admission or something?" he asks.

"Yes, and Chase is going to be there to sign autographs and take photos with fans for a price. Of course all of that was Aimee's idea. It will help the sorority make a lot of money for the foundation."

"Hell, yeah, it will. I can't even imagine all the hot girls that are going to be there. Please tell me that this party is for all students?"

"It is. I'm taking it you plan to be there."

"Are you kidding me? Of course I will be, and so will every other single guy on campus. I mean it's the perfect time to meet single, hot girls. Even if they are there mainly to see Chase, it gives us the opportunity to have a lot of eye candy."

"Maybe you'll find yourself a girlfriend, Matt."

He shrugs his shoulders. "I don't know. Maybe."

We approach the science and math building. I notice that there is a large crowd of girls standing by the entrance. They are all huddled together and laughing. Odd. What are they doing? As Matt and I start to climb the steps, they all rush toward us. My heart picks up pace. Please tell me that what I think is about to happen isn't going to happen.

Before I can even consider another reason for their mad dash, they are swarming me. They are all screaming out my name and questions that I can't even comprehend to answer. Some of them are asking me for an autograph while holding the *Star Gaze* issue that I just finished reading myself. I am overwhelmed and frightened. This is what it feels like. This is what Chase feels like when there is no barrier for him. No protection. I can hardly breathe. I feel like I'm suffocating. Their bodies are all around me, brushing against mine.

Suddenly, I feel Matt's hand reach in for me. A couple of other guys that see the chaos decide to stop and help get some of the girls away as Matt pulls me out safely. He throws his left arm around me, and we rush together for the entrance.

When we get inside I catch my breath and say, "Thanks so much. I wasn't expecting that. Come to think of it, what was that anyway?"

Matt is trying to catch his breath as well and replies, "That was a result of you dating the most famous movie star on the planet."

Yep. He's right. That is exactly what that was. I just never imagined it happening to me. Not like that anyway.

Matt turns to look back through the windows at the girls as they are making their way toward the building. He puts his hand on my shoulder to give me a slight push.

"We better hurry and get to class before they make it inside. I'm sure they'll be looking for you."

We start walking at a fast pace.

"I don't understand. Why now? It's not like Chase and I just started dating last week, and that I haven't been on campus for the last month and a half."

"Maybe it's the fact that the public knows more about you and who you are. It's not every day that a famous star like Chase meets a girl like you."

"Yeah, that's becoming clearer and clearer to me," I say as we near the door to our advanced inorganic chemistry class.

I can't believe it's already Halloween. It's time for the big Zeta eighties party and for Chase to work his heart out in helping to earn money for the Susan G. Komen Foundation. With his love for supporting various charities, I knew when I asked him last month that he wouldn't be able to turn down the opportunity to contribute.

The field house is all decorated and ready for the big event. The Zetas hired a popular band from Charleston called The Diamonds. They play eighties songs and have a DJ that comes along with them who carries a plethora of famous eighties tracks. I notice that all of their equipment has been set up onstage. I also notice that, across the designated dance floor is the area where Chase will sign autographs and take fan photos. The autograph table and photo booth have already been set up and are waiting for his arrival.

As I look around at some of the Zetas doing a few last-minute touches, I begin to wonder why I'm here and Aimee is not.

"Jo!"

Well, I guess I no longer need to wonder, since she has arrived. I turn to face Aimee as she walks over to me.

"Hey. I was wondering when you were going to get here. I mean, geez, I can help you have a great party, but it's not my responsibility to do all the work."

She holds up her hands, and I notice that she is wearing black-lace gloves on both of them. What the hell?

"Okay I must ask who are you supposed to be dressed as? You definitely remind me of some popular eighties pop princess."

I roll my eyes just a little before I answer her. "I tried to dress like Debbie Gibson. Do you like it?" I ask her as I turn to model my outfit. I must admit that I feel like I am rocking the plain, white T-shirt covered with a purple blazer that has the ridiculous giant shoulder pads, suspenders, knee-length shorts with a skirt over them, white Keds, scrunched-up purple socks, and a black bowler hat. You can't get more Debbie Gibson than that.

Aimee nods her head in agreement. "I love it! You definitely look like her in that outfit. Now I know you don't even have to guess who I am dressed like."

No, Aimee, you're right, I don't. She is wearing a black corset dress with black fishnet stockings, black high heels, and several crucifixes around her neck. Her makeup is dark and heavy, and her hair is styled in a messy ponytail. She makes a great Madonna.

"You make a fabulous Madonna, Aimee. I mean, you really look the part."

She smiles real big. You can tell that she is very proud of accomplishing the look. "Thanks! I knew that it would be the perfect outfit for me!"

Yes, indeed. I guess you could say that we dressed the part that suits our personality. I am definitely more of the pop princess, girl-next-door Debbie Gibson while Aimee is the bad girl, troublemaker, spontaneous Madonna.

"So when is Chase going to be here?" Aimee asks as she starts to walk over to the autograph table. I follow her over.

"He should be here any minute. He told me that he wanted to get here a little before the party started so the guys could help him in, and he could be settled at the table before the girls start dashing in the door."

Aimee nods. "Makes sense. Well, it's almost eight."

She spins around and looks past me. A smile forms across her face. "Speaking of … he's here," she says.

I turn around and see Chase heading across the field-house floor. My mouth falls open slightly at the sight of him. He looks so hot with his eighties preppy boy look. It's almost like he came straight out of the movie *Pretty in Pink*. It's one of my all time faves of the decade. He is wearing a turquoise short-sleeve polo with his collar popped, a light-pink sweater draped over his shoulders and tied neatly at his chest, a pair of khakis with a black-and-white striped belt, and his Converses. I can tell that he's even added a little gel to his hair. If he isn't sexy, I don't know who is!

"Wow, Jo, you look great! I love the outfit, and the bowler hat is pretty amazing," Chase says as he walks over to me.

I blush. I really had my doubts on the hat, but now I'm glad I decided to wear it. It really does complete the whole Debbie Gibson look.

"Thanks. You look fantastic! I didn't expect you to dress up, but then again, I'm really not sure what I was expecting for tonight."

Chase grins. "Well, I know what I'm expecting. Chaos. Complete and total chaos. And I certainly hope that you ladies are ready to experience it with me. The guys are here, and Boss has an action plan for the whole party. He and Lincoln will stay with me over at the table, and Zane and Mac will stand guard at the doors. Does that sound okay?"

Aimee and I nod.

Chase cocks an eyebrow at Aimee and says, "You have to be Madonna."

Aimee strikes a pose. "Well, of course. There is no one else I would rather be for a party like this."

I crack a small smile at Chase as he looks over at me.

"Well, I can say that the two of you definitely dressed the right part. Sweet, innocent, charismatic Debbie and boy-toy, rebel Madonna."

I let out a small giggle at his use of the word "boy-toy" and notice a little look of shock on Aimee's face.

Chase holds up his hands in a wait-a-minute gesture. "I just want to take one guess at how Kevin is going to be dressed."

Aimee folds her arms across her chest and lets out a small sigh. "Go ahead."

Chase asks, "Billy Idol?"

Aimee allows her arms to fall and places them firmly on her hips. "How did you know?" she asks.

Chase shrugs his shoulders. "I don't know. I guess because of the similarities. 'Papa Don't Preach' and 'Rebel Yell.' A perfect match don't you think?"

This time I let out an even louder laugh.

Aimee smiles big and rolls her eyes. Ha. "You're too good, Chase. I'm going to double-check with the girls and make sure everything is ready."

She gives us a quick wink and walks away.

Chase reaches and pulls me in for a hug. He gives me a kiss and a smile.

"Thank you so much for doing this. I really can't tell you how much it means to me."

"You are very welcome, and you know that I will do anything for you, love. Anything at all."

There goes that wonderful word again that he likes to call me … "love." The way it sounds as it falls on my ears is just too amazing.

"Now I hope you know that, even though I will be busy with autographs and pics, that I must have a few dances with you tonight. Not having the opportunity is completely unacceptable."

I smile up at him. "Well, we will just have to make sure that we make it to the dance floor before the party is over."

An hour has passed, and I can't even tell you how many autographs Chase has signed and photographs he has taken. The line of girls seems endless. The band is playing on stage, bodies are moving all over the dance floor, and thousands of conversations seem to be going on at once. It is quite loud, and I am just trying to hold myself together through it all. Trying to hold myself together until I have Chase all to myself. After all of this, I know we will both feel the need for some quiet and alone time. I yearn for it.

The band decides to take a break, as does Chase. The DJ gets ready to play a few songs. Boss and Lincoln escort Chase over to where I am standing.

"I need a break. I've only been at it an hour, and my hand feels like it's about to fall off."

I smile at him as he massages his right wrist. "Well, maybe the next couple of hours will go by quickly."

He nods in agreement. "I certainly hope so. I may have carpel tunnel by the time I'm done, but for you it is all worth it."

I blush. "It's not for me. It's for the foundation."

"And you."

We exchange a small smile. Suddenly a song blares from the speaker system. It is the eighties hit, "Is This Love" by Whitesnake. Chase reaches for my hand.

"This is one of my eighties favorites. Will you please dance with me?" he asks.

I nod and take his hand. We walk out to the dance floor. There are numerous couples slow-dancing together. Boss and Lincoln follow us out just a little bit and stay within a reasonable distance in case we need them. Chase pulls me close, and we begin to sway back and forth. It feels wonderful to be here with him. Even if we are surrounded with hundreds of unfamiliar faces, it is nice to just be in his arms, dancing to the music. I can pretend that it is just us. Even if it is for a short moment.

"Don't you have to work tomorrow?" Chase asks.

"Yeah, but I don't go in until right before lunch. I have to close, though, so I will be there until nine or after."

He nods. "I need to be on set around ten in the morning. I might come tomorrow afternoon after the lunch rush has died down and grab a bite to eat."

"That sounds great. I will probably sit with you for a little bit and eat a bite myself. Sundays are pretty busy with the church crowd."

Whitesnake continues to sing as we continue to slow dance. I listen to the words. "Is this love that I'm feeling? Is this the love that I've been searching for? Is this love or am I dreaming? This must be love cause it's really got a hold on me."

Chase and I look into each other's eyes. He softly starts to sing the words to the song. As I gaze into his eyes and listen to the softness of his voice, I begin to wonder if he thinks this is love. Is that what he is feeling? Is this what he has been searching for? For me? For this? Or is it really just a dream that both of us are trapped in? What is this really? So much has happened in a short amount of time. What would we call it? What *could* we call it?

Chase pulls me in closer. He leans his head down to where his right cheek gently brushes mine. I can feel his breath on my ear. It sends a wonderful, shivering sensation down my body.

"Come home with me tonight," he whispers.

I close my eyes at the sound of his voice and at the words that have just escaped his lips.

"Most definitely," I whisper back.

The next couple of hours of eighties hit music, signing autographs, taking photographs, and dancing goes by faster than we anticipated. Aimee estimated that Chase helped raise close to sixteen thousand dollars for the Susan G. Komen Foundation. There were well over three hundred people there, and the majority of them wanted autographs with a photo. Also the admission fee helped boost the total. I was very excited and pleased that the event turned out so successful.

It's Sunday afternoon and the first of November. Time is really going by. The craziness hasn't been too bad at the cafe today. The church lunch crowd is starting to fade. We have had several hangovers from the after-party last night show up for coffee, and there have been some new faces. I'm wiping down a table, and I glance up at the clock. It's two. I am starving. I could sure go for a cup of Ramona's oyster stew and the turkey specialty right now.

The bells over the door ring behind me. I turn around to see who is walking in, and my eyes fall on *him*. I smile. I think back to last night. I think about lying next to him in bed and his arms swallowing me. His lips, his touch, and all of his perfect movements. Why did we have to leave the comfort of his bedroom? I sigh, but still hold my smile.

"Hey, gorgeous," Chase says as he plants a small kiss on my left cheek. Definitely appropriate for the center of the dining room at Ramona's. Customers are watching. I can feel it. I'm blushing.

"Hey. I'm so glad you're here."

He smiles his most wonderful smile. "I was going to text you, but I figured you would be busy, so we just headed over."

Boss and Lincoln are standing at a small distance away. I give them a smile and a nod. They do the same.

"So, are you hungry?" Chase asks.

"I'm about to perish. I also need a break. Do you know what you want?"

He replies, "Not really. What about you?"

"I'm going for a cup of oyster stew and the turkey specialty."

"I'll take the same. I'll go grab us a booth near the back. The guys can sit somewhere close by. They ate earlier while I was filming. They may want a sweet tea or water."

I nod with a smile and head for the kitchen to put in our orders.

Ramona gently places our order on the booth tabletop. The cups of oyster stew are steaming hot and the turkey specialties look so tasty.

"It all looks delicious, Ramona. Thanks," Chase says as he reaches for his napkin.

Ramona gives him a big smile.

"Well, thank you, Chase. You know we love seeing you here at the cafe. It's always a pleasure to serve you."

Chase returns her smile.

"Now you two enjoy your lunch."

Ramona gives me a wink and a smile as she walks away.

"I really like her. She's a sweet woman."

I nod in agreement. "Yeah, she reminds me a lot of my grandma. She was the same way."

Chase reaches for my hand, indicating that he wants to say grace. I take his hand in mine. We bow our heads, and he softly utters words of thanks and praise. It makes my heart skip a beat to hear him say such wonderful things. It is so attractive and even romantic.

"So I stopped by and saw Grandpa Dawson the other day."

I love how he calls my grandpa Grandpa Dawson. My heart is wearing a big smile right now.

"He wants us to eat Thanksgiving dinner with him and Ms. Margaret," he adds.

I take a bite of my stew. I wonder if that is something that Chase wants to do. I'm sure he would rather spend his time off for Thanksgiving with his family.

I swallow my bite and ask, "What do you think? You have plans with your family, I'm sure."

He shakes his head as he also swallows his bite of stew. "I told him that would be wonderful. I'd love to spend time with you and your family for Thanksgiving. I'm working on some big plans for us for Christmas, if that's okay with you?"

I smile at him. How could that *not* be okay with me? Of course it's okay. "Exactly what do you have in mind?" I ask with great curiosity.

"Well, definitely a trip to Denver, but the big surprise will have to wait. I'm not giving that away."

I wonder what he has planned. I'm going to guess something out-of-this-world amazing and romantic. I don't see how he would plan something any other way.

"Then I am going to have a hard time waiting for Christmas to get here."

He nods. "Yeah, but you will be so busy with work and school that it will be here before you know it. You are going to need that nice break. Ramona has always been so nice to let you take off work for us to go places and spend time together. Do you think she will let you take off a couple of weeks during Christmas break?"

I want to choke on my stew. *Two weeks? What in the world could he have planned to where I need to take off that long?*

I shrug my shoulders because I honestly don't know the answer. I'd like to think and say yes, she would not have a problem with giving me the time off, but I know that Christmas is busy, and she needs all the help she can get.

"I really don't know. I'm sure she would love to give me all of that time off, but we get so busy at Christmastime with all the tourists, and then there are several locals that have family visit for the holidays. Ramona usually hires a new waiter or waitress and busboy just to keep things running smoothly."

Chase has a contemplating look. He is trying to figure out a way to make things work. I like it. He is determined, and it makes me feel like, to him, I am worth all the trouble in the world to be with.

"How about I talk to Ramona about you having the time off, and I offer to pay the extra help she hires during that time, and I'll also give her some money for the time that you are gone to help with any inconvenience."

I think about his offer. It could work, but I hate the thought of him doing something like that.

"I really don't know if I could accept you paying money like that just for me to be away from work for two weeks."

"Are you kidding me? I would do whatever it would take to be able to have you to myself for two whole weeks."

I blush a light shade of red. *Yes, please. Take me all for yourself and do whatever you want to me. I am yours.*

"It may be a good idea to add one more thing."

"And what would that be?" he asks.

"Maybe I should offer to work six days a week until Christmas break just to help out as much as I can around here."

Chase shrugs his shoulders and gives a quick nod. "If you feel like that is something you could do. I just don't want you to be overwhelmed with school and so much work."

He's right. I don't need to overdo it. The Christmas break will be a nice way to catch up on rest and other things, but I know that Chase doesn't want me to get burnt out way before the break even gets here. It's still a good seven to eight weeks away.

"Maybe I should just talk with Ramona, and then we will take it from there once we see what she agrees to."

I nod. "Sounds fair enough."

Chapter Eighteen

Writing a paper on *Pride and Prejudice* with my arguing opinion on how Mr. Darcy is without a doubt Elizabeth Bennett's life- and ego-saving hero should not be a struggle for me. But it is. At least for tonight. I sit in my bedroom chair and stare blankly at the blinking cursor. I have so much on my mind. This paper, Thanksgiving, Christmas, lab, work, and, above all things, Chase. If I can just hold myself together until mid-December, then everything will be all right, and I will have a nice break. A break I will honestly say that I deserve. Geez. My brain is going to be fried by then, I just know it.

I try to focus. *How should I start? What would be the most appealing way to hook my professor in the reading of my essay?* The doorbell rings, breaking what little concentration I do have going at the moment. Great. Now I have to get up and answer the door. This is one of those times that I wish Aimee was here.

Before opening the door, I run my fingers over my hair to make sure it is straight and that I look somewhat decent when greeting whoever has decided to stop by. I take a quick peek through the peephole and stare at the godliness that stands on the other side. My mouth starts to water. Chase is waiting patiently. I quickly open the door. He is dressed in a pair of blue jeans and gray T-shirt with a cotton, navy-blue Abercrombie and Fitch jacket and, of course, a huge smile.

"Hi," he says.

I melt. An imaginary puddle has already formed on the floor below me. He will always do *this* to me. There is no question about it.

"Hi," I say back with a smile and a hint of pink on my cheeks.

I hold the door open for him to walk in. I close it behind him, and he takes me in his arms. We share a deep, passionate kiss. I absolutely love the feeling of our tongues dancing together. It's almost as if one is fighting for control over the other. We finally pull away, yet still embraced in each other's arms.

"So what do I owe this pleasant surprise?" I ask him as I keep my hands still on his back.

He gently rubs at my hips with his hands. "Well, first, I couldn't stop thinking about how badly I wanted to see you, and second, I have great news."

A shiver runs up my spine, not only from his touch, but at his confession of how bad he wanted to see me. "Great news?"

He nods. "Actually, you could call it amazing news."

Amazing? I love the sound of that! I have to know. The suspense is killing me!

"So what is it? I'm dying here."

"Wait, where's Aimee?" he asks as he glances around the living room of the apartment.

"She and Kevin are in Charleston, hanging out with some friends. They won't be back until late tonight."

"Oh, okay. Let's sit down on the couch for a minute then."

He grabs hold of my hand and leads me over. We sit, and I start to fidget my fingers around in my lap. I'm waiting, and my patience is getting thin. "Well?" I say as Chase takes notice of my hands. He grins.

"I went to the cafe last night at closing and had a cup of coffee with Ramona."

I know where this is going. He talked to her about Christmas break and me taking off work. I can feel a small dose of anxiety in my chest. My heart is starting to pound. He said he had great—no, amazing news—but he could be talking about something else.

"We talked about you being off for Christmas. I told her that I would gladly pay for someone to fill in for you and for whatever else she would need during that time. She happily agreed."

"Really?" I say out loud as I start to jump up and down next to him on the couch like a little girl. *Okay, Jo, you need to stop. You are acting just like Aimee. Geez.*

194

He laughs. "Yes, really. And she said that you are covered until after New Year's."

I stop bouncing. Wait, what? How is that possible? I didn't expect her to give me that much time off. I am shocked. "How did you manage that?"

"I told her that I had something very special planned for us, and that I really needed you to be off until after New Year's, and, of course, she just couldn't say no. So I've got it all taken care of, and I am in the middle of making some very important arrangements for us."

I am speechless. I really don't even know how to say thanks. Pinch me, please. Someone just pinch me and tell me to wake up. This is all a dream. It has been a dream for the last several months. I am due to wake up at any moment.

"Is this for real?" I ask.

"Yes, love, its real. Very real indeed."

Words cannot express the excitement that has built up inside of me in just the few minutes that I have been sitting here with him. *Do I deserve all of this? Do I deserve him? Why me?*

"Do you have a calendar handy by any chance?" Chase asks.

"Um … yeah, Aimee always keeps one on hand in one of these side tables."

I step over to the side table on the right of the couch and find a small pocket calendar in the drawer. I sit back down next to him and hand over the calendar. He flips through it until he gets to December.

"Okay, so I wanted to show you what all I have planned, just to get your thoughts in case I need to make some changes."

Chase, you can make all the wonderful plans for us that you want to. There is no need for me to make any changes as long as I am with you. I nod with a small smile. He's got this. He's got it all under control.

"I also stopped by and talked with Grandpa Dawson. I hope you don't mind, but I filled him in on all the plans I have for us, and we agreed to have Christmas at his house with him and Ms. Margaret on Friday December 19. Is that all right with you?" he asks as his finger rests on the date.

I gaze up into his eyes and nod again. I'm so mesmerized that he is doing all of this for us. For me.

"Of course. That sounds great."

"Then we will fly out early the next morning for Denver. My family will come see us on Christmas Day. Mom and Dad are going to stay in their rental cabin like they do every year. Mary and Cameron will stay with us for a few nights, since Cameron will be bringing Katherine, and Mary has met a new guy that I am sure will be there. We will return to Folly on Saturday January 3. I figured it would be good to be home, then so we could take Sunday to rest up from all the holiday events and traveling."

Wow! All of this for me? For me? Why? I am falling so madly, deeply in love with this guy. This famous movie star. This guy who is the dream of almost every girl on the planet. He's mine.

"Chase, all of this sounds absolutely wonderful. You don't have to do this. I really don't deserve any of it."

He takes his left hand and gently cups my chin. Our eyes hold in a lock. "Baby, you deserve this and so much more. You deserve everything I have to give. If it can be done for you, then I want to do it. Please come away with me. I want you all to myself for a while. I want to take you away from all of this and just focus on each other."

How heavenly does that sound? And how sweet?

He leans in and places a soft kiss on my lips. I crave more. I need him. Right here. Right now. I look into his eyes for a moment. We do not speak a word. I reach for him. I pull him close to me and kiss him hard. My tongue enters his mouth. His enters mine. Our breathing starts to escalate. Our hands start to explore. He moves his lips from my mouth over to my right cheek, then my ear, and then down to my neck. His lips feel so good. They are so soft and wet. I close my eyes at their touch.

"Stay with me tonight," I say.

He stops and looks at me.

"Please?" I add.

He doesn't say a word. He takes my hand in his and stands up. I rise from the couch and follow as he leads me to my bedroom. Once we enter, he closes the door behind us and locks it.

I can feel a small hint of sunlight caressing my face as it peeks its way through the curtains hanging from my bedroom window. I slowly open my eyes and see Chase sound asleep next to me. The sound of his breathing is calm and sweet. He looks so peaceful. I still can't believe that he is mine.

All mine and right here next to me, wrapped up in my comforter, in my bed, and in my bedroom. I never in a hundred million years would have imagined that I would be here with him like this.

I glance over at my alarm clock. It is seven a.m. I have to be in class at nine. I dread leaving the warmth and comfort of my bed with Chase lying beside me. I wish we could just skip all of our responsibilities and snuggle all day. *Patience, Jo. Be patient. December 19 will be here faster than you realize.* I just hope and pray that the days of our Christmas vacation pass by very slowly.

"Good morning, love."

I turn and face Chase. There it is again. The name he calls me ... "love." I absolutely love it.

"Good morning." I smile at him.

He pulls me close and gives me a sweet, gentle kiss. "Time to start another day."

I nod. "Yes, it is. But the way I see it is I'm working on getting through another day that is getting us closer to our time away together."

He smiles. "That is a great way to look at it. You have to be in class at nine right?"

"Unfortunately so."

"I have to be on set by ten. We are filming late tonight. You want to grab some breakfast?" he asks.

"Breakfast sounds wonderful."

"Does Waffle House sound wonderful?"

I giggle. "It does, actually."

"Great. Let's get ready and head over. I'm dying for some steak, eggs, and hash browns."

Chapter Nineteen

It's the week of Thanksgiving. Time has been flying by, and all I can think about is getting to Denver. In four weeks, I will be snuggled up, all warm and cozy, with the guy that has been changing my life since the night he walked into the cafe. The guy of my dreams. Right now, I just need to focus on studying for my finals. The end of fall semester is drawing closer with each passing day.

I grab my book bag and walk out of my bedroom. I hear Aimee and Kevin in the kitchen, discussing their upcoming trip to Aimee's parent's house for Thanksgiving. I'm sure Kevin is thrilled.

Aimee peeks her head around the doorway and asks, "Where are you headed?"

I set my book bag down in the living room chair as I reach for my jacket. "I'm going to the library to study."

"Oh, okay. Are you going alone?"

"Yeah, why?"

"Well, I was thinking about going tonight and doing a little studying myself."

I'm a little shocked at her statement. Aimee studying? This isn't something that happens very often.

I give her a puzzled look. "So, you are going to leave Kevin here?" I ask.

"Nah, I'm about to head over to Mike's," Kevin replies.

"Do you want to ride with me, Aimee?"

"Yeah, hold on and let me get my stuff."

The heat blowing through the vents in my BMW feels so good. It's actually pretty chilly tonight.

"You and Chase having Thanksgiving with Grandpa Dawson and Ms. Margaret?" Aimee asks.

"Yep. I'm excited about it. Chase and I are going to make a green-bean casserole, and there is a cake he wants to bake for dessert."

Aimee laughs. "I'm sorry, but I still find it quite humorous that he likes to cook and is good at it at that."

I laugh a little too. "Well, it's not exactly the type of thing you imagine Chase Hartford doing, but he is definitely good at it that's for sure."

"I bet he's good at other things too," Aimee adds.

I notice a mischievous grin on her face.

I shrug my shoulders. "I couldn't tell you, but I'm sure he is amazing at everything he does."

"I'm still trying to figure out how at this point you still haven't slept with him. I mean he is so into you, Jo."

"So you're saying that just because he is *into* me as you call it that I should sleep with him?"

She nods. "Of course. Any other girl would. Any other girl wouldn't hesitate."

I roll my eyes and let out a small sigh. "But, Aimee, I'm not those *other* girls. It's all so different for me. I thought with you being my best friend that you would understand that more than anyone."

She turns to face me. "Look, I realize that everything you have been through has been extremely tough, and yes, you've been through some shit, but, Jo, it's time to let it all go. Put it all behind you and move on. Let things happen. Let things happen with him. What are you so afraid of?"

"Love. Being hurt. Being disappointed."

"Ha. Well, guess what? Reality check. That is what it's like for everyone. We are all scared of love, getting hurt, and being disappointed or let down. It's what love is all about."

"I realize that, but I have never had the feelings for anyone that I have for Chase. I mean I had feelings for Jake, but not like this. It's so new to me. Everything is new to me. I just want things to be right. To be perfect."

"And you think that's what he wants too?"

"Most definitely. He's told me. He's in no hurry to make rash decisions and mistakes. He is considerate and understanding. He wants everything that happens between us to be right."

"Christmas."

I give her a quick, confused glance. "Huh?"

"It's going to happen when you go to Denver."

"What makes you think that?"

"Well, he has something very special planned while y'all are away. I just have this feeling that the timing will be perfect when ya'll are there together."

I give a small shrug with my shoulders. "Could be. I really couldn't say right now. I guess we will know when that time gets here."

"I'm just excited for you that's all. I like seeing you happy. It's been a long time since I've seen you like this. To be honest, I really don't remember the last time I did see you this way."

I pull into the parking lot at the library and find a spot as close to the door as possible. I put the car in park and switch off the ignition.

"Thanks. I really appreciate that. I'm fine. Chase is fine. Everything is fine, and it will happen. I'm going to let it happen, and so is he, but on our terms, and when we are both ready."

She nods at me with a small smile. "Good idea. That's the best way to do it. I know I sound pushy and all, but you definitely don't want to go the route Kevin and I did."

She pauses for a moment.

"Geez am I kidding myself? You and Chase passed that mark almost two months ago."

"Ha!" I laugh out loud.

I couldn't control myself. She's right. Aimee and Kevin didn't take things in the slow department by any means.

She lets out a loud laugh as well.

"Let's get inside," I say as I reach for my book bag in the back seat. "I have a lot of studying to get done."

It's Thanksgiving Day. Chase, Grandpa Dawson, Ms. Margaret, and I are seated around the dining-room table. The table is covered with some of the best and most popular Thanksgiving dishes. Ms. Margaret baked a huge, honey-glazed ham, macaroni and cheese, sweet potato soufflé, and country-style biscuits. Grandpa did the cranberry sauce and baked

Grandma's dressing, while Chase and I did the green-bean casserole and cream-cheese pound cake. Delicious. Yes, you could definitely say delicious.

"Grandpa Dawson and Ms. Margaret, this has to be one of the best Thanksgiving meals I've ever had," Chase says as he takes the last bite of his dressing.

Grandpa smiles.

"Well, thank you, Chase. We try around here, wouldn't you say, Margaret?"

She gives Grandpa a smile with a nod.

"If there is one thing I know for sure, I am ready for a big slice of that good-looking cream-cheese pound cake you two baked," Grandpa says, giving a wink.

"Now I can't take any credit for it, Grandpa. Chase is the one that baked the cake. I watched."

Everyone lets out a small laugh.

"You know, Jo, I never thought that you would find a guy that would teach you how to cook some things. I figured you would be doing all the teaching," Grandpa says.

Ms. Margaret looks over at me and adds, "We need to be thankful for these gentlemen, Jo. They are few and far between, you know?"

She gives me a wink and a smile.

"Yes ma'am, I believe they are."

Grandpa adds, "I must admit I'm afraid I may hurt myself with that cake. It just looks too good."

Chase rises from his chair.

"I'll cut everyone a slice. I'll make sure you get the biggest one, Grandpa."

I melt in my chair. I can't even begin to explain how much it means to me and how it makes me feel to hear the way my grandpa and Chase talk to one another. If someone would have told me it would be like this, I never would have believed them. They act as if they have known each other since Chase was running around in diapers.

I also rise from my seat. "I'll help."

I follow Chase into the kitchen. He grabs four small plates out of the cabinet and sets them down on the counter.

"You know I've never told you how wonderful it makes me feel to watch how you and my grandpa interact with each other. It means a lot. The relationship that y'all share almost reminds me of the one he had with Sam."

Chase looks over at me with a small smile. "Oh yeah?"

"Yeah." I nod. "Sam was his little man. They were very close."

"I think the world of your grandpa. He's an amazing man."

I smile back and agree, "Yes, he is."

We stare at each other for a moment without saying a word. Our faces seem to say a thousand words, but there is no sound.

"Thank you. Thank you for everything," I say to him with a serious and appreciative look.

"Always," he says with a small wink.

We quickly slice the cake and carry the plates to the dining room.

"All right, the first and biggest slice goes to you, Grandpa," Chase says as he sets the cake down in front of Grandpa Dawson.

Grandpa has a big smile on his face. "Oh, that looks fantastic."

Chase smiles. "Well, I hope it tastes as good as it looks," Chase adds as he walks over to his chair.

We both sit down as Grandpa takes his first bite of the cake. His eyes close as he experiences the taste of the cream-cheese icing.

"Chase, this is really amazing. Definitely the best cream-cheese pound cake I've ever had."

We all smile at each other.

Ms. Margaret says, "Like I said, Jo, be thankful for the fine cooking this young man provides. Don't ever let him go." She throws me yet another wink.

"Oh, you don't have to worry about that. I won't let him go anywhere."

We all let out a small laugh.

"So, Jo, when are finals?" Grandpa asks.

I take a bite of my cake and reply, "Next week."

"I know you are ready to get them over with."

I nod. "Definitely."

Ms. Margaret chimes in, "When is it again that y'all leave for Denver?"

"We will leave early Saturday morning the twentieth," Chase responds.

"And when will y'all be back?" she asks.

"Not until the third of January," he adds.

She raises an eyebrow and gives us a smile. "Well, that sounds like a nice little getaway for the two of you. Anything special planned? Is your family coming to visit while you're there?"

Chase smiles back and nods. "Yeah, I plan on it being a great time. I have a few things up my sleeve that Jo doesn't know about, and yes, my family will be there to see us on Christmas Day."

"That's lovely. Thomas, isn't it a great feeling to see young people in love?"

Chase and I glance at each other.

My grandpa replies, "It's absolutely wonderful. Especially when one of them happens to be my one and only beautiful granddaughter."

I blush. "Aw, thanks, Grandpa. You know it's a great feeling, Ms. Margaret, to see my grandpa happy. I'm so glad that the two of you met."

"Thank you very much, Joanna. I'm glad we met too. After William died, I really didn't believe that my heart could let another soul in, but Thomas proved that to be wrong. He's a fine man."

They smile at each other.

"You know, I think it would be fun for us to build a fire in the living room and play a game of cards," Grandpa says.

"That sounds like a great idea, Thomas."

"What do you kids think?" he asks, looking up from his empty plate.

Chase and I agree that it sounds like fun.

Ms. Margaret stands from her chair and starts to collect dishes. "I'll start cleaning up a little."

"I'll help," I say as I reach for some of the dirty dishes on the table.

Grandpa also rises. "I'm going to grab some firewood from out by the barn."

"I'll come grab a load with you," Chase says.

Within about fifteen minutes, Ms. Margaret and I have all the dishes up and table cleaned, and Grandpa and Chase have the fire going. We play rummy and UNO for a couple of hours, sharing laughter and conversations about many different things. For our first Thanksgiving together, I believe it turned out perfect.

Chapter Twenty

The weeks since Thanksgiving have flown by. Oh, and how that is *exactly* what I wanted them to do. I made it through my finals with an A+ in all of my courses. Boom! Chase, Grandpa, and Ms. Margaret were all very proud of my hard work. Even sweet Ramona congratulated me on being able to pull off so much while working at the cafe. She was very impressed.

I enjoyed the first part of my break. Chase kept me busy and things interesting. He continued to film on almost a daily basis while taking me out on dates. Very intriguing dates. I suppose that's what you could call them. One night at Chase's, we built forts out of furniture and blankets and then waged war with paper airplanes. Childish? Maybe. Insane? Just a little. Fun? Absolutely! Another time we walked down King Street and the battery in Charleston. It was nice, and Chase was able to see a lot of interesting and historic things. We grabbed a bite to eat at Fleet Landing. One of the most out-of-this-world dates was when we decided to go for a drive, and we agreed to make right turns only just to see where we would end up. We ended up at James Island County Park. It wasn't crowded at all, so we decided to go for a swing on the playground and play hide-and-seek among the trees. Like I said before: childish? Maybe. Insane? Just a little. Fun? Most definitely! The laughter we shared and the time we had together felt so good and meant the world to me.

I hope my time here in Denver goes by very slowly. Chase and I arrived yesterday afternoon. Of course, at first, he gave me the tour of his beautiful log home. It is right around 4,200-square-feet. On the first floor, there is a huge kitchen with an attached dining room and private laundry. There is a half-bath and large living room with a fireplace covered in cobblestone rock that stretches to the ceiling. On each side of the fireplace are doors that open to the back wooden deck. It has a large, outdoor sitting area with a fire pit. Down a short hall there is a small bedroom with its own private bath. At the very end is the master suite with a cobblestoned fireplace as well, its own large private bath, and door that leads to the back deck. Upstairs is a large loft and two more bedrooms, with each having their own private bath. The home is gorgeous, with its sprawling multi-level roof line, heavy log accents and beam work, and expansive large windows. After getting everything settled, we went shopping for groceries. It was nice to be able to go and do this without the guys and to actually shop in the store without being bothered. All I know is that I am excited to finally be here and can't wait to see what all Chase and I will do together.

I hear the beep from the coffee pot as it wakes me from my daze, signaling that it is ready as I stare out the kitchen window. Suddenly I feel his arms wrap around my waist and pull my back close into his chest. I close my eyes at how good his touch feels. How good his arms feel around me.

"Good morning, love," he says as he places a kiss on the back of my head.

I smile. "Good morning."

"How are you feeling this morning?" he asks.

"Amazing. I'm here with you. I couldn't be better," I reply.

"Same here."

I turn around to see his handsome face. His godliness radiates even in the early morning. Complete and total hotness. Boom.

"Would you like some coffee?"

"Please."

"I'll get you some," I say as I head over to the cabinets to grab us both a cup.

"So, did you sleep good last night?"

I nod. I'd say for my first night, it was wonderful. "Most definitely. Your bed is so heavenly. I felt as if I were sleeping on a cloud."

He smiles. "Well, good. That's what I want to hear."

"And being in your arms just made it even more wonderful."

I give him a small wink. I'm proud of myself. This is another accomplishment for me. I've had many of them when it comes to him. He has really helped me come out of my shell. I've tried to be as guarded as possible, but it seems that my guard hasn't been as strong as I thought. I am a book, and the pages inside of me are becoming more open. I am allowing him to read so much into my past and to help write my future.

He smiles again. "Now that's what I really want to hear."

I walk over to the perfectly constructed log island where he is sitting and set down his coffee. "Thanks, love."

"My pleasure. What is on our agenda for our first day together in Denver?" I ask with curiosity.

"Well, I thought we could ride out to Sullivan's Christmas Tree Farm and find us the perfect tree to decorate. We are going to be here for a while, and I would hate for us to go without one. Plus I get one every year before my parents come. Oh, and I meant to tell you that Cameron, Katherine, Mary, and her new boyfriend decided to come early. They arrived last night. They changed their minds and ended up renting their own place closer to the city. They will be here sometime before lunch to help us get the tree back here and to decorate it."

"Oh, that sounds nice. I can't wait to see them. You've seen my and Aimee's little three-foot-tree on a pathetic stand that sits on one of the tables in the living room." I let out a small giggle.

"It's like your typical college-apartment Christmas tree."

"Yeah, I guess you could say that. Grandpa and I put up a tree that has to be at least eight foot in the living room by the fireplace."

"I feel sad taking you away from him this holiday season."

"It's fine. I promise you he doesn't mind at all. I know that he is glad to have Ms. Margaret. I'm glad he has Ms. Margaret. I'm sure he's excited that we both have someone special to spend Christmas with."

Chase nods. "And I want to make this Christmas the best you've ever had."

I have chills. I get more just wondering what he has planned for us. I think back to the conversation that Aimee and I had in my car on the way to the library. Will this be the place? The right time? Are we ready? A big part of me believes that I truly *am* ready. I am ready to take that step. I'm going to have faith in his strength to lead me.

We went to Sullivan's Christmas Tree Farm and found the most absolutely perfect ten-foot-tree. After cutting it down, the other customers had plenty of entertainment watching as Chase, Cameron, and Mary's boyfriend, Ian, tried to load and strap down the huge tree to the roof of Chase's Hummer H2. It was even more amusing for Katherine, Mary, and me as we watched the guys take the tree down from the top of the truck and get it inside by the fireplace to be decorated. Chase admitted to me that every year he would have Sullivan's deliver the tree he picked, and they would also set it up inside for a small charge. I guess this year he wanted his Christmas experience with me to be as normal as possible. I'm sure that Cameron and Ian really appreciated his new decision this year, since they were involved in the most difficult part of getting the tree.

Katherine, Mary, and I are hanging garland on the mantelpiece in the living room as the guys grab some boxes of lights and ornaments from the basement. They walk in and set them down on the large coffee table.

Chase pushes a few fallen strands of hair out of his eyes as he stands upright and looks at me. Damn. Every time I look at him he sends a vibe through me like I have never experienced before. It gets stronger every time. He gives me a wink and a sexy smile. Well, that just made it more intense.

"Ladies, are y'all cool with us guys stringing the lights, and then we can all pitch in on hanging the ornaments?" Chase asks.

Mary, Katherine, and I glance at each other and nod in agreement. I don't think we would object. Stringing the lights is the most aggravating part of decorating a tree; especially one this size.

"When are we going skiing?" Mary asks as she straightens a corner of the garland.

Chase replies, "I was thinking tomorrow."

"We've got to go to Winter Park. They have the best slopes. Plus it's tradition," Cameron adds.

"Well, I'm going to straight up tell you guys that I have never been snow-skiing. Now surfing I know just about every move there is, but skiing is just not my thing," Ian says as he pulls the second string of lights from a box.

Mary gives him the oh-don't-worry-about-that gesture with her right hand and steps back to make sure that the garland looks perfect.

"It's okay, sweets. I'll take you to the beginner's park there. It's the perfect place to learn and practice the basics of skiing."

"I'm sure that if you can surf, Ian, then you won't have a problem learning how to ski. You'll catch on pretty quick."

"What about you, Jo? Do you know how to ski?" Mary asks.

"I can a little. I'm not as great as I used to be. My parents would take Sam and me every winter in Virginia."

"You and I will stick around Discovery with Mary and Ian then. That way you can brush up on your skiing skills," Chase says as he gives me a sweet smile.

Cameron chimes in, "Katherine and I will be up at Mary Jane Mountain. I'm eager to hit some of those jumps. No doubt she is too."

"Oh, I'm definitely ready. By the way, we still have a bet going on from last winter. You may recall the one I'm talking about, Cameron," Katherine adds as she purposefully clears her throat.

Cameron lets out a small laugh. "I know which one you are talking about. You're going down, babe."

She shakes her head and her finger at him. "Oh, no no. You are. I'm going to show you up on Mary Jane this year."

"Okay, we'll see."

We continue talking about skiing and how everyone wants to go eat at Denver's oldest restaurant afterwards. It's called The Buckhorn Exchange, and they serve your original steakhouse foods, as well as some exotic items. They start talking about the elk and buffalo prime rib and how they are cooked to perfection and taste so good. I'm not too sure, but willing to try it. I guess.

The guys finish up stringing the lights and plug them in. The tree is lit and now ready for decorating. Chase opens up a big box full of ornaments. We all reach into the box and start filling the branches of the tree with a variety of ornaments that Chase and his family have collected over the years. They are all beautiful, and to me make the tree look just right. Perfect actually.

Mary stands back and says, "It looks great, Chase. I honestly think it's the prettiest one we've had here."

"It's perfect," Katherine says.

Chase shakes his head. "No, not quite. There's something missing."

Cameron gives him a confused look. "Huh?"

Chase holds up a finger. "I'll be right back."

He leaves us all standing in the living room, wondering what it could be that he possibly needs to make the tree any better than it already is. We look at each other and shrug our shoulders.

Within a matter of minutes he returns, holding three ornaments by their hooks. My right hand quickly goes up to cover my mouth. I am awestruck. Speechless. What? How?

"Where did those come from?" Mary asks as she notices the cross-shaped ornaments in his hands.

Chase walks up to me with a sorrowful yet comforting smile on his face. My heart is racing. I can't believe this.

He replies, "These are personalized cross ornaments in memory of Jo's parents, Sam, and Grandma Annie. Grandpa Dawson gave them to me to bring here to put on the tree for Jo. She has had them ever since they all passed."

I am trying so hard to fight back the tears. Like numerous times before, I'm going to lose the battle. It's okay. It's obvious that I haven't been the best warrior fighting against much these last several months. Everything that he does, every word he says, every movement he makes takes me prisoner. The tears start to fall slowly but surely. I don't care that Cameron, Ian, Katherine, and Mary are standing there watching either. This tender act has touched my heart in a way that no one has ever touched it before. I can't begin to explain it. There's no way he could top this.

I look up into his deep, beautiful blue-gray eyes and wipe a tear from my face. "Thank you so much. You didn't have to do this," I say.

"I wanted to. When Grandpa told me about the ornaments, I couldn't leave without having them here for you. I knew that they would be on your mind; especially spending Christmas somewhere new."

I let out a sob and continue to wipe the tears that are falling. I'm so touched by this moment. I'm not embarrassed for my reaction. This just goes to show how much Chase really cares about me. Not just anyone would do something like this.

"You want to hang them up?" he asks softly.

I nod and give him a small smile. We walk over to the tree, and I gently take one at a time from his hands and hang them in what I feel is just the right place. I gaze at the ornaments and the names engraved as well as the dates of passing on them: John and Victoria Dawson, June 1, 2006; Sam Dawson, March 13, 2009; Annie Dawson, May 23, 2013.

"Now it's perfect," Chase comments.

He reaches over and pulls me in his arms. It's the perfect place to be.

Chapter Twenty-One

It's Christmas Eve. I miss my family. I cherish the memories of the times we shared on this particular day. Sam and I would help Mom bake cookies for Santa. My job was to roll out the dough, and Sam would beat it down and spread it out. Then we would take turns with the different-shaped cookie cutters and place our perfectly cut cookies neatly on the baking sheet. Dad would come in once they cooled down from the oven and help add the sprinkles and icing. He would also gather all the ingredients that we needed for the reindeer-food mixture. Sam loved going outside and sprinkling the lawn with what he just knew was the most favorite food of Santa's reindeer. Sam and I would sleep together in my bed. Before drifting off to sleep, we would talk about what we hoped Santa would bring for us. Mom and Dad would come in several times to tell us to get settled and go to sleep.

Then came the first Christmas Eve and Christmas Day that Sam and I had to spend without them. Grandpa Dawson and Grandma Annie did everything they could to help us find enjoyment in the holiday season. We tried to bake cookies. It just wasn't the same, and we knew it never would be. And then came my first Christmas Eve and Christmas Day without Sam. I didn't even attempt to bake cookies. I didn't even want to bake them with Grandma Annie. I remember sitting in the big chair by the living room window and staring outside, wondering why they all had to be gone. Wondering why my grandpa, grandma, and I had to hurt so bad. And then lastly arrived the first Christmas Eve and Christmas Day that Grandpa Dawson and I had to share without my Grandma Annie. Grandpa was so depressed that I didn't think he would ever come out of their bedroom. I did manage to encourage him to help me put up the

Christmas tree. I did bake cookies. He did eat a few. We exchanged a few gifts and spent the majority of the day sitting by the fire in the living room in silence. I read a book, and he would doze on and off in his armchair.

Now here I am having my first Christmas with Chase in Denver, and my sweet grandpa is back home having his first Christmas with Ms. Margaret. This is how it should be. I know that he is happy. I know that he still has Grandma Annie on his mind. I know that Chase is aware that I still have all of my family on my mind during this important and special time of year. But this is how it should be.

We all did go skiing at Winter Park on Monday. It was very entertaining watching Ian as he tried to learn how to ski. Chase, Mary, Ian, and I did spend the majority of the day at Discovery Park, where the beginners go to learn and practice. We hardly saw Cameron and Katherine. They were keeping Mary Jane Mountain pretty busy with their jumps and stunts. Katherine won the bet. I wasn't surprised after seeing what she could do on her skis when we first arrived. I was very impressed. I knew Cameron had his work cut out for him.

After skiing, we went to The Buckhorn Exchange to eat dinner. The environment was interesting, with its walls of mounted deer, mountain lion, elk, rams, fox, and other wildlife. It wasn't that crowded, which was nice considering that we were bodyguard-mafia-free. I guess being there with everyone made it easier for us to be left alone. I tried the buffalo prime rib, and it was mouthwatering.

Chase and I just finished a wonderful dinner that he prepared. He marinated some beef stew meat and let it cook in the Crockpot all day. He then cooked rice, mixed veggies, and yeast rolls. Our first Christmas Eve dinner together.

I'm standing by the fireplace in the living room watching the flames of the fire. Chase comes in the door from the back deck, carrying a couple of pieces of wood. He walks over and carefully places them on the fire. Once he has it just like he wants it, he stands upright and looks over at me.

"Are you all right?" he asks with what seems like a concerned tone.

I nod. "Yeah. I was just thinking about this week. You?" I ask in return.

He also nods. "I'm great."

He walks over to the sound system unit that is built into the wall. He pushes a few buttons and the sound of "A Sky Full of Stars" by Coldplay begins echoing around the living room. Quickly he turns, heads in my direction, and grabs me in his arms. He starts to move back and forth. I glance down at his feet and realize that he wants to slow dance. I blush a little as I look back up at him and join in the movement. We sway to the music without speaking for a little while.

"Did you enjoy dinner?" he asks.

I smile at him.

"Chase, I enjoy anything that you cook. It's always wonderful."

He smiles back. "Good. So it's Christmas Eve, and tomorrow for Christmas, my family will be here."

"Yeah," I say.

"I want to give you your Christmas present tonight."

"Tonight? Are you sure?" I ask.

"Yes, I'm sure."

"Ok. That's fine. Will you open mine first?"

"Sure."

Geez, I'm nervous. I hope he likes them. I worry about what he has gotten me, and if what I found for him will even compare. It's hard to measure up to someone like him when it comes to buying gifts. However, I know that to him that is not what matters. It's all about the thought being put into what is being given.

I pick up two small boxes and bring them over. I hand him the first box while I continue holding the other. He shoots me a smile, removes the bow, and starts tearing off the wrapping paper. He opens the small box. "Cool. An iWatch. You know I've been wanting one of these. I just haven't taken the time to get one. Very nice. And the color is perfect. Thanks so much."

Good. He likes it. I smile. I mean I really had no clue what to get him. He can get just about anything he wants.

"And then this one," I say as I hand him the box that's just a little bigger.

He gently takes it from my hand and opens it. He pulls out a piece of paper a little bigger than a coupon. He reads what is on it and lets out a small laugh.

"Seriously?" he says as he looks at me.

I nod with pink cheeks.

"Chase, I honestly have had the hardest time finding you the right gift. The iWatch I thought you would really enjoy and could use. I was excited when I thought of that, but then afterwards I was at a loss. So that is what I came up with. It's really hard to buy gifts for the guy who has everything or can afford anything."

The small paper has been decorated and written from me to him. It is a coupon saying that he will either allow me to cook him a meal or pay for a dinner out together. It is something I haven't done yet. It may seem like a crazy gift, but I liked that it was different. Besides, I *really* couldn't come up with anything else.

"So you want me to cash this in to let you either cook without my help or pay for dinner out?" he asks.

"Yes, that's exactly what I want you to do. It's your choice, but you have to let me do one of them."

"Okay, so if we swing by McDonald's and grab a Value Meal, I can use it so you can pay for our food?"

I cross my arms across my chest. "No, silly. I won't allow you to use it somewhere like that. It has to be a place that is very nice. I would like to pay for dinner somewhere elegant."

He chuckles. "And if you cook dinner, it can be, like, a ham sandwich and potato chips?"

I sigh with a smile on my face. "Are you kidding me? No, it has to be a big meal, and I also pay for everything I cook."

He shakes his head at me with a smile. "Jo, you are something else."

I shrug my shoulders in a playful way. "Well, I really didn't know what to get. You have everything, or so it seems."

He sets the paper down on the coffee table and reaches for my hands, taking them into his own. I notice that Coldplay is now being replaced with the charismatic, soft voice of Jason Wade from Lifehouse singing "Everything."

"I have everything now. There's nothing else in this world that I want, Jo, as long as I have you. Nothing can make me happier than to have you by my side always."

My cheeks are an even brighter pink than before.

"Now, my love, it's time for you to open my first gift to you."

He lets go of my hands and steps over to the tree. He reaches down and picks up a small box with green wrapping paper and a red bow with a ribbon. It's really small. Oh, geez, I'm nervous. I'm nervous about what's inside.

He walks up and hands the gift to me. I slowly take it from his hands and look up at him.

"I'm nervous," I say.

He nods and runs his right hand through his hair, pushing a few strands back.

"Oh, you have no idea," he agrees. I watch as he swallows a small lump. He's just as nervous as I am, if not more.

I remove the bow with the ribbon and wrapping paper. I stare at the box in my hand. It's amazing how something so small can feel so big. So important. Special. Whatever is inside, I truly believe that it is something that Chase chose just to show me how much meaning our relationship has. Something from the heart. If he is showing signs of nervousness as strong as he is, then it has to be something big. But what?

I slowly remove the box lid, and inside sits a somewhat smaller box with my name monogrammed on the top. I glance up at Chase. He smiles.

"Go ahead. Take it out and open it up," he says.

I take the smaller box out. He takes the bigger one from my hands and sets it down on the coffee table. Now my nerves are really shot. I don't know what to expect. I can't even try to name the one thing that could possibly be sitting inside this small, square item. The one that I am holding and hesitating to open because I am terrified. The anticipation of not knowing is comforting and nerve-racking at the same time. *Open it, Jo! Just open the box! He's waiting, for crying out loud!*

I take a deep breath and pull the top back. My eyes widen as I gaze upon what's in the box. My mouth falls open as I turn my attention to Chase. He is focused hard on the expression on my face. I truly never knew what being lost for words was all about until now. I don't even know how or where to start. Do I comment or ask questions? I look back down at the item in the box that holds so much sentimental value to my heart, and then I turn my attention back to Chase. He waits.

"May I?" he asks as he points to the contents.

I nod and suddenly feel emotional. I want to cry. I want to cry in a way that shows my heart is happy. My heart is feeling things that I never knew possible. Chase reaches in and gently takes Grandma Annie's wedding ring out. I am still finding it hard to speak. He takes my left hand in his. My heart is beating so hard it feels like it could break right through my rib cage.

"Jo, you make my heart feel things it never has before. I was swept away the very first night I met you at the cafe. I knew you were different. When I left I couldn't get you off my mind. I thought about you constantly, and that's when I knew that I had to see you again. I wanted you to know that you had done something to me that I couldn't explain. That's why I sent you the flowers and came to ask you out to dinner. I also found it coincidental that I ended up at your grandfather's rental house."

He continues, "I remember that on my first night here after leaving the cafe I stopped to meet and talk to Grandpa Dawson. I was carrying on and on about you and how I was so amazed by your presence and strength through everything you had told me you had been through. When he told me that you were his granddaughter, I was floored. I couldn't believe it. That's when I really knew that my life was about to change, and that I would do anything to make yours as wonderful as possible."

My tears have been released. They are slowly falling down my face and caressing my chin.

"Grandpa Dawson and I have had many talks. We have shared many nights sitting outside on the porch discussing things and sharing stories. He would tell me a lot about the relationship that he and your Grandma Annie had together. It was the type of relationship that any man and woman could hope and dream to experience. One of true love. One of true companionship. I want that with you."

I smile at him through the tears that continue to fall.

"Grandpa Dawson gave me your Grandma Annie's wedding ring because I have confessed to him how I feel about you in the five months that I have known you. I told him that you are like no other girl I have ever met. You are someone that I could never hurt and could never be without. So I'm giving you her ring as a promise that I will always be here. I will be here for anything you ever need. I will be your strength. I want to be your everything. I love you, Joanna. I want you to hear it. I want you to believe it. I am madly and deeply in love with you. I'll always love you."

He slides the beautiful antique wedding ring on my finger. It's a promise ring. All of his promises are wrapped around my heart. He has told me how he feels about me. He loves me. He truly loves me. He wants to be with me. I will have faith in his strength. He can be my everything just as I want to be his.

"I love you so much, Chase," I say with a confidence that I have never known. It is true. I love him. I love him.

We smile at each other. He takes my face in his hands and gives me a gentle kiss. He pulls away and looks into my eyes. We don't have to speak. Words are not needed. He pulls me up into a threshold and walks toward the master suite. As we go through the door, I notice there is a fire roaring in the fireplace. The bed has been turned down. The only light in the room is coming from the dancing flames.

He carries me over to the bed and helps me stand by making sure that my feet land firmly on the floor. We embrace each other and engage in a deep, passionate kiss. He grabs the bottom of my shirt and pulls it over my head. I then help him remove his own. The desire for each other is so strong and intense that we waste no time. He reaches down to the button of his jeans and quickly has them on the floor and me on the bed. While kissing erotically, he unbuttons my jeans and then stops to slide them down until they reach the floor. I am lying flat on my back with my right leg propped up, bending at the knee. He lies on his right side keeping himself up with his right elbow. He takes his left hand and slowly runs it from my right knee down to my thigh. He plays gently with the side of my panties at my hip and then runs his fingers along my waistline. A shiver starts in my head and runs all the way down to the tips of my toes. His hand spreads as he tenderly rubs my stomach.

He looks down at me with the same sexy gaze that never fails to numb every part of my body. "I'm so glad that you're here with me," he says in a whisper.

I reach up and caress his left cheek. It's so soft under my fingers. "I don't want to be anywhere else but with you," I say to him.

I reach and pull him down to me and my lips cover his. Our tongues explore as well as our hands. I run them down his naked back as he pulls me into him. I want to get closer. His hands move up. I want him to touch *them.* Caress them. They are stimulated just from him being on top of me and lying in between my legs. But he refrains. His lips move from my lips, down my chin, to my neck. I lean back and enjoy the feeling of them pressed against my skin. I can feel his tongue. Oh, the places I want it to be! My neck is only one of them! I moan softly at the touch of his mouth. His hands.

He moves back up and inserts his tongue into my mouth. I take my left hand and run it up his neck into his hair as my right hand pulls gently on the waist band of his boxer briefs. He reaches back and grabs my right hand, pulling it up close to us, our hands intertwined, and the presence of our bracelets in the dimness of the light that radiates from the fireplace. His breathing is increasing.

He says through kisses, "I want you so bad, Jo."

Oh, I want you too! This is right where I want to be. Underneath him, experiencing every touch, kiss, and breath.

He sits up and pulls me into his lap. I wrap my legs around his waist. I caress his bare back, loving the sensation of his skin under my hands. He moves his lips down to my neck again as he pulls me even closer. I lean my head back and feel the strands of my long, brown hair brush against my shoulders and back. He slowly starts to kiss further down near the top of my bra right above my boobs. I take my hands from his back up to stroke his head. His dark, messy strands fall smooth through my fingers.

He moves back up to my neck. Our breathing escalates.

"Chase, please," I whisper.

"Please what?" he whispers back through each kiss.

"Please take me. Make love to me."

He stops and looks into my eyes for what seems like an eternity. We know that we're ready.

He gently unsnaps the clasp of my bra, removes it from my body, and throws it on the floor. A few strands of my long, brown hair cover my nipples. He pulls me in to him and kisses me as my boobs brush against his chest. We moan and breathe heavily through each other. We lie back with him on top of me. I feel like I can't get close enough to him. I run my right hand down his side to the waistband of his boxer briefs. I begin pulling on them, expressing my desire to remove them. The next thing I know he is sitting up to slide them off. My heart is pounding. Within a matter of seconds he is naked and exposed.

He lies back down in between my legs and presses against me. Our tongues tangle. I moan through our passionate kisses. My body yearns to be one with him. I want him to fill that sacred place. I want it to be his.

"Please. I need you so bad," I whisper to him as he kisses my face.

"Oh, baby, I need you too. More than you could ever know."

Slowly and gently we become one. I want to feel this way forever. I never want to stop. I want us to make love to each other every second, every minute, every hour of every day. Our lips and tongues are going mad over the uniting of our bodies.

There in his suite, in his bed, we make sweet, passionate love. We make love to each other at the right place at the right time.

Chapter Twenty-Two

It's Christmas morning, and the greatest gift I have ever received has me wrapped in his arms. The warmth of his body and the sound of his breathing are indescribable. I look over at my finger that wears the promise ring. Despite everything we have done together, I never imagined Chase doing something like that. At least not now. I never imagined him pouring his heart out to my grandpa about how he feels about me. And what's more, I never imagined that my grandpa would hand over an item that he held so dear to his heart. The ring that belonged to my dear Grandma Annie. The ring that symbolized their love and all their years of marriage.

I smile as I think about what it means to me. Yes, it belonged to someone near and dear to my heart in so many ways, but now it has even more sentimental value. It was given to me by the one person that is changing my life in so many ways. Someone who has helped me open up and trust. Someone who is slowly but surely taking away all the pain that I have been enduring. The wounds are healing.

Chase starts to move beside me. He pulls me closer to him tightening his grip. I can feel his nose buried in my hair. "I feel like I'm in heaven. It is so amazing to wake up next to you and take in your sweet smell."

I close my eyes as I listen to his tender words fall upon my ears. *Yes, Chase. It is so amazing.* "I just want to stay here in your arms. I want to spend Christmas in bed with you," I say.

"That sounds wonderful."

I turn around to see his gorgeous face. He holds himself up and looks down at me.

"Merry Christmas, love."

I smile at him. "Merry Christmas to you."

He takes his left hand and pushes a few strands of hair back from my forehead and smiles. "You are so beautiful. Every part of you, everything about you is so beautiful and perfect. You are everything I've ever wanted and everything I need."

I shake my head in disagreement. "No, you are. I should be saying those things to you."

"Now why would you say something like that?" he asks.

"Because you are the only one that could reach me."

He gives me a deep, serious look.

I continue, "I have been broken for quite some time, and you are putting all the pieces back together."

He gently strokes my right cheek. "It makes me happy to know that I'm the one that can do that."

"The only one," I add.

We smile at each other and embrace in a deep kiss. He slowly pulls away and looks down at me.

"We have a busy day ahead of us. Mom and Dad should be here right after lunch, and then Mary, Ian, Cameron, and Katherine. I'm sure we will exchange gifts before we eat dinner tonight. Are you in the cooking spirit?"

I widen my smile and nod. "Of course. I'd like to call and wish Grandpa a Merry Christmas this morning."

"Sounds great. Shower first?"

"Definitely," I reply.

"Together?"

Oh, why the hell not? I am ready for anything. Anything with him. He has opened the door to the desire to be with him in all the ways that two people in love could be.

I throw my arms around his neck, pulling him in close to me. "Yes, please," I say as his lips touch mine. Hopefully we will make it there.

"Merry Christmas, Grandpa!" I shout into the phone as soon as Grandpa Dawson answers hello.

"Merry Christmas, Jo! I'm so glad you called me," he says. I can hear the excitement in his voice.

"Now, Grandpa, you know it wouldn't be Christmas if I don't get to hear your voice."

"Oh, well, it sure is great to hear yours. How's it going, sweetheart? Are you enjoying your time with Chase in Denver?" he asks.

I smile and nod, as if he can see me. "Oh, it is wonderful. It's absolutely beautiful here. We went skiing and picked out the perfect ten-foot Christmas tree. Chase surprised me with the ornaments."

"I'm so glad. I knew that, since we weren't going to be together for Christmas, that it really wouldn't be the same for you if you didn't have those keepsakes to hang on the tree."

"I really appreciate you thinking of me. I wish that you would have at least kept Grandma Annie's to hang for yourself. I must admit that I thought about the ornaments when I saw that you had already put your tree up when we came to visit before we left for Denver. I noticed that they weren't on the tree and was curious. I decided not to mention it to you. I didn't think about you giving them to Chase to bring here, though."

"I'm glad you're not upset with me. I just thought that you might like to have them there with you."

"Oh, I could never be upset with you over something like that. It was a sweet and emotional surprise. Thank you."

"You are very welcome, dear. So what do you and Chase have planned for today?"

"His parents are going to be here this afternoon. We are going to cook a big meal for them as part of their Christmas," I reply.

"That sounds nice. I know I could sure go for a big slice of Chase's cream-cheese pound cake right about now."

We both let out a small laugh.

"Well, he will have to bake you one when we get back to Folly. I know he'd be happy to."

"I look forward to that. So, anything special besides the ornaments you would like to tell me about?"

He's talking about the ring. Grandma's ring. He wants to know about it and how I feel. How I reacted, maybe.

"Well, last night Chase gave me Grandma's wedding ring as a promise ring."

"Yes, indeed he did. And how do you feel about that?" he asks.

"Amazing. Shocked," I answer.

"Shocked? Shocked in what way?"

222

"Well, I honestly didn't think you would ever give someone something that had so much meaning to you. I mean it's Grandma's wedding ring. You gave it to her to signify your love. Your devotion to her."

I make sure that the tone I take with my grandpa is sensitive and compassionate. I don't want him to feel that I am angry or upset in any way over the fact that he gave such a precious, antique valuable to a guy that I have known for only five months. Even if we are talking about *the* Chase Hartford.

"Who has the ring now?" Grandpa asks.

"Me."

"Exactly. I gave it to a very special young man to give to my one and only granddaughter. The one person I have left on this earth that means more to me than I could ever explain. Your Grandma Annie wanted you to have her ring. It was in her will. She wanted it to be passed on to you and then to your daughter if that's what God has planned for you."

"Oh, Grandpa," I say as I try to fight back the tears that are forming.

"I promise you I knew what I was doing when I gave it to Chase. I was in the right state of mind. We all need to enjoy that while I still have it."

He lets out a small chuckle.

He continues, "I think a lot of Chase. He's a wonderful young man, and I hope that this relationship that the two of you share will continue to grow, and you will have a bright and promising future together."

"This all means so much to me. I can't thank you enough for everything."

"I just want you to be happy, Joanna. After all the heartache you have endured over the years, you deserve so much. You are an incredible young woman. I'm so blessed to call you my granddaughter."

"And I'm so blessed to call you my grandpa."

Chase's parents have arrived. I haven't seen them since before Halloween. I am nervous again. So much has happened between Chase and me since then that I am not sure how to act. I know that I need to be myself, but now with the promise ring that I wear on my ring finger, I wonder what will be said if and once they notice. I look down at it and take a deep breath. Chase walks over to the door to welcome them inside.

"Mom, Dad," he says as they walk in.

"Hey, bud," Mr. Hartford says as he reaches to give his son a hug.

"Hey, sweetheart," Mrs. Hartford adds as she also receives a hug.

"I feel like it's been forever since I've seen y'all. Merry Christmas."

"Merry Christmas," they both say in unison.

Mrs. Hartford turns her attention to me.

"Oh, Jo, darling. It is so wonderful to see you again." She walks over and embraces me.

I smile as I embrace her in return. "It is wonderful to see you as well, Mrs. Hartford."

"Jo. Great to see you," Mr. Hartford says as we also exchange a hug.

"Thanks, Mr. Hartford. So glad that y'all are here with us."

"When will Mary and Cameron be here?" Mrs. Hartford asks as she removes her coat.

"I suppose anytime. They had planned to be here around the same time as the two of you."

Chase takes his mother's coat and places it on the coatrack.

Mr. Hartford asks, "Okay, I have to know what you think about Ian."

Chase nods his head. "He's pretty cool. I like him. Skiing isn't his thing, though. He definitely needs to stick to surfing."

They let out a small laugh. I smile.

"Well, Mary sure is crazy about him, I know that," Mrs. Hartford says.

"Yeah, I can tell. Let's go sit down in the living room. I've got a good fire going."

"Mr. and Mrs. Hartford, would y'all like a cup of coffee? I was just going to make a fresh pot," I ask as I point toward the kitchen.

They both nod and answer with a "Yes, thank you."

"I'll come help you in just a minute. Mom and Dad take their coffee the same way we take ours." He smiles and gives me a wink.

I nod and smile back. "Okay, great."

I turn and head for the kitchen to start brewing the coffee.

We are all sitting around in the living room, enjoying a nice, hot cup of coffee. Thankfully the large wraparound couch provides enough seating for all of us. Mary, Ian, Cameron, Katherine, Chase, and I are seated from one end to the other, while Mr. and Mrs. Hartford are seated comfortably on the love seat.

"All right so I'm going to be the one to say something. You know you guys can always count on me for that. You have to tell us about the ring, Jo. I'm dying over here," Mary says as she carefully sets her cup down on the coffee table.

I glance around the living room at all the eyes that are resting upon me. Oh, goodness. I have been thinking about the ring and how I would explain it, but I wasn't quite sure when the topic would arise. *Well, Jo, here it is. The moment. Fill them in. They are all ears, I assure you.*

I look over at Chase. He smiles and gives a quick nod of approval, and seems to me to be somewhat encouraging.

"Well, um ... it's a promise ring that Chase gave me last night. It belonged to my grandmother. It was her wedding ring."

"So, y'all aren't engaged?" Mary asks.

I glance at Chase and shake my head. "No, not at all."

Mary sighs, "Seriously? I was really hoping you were going to tell me that Chase proposed to you."

I'm touched that she is so accepting of the idea. I smile at the thought at how it could happen one day. One day in the far, far future.

Chase jumps in to say, "Mary, I gave her that as a promise to be here for her always. I wouldn't want us to jump into something like an engagement too quickly."

Katherine decides to add something to the conversation, "True. How long have y'all been dating now?"

Chase replies, "Well, we met at the end of July when I arrived at Folly to start filming. I can honestly say that I was overwhelmed with emotions I have never felt before the very first night I met Jo at the cafe."

He looks over at me and smiles.

"So that's been five months ago. Heck, in the world of Hollywood that's plenty of time to fall madly in love and announce an engagement," Mary remarks.

Chase shakes his head. "Oh, come on, Mary, I thought you knew me better than that. Being engaged is not something I take lightly. That's a serious step. Jo and I are working on a future together. We just want to do it the right way. She knows that I love her, and I know she loves me."

Mary swats her hand at him as she leans over to grab her coffee cup from the table.

"Oh, whatever. I do know you, little brother. I know that I have never seen you act like this over someone. Ever. Just cut to the chase, Chase," Mary says as she gives him a wink.

"Son, I just want to say that your mother and I are very proud of you. Despite all of your success, you have really grown into a fine young man. We appreciate the outlook you take on things and how you want to make sure that you are making good choices. And, Jo, we couldn't be happier that Chase found a sweet, intelligent, small-town girl like you. I pray that the love you two share will continue to blossom and that there will be many wonderful things ahead for you both in the future. Even though we already consider you a part of the family, we look forward to the day that we can make it official. Of course, if that's what's in God's plans for the two of you," Mr. Hartford says.

I smile over at Mr. and Mrs. Hartford. His words have so much meaning to me.

"Yes. I couldn't agree more. This is such a blessing, and I pray daily that your relationship will grow and be strong enough to handle any battle that comes its way. I have faith in the both of you. We think the world of you, Joanna," Mrs. Hartford adds.

If I have ever had any doubt about how Chase's parents feel about me, then that has been washed away. I know their feelings and how they hope that Chase and I can stay together through all the bad obstacles that may and will eventually present themselves to us.

"Well, I know one thing. That promise ring is really going to have the magazines talking. Stacey Phillips is going to be all over that," Mary adds.

Chase shrugs his shoulders. "She can knock herself out."

Cameron says, "I can see the magazine cover now. Oh, and wait until Claudia finds out! Ha. I wish I could be a fly on the wall when she sees it for the first time."

"Who cares what Claudia thinks or how she reacts. She is old news. Our relationship was not meant to be. I knew that from the start. I'd like to give myself a good kick in the ass for allowing it to go on as long as it did," Chase says.

He reaches over and grabs my left hand, taking it into his. "I know a good thing when I see it. Most importantly, I know a good thing when I feel it in my heart."

We smile at each other. I can't describe how it makes me feel when Chase expresses his feelings for me in front of others. My heart swells. It beats faster. It's embarrassing yet wonderful. I was raised to believe that if a guy can pour his feelings and heart out about you in front of an audience, then you mean something more than you ever thought. I don't ever want the feeling of knowing that I am something so very special to Chase to ever go away.

We devoured and enjoyed the huge meal that Chase and I prepared for Christmas dinner. Prime rib, baked turkey, fried chicken, mashed potatoes with garlic and butter, rice and gravy, peas, corn on the cob, hash-brown casserole, green beans, and homemade biscuits. It was fun cooking such a large meal together, and I learned some interesting tips on frying chicken and cooking your own prime rib. It had to be one of the most delicious home-cooked meals that I have had in a long time. For dessert, Chase and I baked extra-large chocolate-chunk brownies and served vanilla ice cream on top.

The large dinner table was filled with conversation and laughter. We heard stories about Mary's, Chase's, and Cameron's childhoods. Mr. and Mrs. Hartford talked about how they met and fell in love. It was entertaining and wonderful to be a part of something so special with such an important person in my life and his family. I don't see how I can allow anything or anyone to ruin this happiness.

Chapter Twenty-Three

My time here with Chase in Denver has been a dream come true. I wish that the last few nights would slow down, but the reality of going back to Charleston and getting ready for my last semester at the College of Charleston is getting closer and closer. A part of me dreads finishing, while another part of me is so excited that I will finally move on to MUSC. This just means I'm getting closer to experiencing my purpose. My purpose for Sam. My purpose for all the other sweet and innocent children who have cancer. My purpose in life.

It's 11:30 on New Year's Eve, and Chase and I are standing with Boss, Lincoln, and Mac on Sixteenth Street in downtown Denver, waiting for the spectacular midnight firework show. Chase thought it would be neat for me to experience the yearly event that brings locals and tourists by the hundreds. While we wait, there are magicians, mascots, balloon artists, stilt walkers, and comedians interacting with people in the crowd. It is very entertaining to watch. I know that Chase would like as few people as possible to notice him.

"You are going to absolutely love the show. The fireworks are amazing. They get better every year," Chase says.

"It's exciting. I've never seen fireworks on New Year's Eve before. Only over the beach at Folly for the Fourth of July celebration. We would go every year."

Chase nods. "That sounds like something we need to plan for next summer."

We smile at each other.

"I thought that after the show we could go back to the house and have a glass of wine. Does that sound good to you?" he asks.

I nod. "Definitely. I look forward to being inside and warm by a fire."

"Me too," he says with an even bigger smile.

The Denver cold is no joke. I've never experienced anything like it. It's a whole different world, but such a beautiful one.

Chase and I glance over the crowd at all the activity that is happening around us. The guys are standing close. We know they are there if needed.

Chase says, "Don't look now, but we have company."

I look at Chase with a confused look on my face. I'm not sure what he means. Company? "Company? Who?" I ask with a little concern in my voice.

"The one and only Stacey Phillips," he replies.

I knew it. Why did I even ask? "Are you serious? Where?"

Without looking or pointing, he answers, "Over to your right, standing by the planter and the bench."

I try to act cool as if I am observing what is happening around me. I slowly turn my head in her direction. He is right. There she stands in all her star-reporting glory. Her huge camera hangs perfectly around her scrawny neck. She looks like a tourist. She pulls off the look nicely. I can't wait to read the next issue of *Star Gaze*. I'm eager to see what all she will write and what pictures will make the front page this time. She happens to turn her attention toward me. I quickly look in the opposite direction.

Chase looks down at his iWatch. "It's just about that time. The fireworks should be starting any minute."

He pulls me close. I rest my head on him. My forehead touches his neck. I'm ready now more than ever to get back to his house and be alone.

Suddenly there is a male voice that bellows from an intercom system. "Happy New Year's Eve, everyone! We are honored that you all joined us tonight for such a wonderful occasion. We hope that your experience with us will have you coming back for years to come. It is almost time for our fantastic New Year's fireworks celebration. We will start the countdown in the next few minutes."

We continue standing there, observing those around us. I can still see Stacey out of my peripheral vision. She hasn't moved an inch. She is obviously waiting for something big to happen. A fan riot? A big New Year's kiss? Oh, that has to be it. The big kiss to bring in the new year.

Her camera will be aimed and ready. No doubt. She won't miss it. After all, she is a professional. Always on her A-game.

The male voice echoes again over the intercom system. "All right, everyone. It is time for the countdown."

I lift my head and look over at Chase. He continues to hold me close. The mass of people around us start to count simultaneously down from thirty.

Chase and I smile at each other and join in.

"*Ten! Nine! Eight! Seven! Six! Five! Four! Three! Two! One! Happy New Year!*"

Beautiful fireworks of every color imaginable light up the cold, Denver night sky as Chase pulls me in for a kiss. A long, sweet kiss. For a moment, it feels as if we are the only ones there.

He slowly pulls away, yet stays close and says, "Happy New Year, love."

I smile at him.

"Happy New Year to you."

The fireworks were just as Chase said they would be … amazing. And now, being in the warmth and privacy of his house is even more amazing. The hot shower I just finished helped thaw me out. Chase and I are snuggled on the couch by the fire with a nice glass of wine.

"I have really enjoyed every minute of being here with you," Chase says as he wraps his arm around my neck and rubs my arm.

"I wish it didn't have to end."

"I know. I feel the same way. But we have many more times like this ahead of us."

I smile at the thought.

"There are so many places I want to take you and things I want us to see and experience together. This is just the beginning."

It sounds wonderful. Every bit of it. Wherever he wants to go. Whatever he wants to do, I will be right there with him.

"The next thing on my to-do list is to start planning something special for Valentine's Day."

"Chase, why don't you let me plan something? You have done so much for me and have done so many amazing things. I would really like it if you would let me do something for us for a change."

He smiles at me with a look that pretty much says he's not sure he can allow that to happen. "Nah, not for Valentine's Day."

"Oh, come on, please?" I beg.

"But that's the most romantic day of the year. You have to let me keep that date. How about you plan something special just for me on my birthday?"

I poke my bottom lip out just a little with a pouty look.

"Ah, please don't make that face. I really don't want you to do that. It may convince me to change my mind. I already had some great ideas, and I really want to do it. We can trade up, and you take over the next Valentine's Day."

I love the fact that he is thinking about Valentine's after next. I can tell that it would really mean a lot to him to be able to go forth with whatever ideas he has in mind. I can't argue. I must surrender. "Okay. You go ahead. But next Valentine's, don't forget who makes the date," I say as I point a finger at him.

He nods in agreement. "You got it. It's all yours."

I give him a victory smile. "Yay, thanks."

He sets his wine glass down on the coffee table next to us and then grabs mine from my hand, placing it next to his. He leans in close to me. "But right now I'm the one that planned this getaway, and I still have many great things in mind for us to do together."

He gives me a mischievous grin and starts to kiss me. I pull him close. I slowly lie back on the couch with him on top of me. Our kisses are long. They are passionate. I grab hold of the bottom of his white T-shirt and pull it over his head. I toss it on the floor. The feeling of his skin underneath my hands and fingers is wonderful. I caress his back as he moves his lips down to my neck. I lean my head back and close my eyes as I savor every kiss. He trails the kisses down to the V-neck opening of my T-shirt. Quickly he sits back and helps me sit up to where he can remove it. I lie back down, and he takes no time to untie the string on my jogging pants. I lift up as he pulls them from my waist. He stands next to the couch, and, staring down at me with a serious and sexy look, a few of his bangs caressing his brow, he unties his own jogging pants and pushes them down to the floor. Armani again. Why, yes, indeed. Gray. Dark gray. He reaches his right hand out for me to grab. I'm not sure what he wants to do. Does he prefer the bedroom?

I take it, and he gently pulls me up. He then sits back down on the couch and pulls me on top of him. My knees touch his sides as I straddle him. My matching Victoria Secret tan sports bra and panty set look amazing on my tan body. I feel so confident around him. So much more confident than I ever thought I would. More confident than Christmas Eve night when we made love for the first time.

His bare, tan chest is there for me to touch, and his muscular arms there to hold me close. I run my right hand over his smooth chest as the fire gives off just enough light in the living room.

"Let me look at you. Let me sit here and take in how beautiful you are," he says to me.

He lifts his left hand up and gently touches my right cheek. I close my eyes at his touch. It always feels so wonderful. I know, with each touch, that I will never get enough. He pushes a strand of my hair behind my ear. I open my eyes to look at him.

"I love you, Joanna."

I don't know why, but hearing my full first name escape his lips does something to me that I can't explain. "I love you too, Chase."

I lean forward and press my lips softly against his. The kiss we share is gentle. I pull away just far enough to look into his eyes. I love the blue-gray. Our eyes speak a thousand words to each other. We begin to kiss again, but this time with more intensity. We wrap our arms around each other. Our hands caress and explore. Our breathing starts to escalate, as well as the beating of our hearts. It is moments like this that I want to experience with him forever. I want him, and I want him to take me. To make me his. For he is the only one that can ever reach me.

I walk into my and Aimee's apartment. I wonder if she's here. Her car is parked outside. I set down my suitcase and glance around. It's too quiet.

"Aimee?" I yell.

I wait, but there is no response. Maybe she isn't here.

"Aimee?" I yell once more.

Within a matter of seconds, I hear a door swing open down the hall. Aimee makes her appearance. She obviously just got out of the shower. Her hair is wrapped in a towel, and she is wearing her bathrobe.

"You're back!" she screams at me in excitement.

She steps into a light run, and once she reaches me, she gives me a big hug.

"I missed you so much!" she says.

I let out a small giggle. "I missed you too."

She steps back and looks me up and down. "You look different."

I glance down at myself and then back up at her. *What? How?* "Well, I certainly hope you mean in a good way," I say.

She nods.

"Oh, definitely. It's a good different. I can look at you and tell that something has happened. Something wonderful. I see it in your looks and in your movement. I mostly see it in your eyes."

I cock my head to the side and place my hands on my hips. "Oh, really?"

"Yes," she replies. "I know what it is. You've had sex!"

I smile at her and try so hard not to blush at the words that have just escaped her mouth, but it is a tough battle to fight. Of course I lose.

"Well, I wouldn't say I had sex, but I will say I made love."

"What? Really? It really did happen?" she screams.

I nod and laugh at her. "Yes, it did."

She starts to jump up and down. It reminds me of how she acted when Chase and I first met and shared our first kiss. "Oh my God, this is the best news ever! Okay, so spill it. How was it?"

I give her a contemplating look. "Which time?" I ask.

Her eyes widen like golf balls, and her mouth falls open. "Oh my God, Jo how many times did y'all do it? I mean, dang, it sounds like you really laid it on the guy."

I decide to play around with her. I am thoroughly enjoying this right now. "I'm really not sure. I kind of lost count."

"What? Okay this is scary. You're starting to sound like me."

I shake my head. "Oh, no, Aimee. I don't think so. I'm just joking, but I really am not going to tell you how many times we were together. All that matters is that we were, and it was beyond amazing. Beyond anything that words can describe."

She folds her arms across her chest. "Oh, I bet it was. Okay, so onto the more detailed questions."

I shake my finger at her. "Oh, no, no. There are things for only me to know and you to never find out." There is absolutely no way I am going to tell her anything about positions and size and all that stuff her sex-crazed imagination would like to know.

She rolls her eyes and sighs. "Really? You're going to do your best friend that way?"

I throw my hands up and wave them while shaking my head. "Nope. Not going there."

She studies my hands for a moment. She stares real hard, and then I realize what she is looking at. She has noticed my promise ring.

"Oh my God, Jo, you're engaged?" she yells.

I look down at my promise ring and reply, "Oh no. It's not an engagement ring. It's a promise ring. Chase surprised me with it on Christmas Eve."

She steps closer to me and takes my finger in her hands to examine the ring up close. "A promise ring? What the hell? It's on your ring finger on your left hand, for crying out loud! Don't you realize that everyone is going to think you are engaged?"

"They can think what they want. I'm telling you it's a promise ring, and that is the finger he put it on."

"It looks old. Like it's an antique or something. Where did he get it?" she asks.

"It was Grandma Annie's. Grandpa Dawson gave it to him to give to me."

She looks up at me with a small look of shock. "Are you serious?"

I nod and respond, "True story."

"You know this is going to drive this town and the world of Hollywood crazy right?"

"Yes, I'm very aware of that. They can go as crazy as they want, think what they want, and say what they want. I don't care," I say with a confidence that I am very proud of. I really don't care. I'm learning. It's taking me some time, but I'm learning that I can't let them hurt me and all that matters is what Chase and I know. What we share."

"So where is Chase?"

I grab the handle of my suitcase to head for my bedroom so I can unpack. "He had a meeting with James. He called him before we left and said that, as soon as we got back, he needed to meet with him and the cast members."

"You ready for our last semester?" she asks with a smile on her face.

I nod and think about how, in May, we will be college graduates, and then how I will have only four-to-six years left of school before I will hopefully be at St. Jude, working with precious terminally ill children.

"Yeah, I'm ready. I can't believe it's so close."

"Yeah, I know. I'm going to be student-teaching at Harbor View Elementary School. I'll be working with Mrs. White. I am supposed to go and meet with her this week. I hope she's nice."

"She'll be wonderful, and you'll do great. No worries."

"What about you? What's going on with you this semester? I feel like we hardly have much time to talk to each other."

She's right. We have both been so occupied with finals, the guys, and the holidays that we haven't had the time to sit around and talk like we used to. I know this has been a big adjustment for Aimee. I was always here, and she was always coming and going.

"I know that I will have some research to do before graduation, but I am also supposed to meet with my advisor about volunteering some at the children's hospital at MUSC."

"Oh, cool. So what will you be doing while you're there?"

"I would like to help organize the play activities with them. And I would also like to work with the nurses and doctors about some of the illnesses and treatments they have there. Maybe focus on a few particular patients."

"But I thought you wanted to work with children who have cancer?"

"I do, and I am, but just having the experience of working with children who suffer from a variety of illnesses or diseases will be beneficial for me."

"True. So tomorrow is Sunday. Are you off?" she asks.

"Yeah. Tomorrow is my last day to relax, and then it is back in the swing of things. I'll be glad to get back into my routine, though. I miss Ramona, and I'm so ready to get this semester over with."

"Okay, well I'm going to go and finish getting ready. Kevin and I are going to a party. If you and Chase get together tonight and want to come, just holler."

"Great. Thanks."

She turns and heads back down the hall as I walk in the same direction to my bedroom to unpack.

Chapter Twenty-Four

As I am unpacking the ridiculous amount of clothes and items that I took with me to Denver, my Galaxy rings. I glance down at it lying next to my suitcase on the bed. I smile and quickly grab it.

"Hi, Grandpa."

"Well, has my girl made it safely back to the East Coast?" he asks.

My smile widens. "Yes sir. I am home and unpacking right now as we speak."

"That's great. I'm glad you and Chase are back."

"I am too, in a way. I missed everyone, but Denver sure was nice. I wouldn't complain at all if he wanted to go back right now."

Grandpa lets out a small chuckle. "Oh, I'm sure it wouldn't take you no time to throw everything right back in your suitcase."

I giggle back. "How are you doing?" I ask.

"I'm great. I know you have a lot coming up soon with your final semester and work and all, but I just wanted you to know that I'd love to see you. I sure have missed you the last couple of weeks."

"Actually I was going to call you as soon as I finished unpacking to see if you would be home tomorrow evening, so I could ride over and visit with you for a little while."

"Darling, you can come any time you want to. Margaret and I are going to the senior center tonight, but there isn't anything going on tomorrow except church. Are you going to be working?"

"No sir, I'm not scheduled to. It's my last day off for a while. I'm going to spend it around here doing laundry and running some errands. I have several things to do this week, and class starts the next week, so I figured I'd better get busy."

"Yep. I can't believe it's almost that time. Soon you will be a college graduate."

"Yes sir."

"Well, you just come on over tomorrow evening when you're ready. I'll be here. Margaret may be here, but I know she would love to see you too."

"I'd love to see her. I'll call you before I head that way."

"That sounds good. All right, dear, I'll let you get back to unpacking. I know you are tired from all the traveling. Get some rest, and I will see you tomorrow sometime."

"All right, Grandpa. Have fun tonight. See you tomorrow. I love you."

"Thanks. I love you too, sweetheart. Bye."

"Bye."

I hang up the phone and continue unpacking.

I'm sitting on the couch in the living room with the TV remote in my hand. I have been flipping for the last ten minutes. So far, nothing on the guide has satisfied me enough to hit the select button on the remote. *Oh, wait. It's time for the 6:00 news.* I quickly turn it to Channel 3.

The Samantha Stone is sitting pretty behind her big news desk. Her long blonde hair flows, and big blue eyes shine bright. Her pantsuit top is gray, pinstriped, and cuts low enough that her black camisole makes itself known in the center of her chest. Too bad the male viewers only get a small glimpse of some cleavage.

"People are going crazy over the new issue of the famous gossip magazine *Star Gaze* after it hit stands this morning. The front cover consists of another inviting look inside the relationship of young movie star Chase Hartford and his girlfriend, Joanna Dawson. It has been reported that they enjoyed a Christmas vacation in Denver, and that Miss Dawson is wearing a beautiful antique ring on a particular finger. A lot of buzz is circulating about whether or not Chase popped the question over the holidays. Sorry, ladies, if this is true, then he is definitely off the market. I guess this goes to show what effect a small-town Southern girl can have on someone as famous as Chase Hartford. Currently, he is still filming in Folly and Charleston and will be here for several more months. We will keep you updated on this story and more."

Dang, that was fast! They waste no time getting the news out about us, do they? I sit and wonder if Chase has even heard about the new issue yet. He is always on top of things, and knows about them before I do. It is in his nature to be cool and calm, and he wants me to be the same. He understands that it is harder for me, but I am really doing better. I am feeling a little overwhelmed about the situation now that it has been publicized. I guess only because I'm afraid of what or who I could encounter on campus when class starts back. I already had to have help fighting off a mob of girls when they found out for sure that I was the girl in the magazine. Now I have a ring on my finger, and no one yet knows the truth, except for a select few. And even if the public did find out that it is just a promise ring, will they even believe it?

A text message beeps through. I keep my eyes on the news as I reach beside me on the couch and pick up my phone. It's Amanda. She's sick with a stomach virus. She's asking me if I could cover for her tomorrow at work. I sigh. I really want my last day off. I really feel like, even though I have been off for the last two-and-a-half weeks, I need just one more day to be home and get things done. She would do it for me though. She would help me out if I really needed it. I guess I'll just start my laundry tonight and do what I can around here so I can work tomorrow. I send her a message back telling her that I will be happy to cover her tomorrow at the cafe, that I hope she feels better, and to let me know if she needs anything at all. I go ahead and make myself get up to start my first load of clothes.

I'm sorting through my lights, darks, and whites when my phone rings again. Man, my line is hot tonight. What on earth? I look down and see his name. It takes no time at all for me to have the phone next to my ear.

"Hey," I say with an excitement like I haven't seen him in days.

"Hey, love. What are you up to?" he asks. I notice that he doesn't sound as peppy as he usually does. He almost sounds like something is bothering him.

"I'm sorting through my laundry. I have to start washing clothes tonight."

"I thought you were going to do that tomorrow?"

"Well, I was, but Amanda texted me and said that she is sick with the stomach virus. She asked if I would cover her tables tomorrow at the cafe, and I told her I would."

"Ah, that sucks. I'm sorry she's sick. I know you really wanted to have one more day."

"It's okay. I still have time to get things done. It's just me and how I am about things, but it will be fine. What's going on with you? Are you all right?" I ask with compassionate concern.

"I'm … okay. I just left my meeting with James, and I'm headed home to get some things done around the house. Something has come up that I really want and need to talk to you about. Some changes were made to the show over the holidays, and I'm not thrilled about it at all. I'm pretty pissed actually, but I know that I have to be positive and remember my strength. I have to keep my strength up for you."

I'm scared. What is wrong? What could possibly have changed while he was gone? Why would they even make changes without talking to him first? He's the main character of the show, for heaven's sake. This is crazy.

"Is it bad, Chase?" My heart races because I'm terrified of the answer he may give me. I know I shouldn't feel this way because he has already said that he will always be here for me.

"Well, let me just put it this way … I'm pissed because the change is a huge problem for me. I'm pissed because I should have been notified before anything was decided. I made that very clear to James when I left just a few minutes ago. He and I have been close for years, and I am hurt that this type of thing would happen without me being part of it."

"I really wish you would tell me what's going on. This is bothering me."

"I know, baby. I want us to sit down and talk about this, though. I'm good. I can handle the situation because I know it's part of this business, and it's what I have to do. My main concern in all of this is you. I'm worried about you. I'm worried that, even though your faith has been so strong in me the last several months, that this is going to cause it to fade. I don't want that to happen. I don't want to doubt how you feel. I don't want you to doubt how I feel. I know that this is news you are not going to take lightly."

"Well, when do you want to talk?" I wish we could do it right now. I need to know. I don't even know if I can sleep not knowing what is going on. What could it be? How is it going to affect me?

"Baby, I really want to see you right now, but I have to be on set at two a.m. Which is something else I wasn't expecting coming back from the holidays, but it is what it is. Are you closing tomorrow?"

"No. I'm going to clock in at nine thirty, and I'll get off around four o'clock."

"Did you have anything planned after work?" he asks.

"I talked to grandpa earlier and told him that I would come by to visit for a while, but I didn't give him a certain time."

"Okay, let's do this. Why don't you go ahead and see Grandpa Dawson after work and then just come on down to the house when you leave. I'll be there waiting for you."

"Okay. This is difficult. I'm scared. I don't know if I'll be able to sleep tonight. I'm very worried."

"Listen, baby. Don't be. I don't mean for you to feel that way. What I should have done is just waited until tomorrow to talk to you about this to save you from worrying, but you are heavy on my mind and heart since the meeting. I won't and can't exclude you. I will not leave you out. You are such a huge part of my life. Even though I'm upset and pissed off, everything will be all right. Faith and strength. I made you a promise, and damn it, I'm going to keep it. Please don't worry. Okay?"

I sigh. He's right. Faith and strength. He is going to be here for me, and I am going to be here for him. Always. Nothing will change that.

"Okay," I say softly into the phone.

I think back to the big-news announcement about the two of us going to Denver and the supposed engagement ring on my finger.

"Did you get to see the news?" I ask.

"No. Why did something happen?"

"Oh, well, Samantha Stone talked about the new issue of *Star Gaze* that hit the stands this morning, and how people are all over it because of our trip to Denver and the ring on my finger. They showed the cover of the magazine, and it shows us at the New Year's Eve firework show, and, of course, Stacey snapped a good shot of my hand with the ring."

He laughs. "Of course she did. She's good at stuff like that. Remember, we can always count on her."

We both let out a small laugh together. It feels good to do that, despite the lingering fact that I have no clue what problem has arisen for Chase. For me. For us.

"All right, now listen: go ahead and do what you need to do and try and get some rest. I'll see you tomorrow. We'll sit down and talk about what's going on. Promise me that you won't worry, and know that everything is going to be all right."

"Okay. I promise I will try."

"I love you, Joanna," he says softly into the phone. I can almost feel his words caress my ear.

"I love you too, Chase."

I look down at my watch and notice the time. It's twelve thirty. The lunch rush has been tiring, and we still have a little while to go before it's over. It seems that my time off has caused me to forget just how busy Ramona's little cafe can get. In a way, it is making the time go by quickly, yet at the same time it also feels like it is dragging. I'm ready to see Grandpa and to go see Chase so we can talk. I'm anxious to know what is going on. A small part of me wants to be upset with him for not rushing over last night to talk. It just seems like what he would have done. I have to realize that it just wasn't the right time. It's not fair to him for me to feel that way. He did call me to tell me that something serious had come up at the meeting with James, and that he needed us to talk.

I'm at the register, checking out a customer when Ramona walks over to me. I have missed her.

"Thank you so much, Jo, for covering for Amanda. I know you probably had things to do today since you just got back, but it really means a lot to me that I can count on you for help." She gently pats my back.

"Ramona, you know that you can always count on me. I don't mind at all. You gave me all that time off so I could go and enjoy myself with Chase. I owe you a lot just for that."

She waves her hand in a "nonsense" gesture. "Oh, sweetie, no, you don't. It was my pleasure. You deserved it, and so much more."

Everyone keeps saying that. Geez. I enjoy hearing it and everything, but people can go through tough times in life and not feel like they deserve the best of all things.

She winks at me as I give her a small smile.

"It's been real busy today. I'm certainly not complaining or anything. I'm used to us having busy Sundays, but today just seems different," she says as she looks around.

"Yeah, I know. My first day back from vacation is putting a whooping on me."

Ramona chuckles. "You're doing great, dear. No worries. You got this. Oh, and you have two new customers at table twelve. One of them requested a back corner booth, so I sat them there."

"Okay, thanks, Ramona."

She heads toward the kitchen as I finish checking out my customer. I tear the receipt from the register and stick it inside my waitress caddy.

I walk over to my customer and say, "Here is your ticket. I'll take it when you're ready. No hurry, and thanks so much for coming in today."

I give the old man a smile and pull out my waitress pad to go welcome my new customers and take their drink order. I turn and head to table twelve. Once I get close enough to see who is waiting for me, there are only two words that hit my mind faster than a bolt of lightning: *oh, shit!*

About the Author

Most girls fantasize about being swept away from devastating situations in their life by a Prince Charming. He could be anyone from the boy next door to a famous actor or singer. Stephanie would imagine this same situation happening to her when she battled several obstacles as a teenage girl. She realized that, at some point in time, most girls dream of a guy that will rescue them. So she brought the love story of Jo and Chase to life. Writing is something that she loves because she can see her characters and their stories evolve at the tips of her fingers. Stephanie lives in Statesboro, Georgia. She is a middle-school reading and writing teacher. She is married and has three children.

Printed in the United States
By Bookmasters

Printed in the United States
By Bookmasters